Threads

a novel by

Lindsay Gault

Threads First Published September 2019

ISBN paperback 978-0-473-49753-8

Chapter One – Alice Springs

White tracks snaked through salt bush. A trail of dust drifted lazily behind the bike. Maddie Jacobs eased into the turn, lifting the front wheel slightly. Ancient rock biting securely into soft rubber. She loved the feel of the rocks' pitted dry surfaces. Safe and solid. She glanced over the crest to the view of the valley floor below. Beautiful country. Greens in multitudes of hues slashed by the white of ghost gum trunks. Reds and oranges framed by a deep blue cloudless sky. A roo poised for flight beyond the dry brush to the left. Tight turn to the right lifting a plume of sand from the back wheel. Concentrate! Watch that steep drop! Slight wobble in the front wheel rolling on loose rock. The drops getting steeper, forks almost bottoming out. Right, left, left again, tight. The mulga whipped against her boot.

A few tracks from other faster riders lined the creek-bed sand. Ahead, an orange race marker dangled from the branch of a gum. Power on. The sand turned to rock, a dark green pool hugging the shade. A shard of sunlight lasered across her face. The tracks turned sharply right, a steep climb, the secure rock surface gripping the tyres. The change down was smooth, perfectly timed. Maddie felt relaxed, intensely alive and focused, standing on the pegs now to crest the sharp peak and into another steep drop. The brow suddenly revealed the run to the finish. Parked cars glinted in the sunlight, sponsors' tents with bright banners under the mulgas.

She saw a slight plume of dust below. The excitement translated into almost reckless speed down the slope. The rider ahead turned his head as he hit the sand of the creek bed. A slight loss of momentum, enough for Maddie to power past for the run to the finish. She coasted through the tents and turned to check the rider behind. Ryan Mulligan, National Junior Champion. Maddie pumped her fist.

Ryan pulled alongside. Maddie's long blond hair spilled onto her shoulders as she pulled off her helmet. She turned to offer a high-five. Ryan swore, and accelerated past. Maddie shrugged and headed slowly back to her support crew. Grant and Mary were beaming beside the trailer. They both hugged her.

"Three hours and five. Incredible time Maddie!" Grant wrote the time in his diary.

———

Dave Mulligan stood six foot three, a bull of a man. Huge in statute and girth. He owned a big Queensland trucking company and was a major sponsor of the race. He mistook owning a trucking company for owning most things. He listened intently to his sulking son. His anger fired quick and blind. He strode to the organiser's tent at the finish line.

"I want that Jacobs girl disqualified. Ryan saw her take three or four short cuts on the course. She's a bloody cheat."

———

Maddie stared at the results list for a long time. A red line obliterated her name and the word "*disqualified*" was scrawled beside. She walked slowly to the officials' tent. She asked the reason for her disqualification, then responded calmly: "I rode every inch of that course today. Ask your marshals. Mulligan was never behind me from the start, so how the hell could he have seen me on the course?"

She looked at each of the officials in turn, a long steely gaze which none of them could hold. She then walked over to the Mulligan Trucking Tent. Ryan sat exhaustedly on a canvas stool. He looked up briefly then turned away.

3

Maddie simply asked, "Why?" Anger fired her gaze, she stood for a full minute then strode away. "Gutless!" she muttered.

Grant had heard the news from another rider, but he took his cue from Maddie's cool reaction. "I am staying here until this bullshit is sorted. But you my girl have a birthday present from us all." Grant unwrapped the cover from the other bike in the trailer. It was his own BMW Dakar F650. His pride and joy. The big bike gleamed. "Happy seventeenth. You can ride this home, with the blessing of your Mum."

Maddie looked at Grant then back to the bike. It seemed impossible, nearly two thousand kilometres across magic country. "Are you sure Grant? You love this bike. What about fuel and …" Excitement replaced the doubt. She raced across to hug Grant then Mary. "Thank you thank you both, this is amazing!"

Grant held her shoulders. "I saw the anger in your eyes. Don't let it drive you. Use these next few days to put it in a useful place or discard it."

Maddie glanced in the mirror as the last buildings of Alice slid behind a rocky cutting. The bike seemed so quiet after the staccato of the race two-stroke. She eased into a sweeping bend and it felt great. Heat mirrored oily waves from the road surface, but the air was cool on her cheeks. She noticed something on the left, not far ahead. She slowed into the pull-off. Tropic of Capricorn, the plaque below the steel frame globe told her. Long curly horns on the goat pictured on the red plinth. Maddie stretched her arms to the sky. She was on her own, exploring this huge space. Freedom!

Gemtree Caravan Park appeared in minutes it seemed. Maddie's arms and legs ached. She tiredly dragged her leg over the seat. Alongside an elderly coupled appeared at the door of their caravan. "Gosh my dear, where are you heading? Are you all alone?"

"Yes, I am on my own and heading for Ayr." Maddie felt a surge of pride as she said the words. An adventurer, for real.

"You know it's all bull-dust and sand after Gemtree? Are you sure you will be alright?"

Maddie smiled. "I am looking forward to that bit".

Maddie hit the dust soon after sunrise. It flew in a plume from her back wheel. The big bike felt smooth despite the odd suck from sand patches. The Harts Range to her left blazed in pure orange. She pulled up and breathed in the beauty of the rising sun. The road began to take more of her attention. It was fun and she began to sing into her helmet.

A plume of dust appeared on the horizon, perhaps five kilometres ahead. *A road train, three or is it four trailers?* A slight westerly drifted the dust cloud slowly off the road, but the plume from the tractor unit engulfed the width of the road. On the same straight now. Maddie scanned ahead - an old stock track made a faint indent in the bush. She changed down, braking briefly, then gunned over the roadside rock pile. The track bounced the bike and she dropped gears again, braking to a crawl.

The horn-blast of thanks from the big Kenworth startled a flock of gallahs and they scrambled above the billowing red cloud, screeching. Maddie sat on the bike, the acrid musty taste of dust on her tongue. She turned off the bike as the rumble of the big unit faded. Oranges in her panier were a gift from the couple in the caravan. The sweet juice dribbled down her chin.

———

One of the ancestors pointed to the billowing serpent of Maddie's dust-cloud, drifting over dots of witchetty and mulga bush. Most of the visitors had begun to see the country. They were from the European Impressionist School. They saw the colours, the ochre, the red, the space. The native palette came from Walgi Mia in Western Australia, but the Impressionists had expanded the colour range in a fusion of styles.

One French painter stubbornly pined for the greens of his forest garden. Totally oblivious to the possibility of the local heritage. His works focused on feline studies in improbable forest settings. The critics described each as "flat and lifeless", perhaps unsurprisingly, since the models for his work came from feral road kill. His studio-cloud resounded with the calls of scavenger birds.

A local mentor looked over his shoulder with a long sigh of resignation. She needed a break, so descended to follow Maddie's dust cloud.

First, she felt the joy of the flow, then she began to detect Maddie's anger.

Really unfair. What was Grant trying to tell me? Forgive? Forget? Never!

She directed Maddie's eyes to the blue sky down to the merging purple of Harts Range. *Feel the purity of the space*, she urged.

———

There was silence now. Bush peace.

The sun had dropped low on the horizon and directly into Maddie's eyes. She hauled the handlebars, trying to keep a line in the wheel ruts. Her arms ached, her legs ached, everything seemed sore. Her eyes were red with grit. She looked at the odometer again. *Surely that's four hundred kilometres? Where is Tobermorey Station?*

The headlight struggled to light the road, with wind now swirling the dust from behind. *This is crazy. I should have stopped at Jervois Station. No, not far now, just stick it out.*

Two big red eyes. Huge eyes. Maddie blinked and slowed. Helicopters, two plastic domes reflecting the last of the sunset. Tobermorey helicopters. The tension in her body dissipated. *Nothing is impossible.*

Chapter Two - Dida Galgalu

Harsh volcanic rock had cut deeply through car tyre sandals and deep into flesh. The pain merged with the medley of general discomforts. Heat nagged his raw dry throat constantly. The twenty-litre plastic container swished with the dregs of the dwindling water supply. The infant started to fade, no longer able to audibly cry. The Dida Galgalu desert horizon shimmered in heat haze.

The journey had begun before dawn two nights ago. Wani had woken to the clatter of automatic weapons. Distant screams. Beside him, Akeyo's long-lashed eyes flickered, her beauty momentarily distracting him from the approaching menace. The baby blissfully gurgled in her cot. He grabbed the backpack and gently woke his wife, pressing her lips for silence with a firm hug of reassurance. The water container and heavy backpack were the only material memory of the eight years spent in the comfortable Moyale government bungalow as they slipped out into the golden beauty of the desert dawn.

Trouble across the nearby Ethiopian border had been brewing for some months. The local Governor had warned his staff to be prepared, but time had passed, and the threat had seemed safely distant. Isolation still kept the outpost poorly informed. As they reached the bottom of the first steep sandy slope, Wani glanced back at the familiar outline of their little home silhouetted in an orange glow; the clatter of AK47s continued along with the screams.

The baby had woken, Akeyo muffling the early cries with her scarf. They were moving fast through the low bush, thorns tearing at their clothes. Wani navigated nearly a kilometre away from the road south, but parallel, a course into the heart of the desert. He knew the rebels would be on the road as soon as Moyale was ravaged.

During daylight they sheltered under the meagre shade of thorn bushes. They ate sparingly, dry food which gagged in dry throats. Akeyo felt the deep fear, floods of childhood memories, hiding in terror from South Sudanese rebels in her home town. Her eyes haunted Wani - he desperately wanted to keep her safe.

Moving fast in the early light they covered the ground quickly. A cloud of dust a few hundred metres away had the family crouched against a thorn bush in terror. Footsteps, then the unmistakable snort of camels. To their relief, it was a small wild herd.

Wani spotted smoke from the direction of Sololo. He knew that the smoke meant the rebels had already reached the village, but the family needed water urgently. Leaving mother and baby sheltering, he cautiously approached the settlement. Thick and pungent smoke billowed up; the first hut also reeked of recent death. Flies swarmed from the bloated corpses.

Wani crouched in the garden, listening intently to the sounds of the ravaged village. Five minutes and nothing vaguely human. He moved quickly and quietly towards the water tower that dominated the landscape with its thirty-metre tower. The water tap at the base gave an alarming creak as it opened. Wani froze, but the village silence remained. A trickle of perhaps half a litre of water. High above, the bottom of the huge tank had been peppered with bullet holes, the few remaining water drops escaping in tiny pings onto the cross beams. Wani swallowed his frustration and fear.

Across the road the blue and white Al Hamou Hotel looked relatively unscathed. The floor inside glistened with a sea of broken glass. The freezer lid was ajar, precious fluid. A mixture of beer, soft drink and melted ice lay in a sludge at the bottom. Carefully Wani scooped up nearly two litres and reached down for another cupful when the sound of a vehicle split the silence.

11

———

Akeyo draped her headscarf over the lower branches of a scrubby acacia bush. Baby Dafina slept fitfully as her mother gently fanned the hot air. The tiny beads of sweat on her brow had now disappeared as the little body locked remaining fluid deep inside her body. Dafina was their true treasure. Her birthdate coincided with the day Akeyo had agreement from the local administration to trial her reforestation plan. She embraced motherhood with the same enthusiasm she tackled everything in her life. The dream of a micro green centre in the desert of Moyale had seemed crazy to many. A justification for some to plunder her modest aid funding on the way through the bureaucratic chain.

Akeyo closed her eyes and drifted back to the magic of the forest around the cottage in France and the cool waters of the River Vienne. She made her fairy tale haven amongst the trees of the forest. Green intensity so far removed from the Sudan of her childhood it seemed impossible. She cherished a weekly escape there from the rigorous study programme at the prestigious National Centre for Agricultural Research.

She fondly reminisced about the ancient cottage in Thure near Chatellerault. History as deep as the stone block walls. The cottage housed an improbable quartet: Dave, the highly irreverent, fun adventurer from Winton in the heart of the Queensland outback, his roughness hiding a deep gentleness and fierce loyalty; the French duo of Simone, the elegant, aristocratic party girl, and Bruno, the French farmer's son, flamboyant and crazily adventurous.

———

Saturday morning. The four decided to head to the town of Loches, a couple of hours drive away, across the other side of the Vienne Valley. They loaded up Bruno's green Citroen with essential supplies. Simone had a friend who lived in Loches and had invited them to a picnic in the grounds of the old walled city overlooking the village. Picnic days had evolved into an orderly routine. Bruno on food, Simone on wine and picnic blankets, Dave on navigation, and Akeyo looking after the morning dishes and clean-up to free the others.

The old Citroen spluttered into life, the air suspension hissed and lifted the passengers a few centimetres, and the journey began.

In the back-seat Simone reached for Akeyo's hand, "Thank you my friend, you have freed me from my worst self."

The two women were talking quietly, huddled head to head in the back seat of the Citroen. Akeyo had commented: "I don't think I will ever marry. I have too many important things to achieve with my life".

Simone swallowed; she knew she had to approach gently but directly. "Is there something that happened in your past?"

After a long silence, Akeyo whispered, "When I was twelve years old, soldiers came to our village. They took all the young girls. Some they killed afterward. I remained in the corn field. Then I was with child. When she was born, my mother took it immediately to an orphanage. We were too poor to feed another mouth. When I see some men I feel the pain again".

The brevity sent Simone's imagination into overdrive. The words were like a film of plastic cling-wrap over a pit of horrors. Simone knew that the lack of detail provided Akeyo's defence, she never wished to relive the detail beneath. Simone had no words; tears were streaming silently down her face. She hugged her friend tightly. Finally, she whispered back, "Let me show you there are good and gentle-men in the world".

Dave leaned over from the front seat: "There is a beautiful sunflower field I found on my bike the other day. I would like to stop and take a photograph if that's OK?"

The beauty of the field revived the women. They ran hand in hand into the deep rows, sunflowers above their heads. Dave laughed and took photographs. Bruno filled the Citroen with large flower heads. The picnic mood restarted.

———

Akeyo felt the love of the group block out the desert heat. Cool green fingers of French oak and laughter enveloped her. She felt then, the little cough as her beautiful daughter slipped away.

———

Wani sat, trapped deep in the tall blackened corn plot. Black ash cloaked him. The drunken sounds of the rebels were perhaps two hundred metres away, but he was trapped by the open ground between the two roads. The laughter, nonsense and trash talk were intermittently punctuated by the crash of broken bottles. The waves of sound were punctuated by sharp bursts of automatic gunfire. A tinny electric rhythm pounded in the background.

15

Pink hues glazed the early dawn. Morning birdsong replaced human noise. Wani eased cautiously to a crouch. His joints ached from the prolonged stillness. Moving with exaggerated slowness he eased in a long arch into the darkened west. Only once the tall water tower was barely visible on the horizon did he start to head south east into the sun.

He fought his panic at the sameness of the terrain, desperately scanning for familiar clumps of acacia. The road and the ruined village were his only reference. He had to risk getting back to the road.

The sun burned and passed its peak. He had come back as close to the road and village as he dared. His path now swept in long searching arcs, carefully checking for his path markers. He made sure each sweep allowed a view of his last, but nothing.

The sun turned deep golden, then the cool blackness shut down the day. Wani sipped from the sweet cocktail in his plastic container. His mind forced shutdown of thought; only the rustle of a passing snake and the muscle twitches of semi-sleep marked the endless darkness.

The cool dawn awoke with shafts of orange. Wani was finally able to stand and stretch. His eye was immediately drawn to the orange flag not two hundred metres to his left. A fluttering reflection of golden dawn rays. He moved quickly. Perhaps fifty metres away the hump below an acacia took form. A jagged steel band of pain and fear gripped Wani at the throat. His feet dragged the last few metres. A strangled sound, half-scream, half-sob, escaped.

Late in the day the ancestor spirits gently lifted Wani into action; they separated the empty shells of life and the deep love that would remain forever. The pile of sharp black basalt rocks grew around the bodies of mother and child. They would remain with the desert. He took the scarf, sweet with the scent of Akeyo, and moved quickly south into the desert.

————

From the blurred sheen of the desert the white figures of an old man and his donkey emerged. He motioned Wani to tie his small load to the donkey. They moved off in a slightly different direction to the one Wani had been following. At dusk, flashes of small water puddles appeared. Wani drank fully for the first time in four days. The old man handed him some dried corn - mixed with the brownish water, the corn swelled yellow and tasted sweet.

The old man was gone. Sleep blanketed him in seconds. Akeyo's scarf gently kissed his cheek.

———

Mother Madeline headed early to the Marsabit market. She walked quickly, treasuring the company of young Sister Evelina. Evelina had a bubbling cheeriness that never failed to distract Madeline. Her fun and laughter filled the Presbytery. A gift. The sandals of the two nuns puffed dusty red footprints down the rough hill to central Marsabit. Madeline glanced through the morning bustle to the rise of the main road stretching into the dessert. She recognised the signature of movement of the figure heading out of the morning sun even before he became fully visible. 'Signature of Movement' was her own term from the long walks to and from the village well as a child. She trained herself to recognise fellow villagers from exceptional distance by subtle differences in their movements. The game distracted her from the pain of the long walks.

She knew the figure hobbling towards her as Martin. She could trust Martin as an ally and friend on the Regional Council. He always acted fair and straight with no tolerance for the pack of corrupt, weakling hyenas who scavenged personal gain from political games. Madeline felt the pain instantly - Martin was in desperate need. She startled Evelina by breaking into a trot towards a figure still a hundred metres away.

The two nuns arrived simultaneously at Martin's side, breathless. A wave of Evelina's arm summoned a shopkeeper's pickup truck and within minutes the dusty ragged figure was laid out on the crisp white sheets of a Presbytery cell bed. Nursing Sister Agnes moved into action, quickly assessing the medical priority.

———

Wani could only see white. Mysterious figures floated across the white. He had died peacefully – but the pain remained. His brain struggled briefly with the thought then slid back into unconsciousness.

Two weeks later, something emerged from the white fog. A cross, a simple wooden cross. Wani turned to his left and stared at the metal stand, a plastic bottle dangled below. It took five minutes before he recognised the saline drip, his eyes following the plastic tube down to the bandage on his arm. He turned to the other side into a set of familiar, kindly brown eyes. "Akeyo?"

Another month passed. The pieces of memory jigsaw began to join back. It took hours of gentle listening from Madeline. With the memory came renewed pain and grief.

The Presbytery became a safe haven, a gentle recovery shell. No responsibility. Wani spent his days sitting in the sun and eating with the Sisters. He never ventured outside the gate.

Mother Madeline quietly said one day, "You have nothing, Martin. You start again from nothing, you are born again." But it took the cheery Eveline to restart life for Wani. She told her story. At seven-years-old she had witnessed her entire family shot by bandits. They had been heading for a new life in Nairobi. She had only survived by being buried beneath the bodies of her elder brother and younger sister. She recounted the story in a matter of fact voice, but her eyes betrayed her. "My brother gave his life for me Martin, so I must celebrate that every day. They were never sad so I must always be happy for the three of us."

———

The bus slewed through the sand, headed for Isiolo. Wani sat with his head against the window, watching the plains and shimmering acacia trees bounce past. He screwed his fist into his palm until it hurt. In Nairobi he could reassemble the threads of his life.

Chapter Three – Boulia

A mule stood beside the road in the fading light, pink against the Gibson Desert. Dave slowed the Landcruiser to take in the surreal light and ungainly visitor, but quickly gunned the truck before the cloud of his own red dust engulfed him. The light faded rapidly to a faint glow in the west as he turned onto the Developmental Road close outside Boulia. A cluster of twinkling lights appeared in the huge river bed - camp fires, and a village of grey-haired campers telling stories of tyres blown on the route from Birdsville or Tobermorey.

The Boulia Pub lights blazed brightly. Rowdy voices and music boomed from the bar. Dave backed the Landcruiser into the dusty car park at the rear. Friday night and the voices were loud. A chorus of "Gidday Mate" crossed the crowded bar. Matty thrust a frosted schooner glass into his hand as he reached the bar. The red-faced publican also handed him a room key with a small green tag. "Number three, mate, the quiet one at the back." The schooner clinked against a dozen offered glasses as he made his way to a quieter corner of the bar. He savoured the cool beer. He chose Arno for company.

Arno reputedly emigrated from Estonia many years before, but kept his true past confusing and interesting, varying the story with each telling. His years as a miner had made him one of the best, but perhaps even more skilled as an engineer. His ability to construct or reconstruct machines currently kept him busy drilling bores. Dave had employed him a few months ago, extending his artesian bores by nearly two hundred metres to reach the shrinking artesian water table. Arno laced the conversation with his keen perception and wit. His moderate wine-sipping ensured the conversation didn't deteriorate to a slurred gabble.

"Your grief is under control, my friend?" Arno enquired. Dave reeled a little at the directness and at the emotion it immediately invoked.

"Getting there, Arno, getting there." Dave raised his glass to hide behind a large swallow from his schooner.

Arno quickly followed up with a long description of his current project, and Dave relaxed and added the odd comment in the comfortable space Arno created. The two men chatted for an hour, until Dave excused himself and headed to the bar to order a steak. He took the steak and a large glass of Clare Valley Shiraz out to the empty dining room. Cool, quiet and almost peaceful; he shut out thought, savouring the Shiraz. For an outback publican,

Matty had an astute appreciation of better wines and a very good cellar.

The quiet outside in the main street of Boulia enveloped Dave with a sense of nostalgia. Most of the shop fronts were without light. Dave looked at each one with fond familiarity, knowing where to find things in almost all of them. Trips to town required planning and long lists which needed to be quickly filled. But that had been Sue's domain. The thought of her meticulous lists jolted emotion and tears, and his head jerked back. The stars above the Boulia main street became misty and blurred.

—

The hotel room filled with early morning light. Dave felt rested and comfortable. He quietly filled the Cruiser tank from one of the forty-four-gallon drums he had securely strapped on the tray. Heading out through Boulia, he took a long look at each of the places he had passed on his evening stroll, wondering if he would see them again. The long straight out of town lifted his spirits with a sense of adventure. Roos beside the road held his concentration until the rising sun sent them to their day time shelter.

He arrived at Winton with the same sense of familiarity he had felt reaching Boulia the night before. A few waves from familiar faces. He liked the café alongside the saddlery store, and lingered over breakfast, sipping a strong coffee. On the road out of town he stopped at the brightly-painted steel drums, a quirky percussion park – it invoked a tradition he wasn't going to miss. Sue had a musician's ear and, after a few clues dropped, he could always pick the beat she played on their ritual stop. He happily bashed a few resounding beats on the battered drum.

"Celebrate the good times," everyone kept saying. Today he found a few memory moments without the jagged dagger in his chest.

The road east continued on to Hughenden. Celine Dion soared from the cruiser speakers, her voice clear and strong. Dave harmonised loudly and Celine cringed. Hughenden bakery supplied a pie and a strawberry milkshake for his late lunch. Dave paused with the key, about to open the truck door, and glanced across the road to the big old hotel with the wide sweeping verandah. Sue had often said, "Wouldn't it be great to sit out with a beer on that verandah?" – but the long miles ahead had always kept them on the road.

At the hotel reception, a woman named Maria greeted him. Rounded face of pure outback leather, framed by jet black hair pulled into a tight bun. "Lovely to see you." Her eyes smiled deep.

"Thank you – that's a great welcome." Dave held the deep brown eyes for as long as he could, then asked for a room on the verandah.

"Come up and choose – we have recently refurbished them."

Everything felt good: the sweeping polished stairs, the wood-framed sepia photos, the polished wooden floors. They walked into the first room, a huge airy room, verandah doors wide open framing the sky.

"This is great, thank you."

"I knew you would like it. Make yourself at home. Dinner any time from five."

Dave sat on the huge old sofa on the verandah, commanding a view right across Hughenden and the late Saturday afternoon small-town bustle. The beer tasted good, and the shower had provided a powerful burst of hot water so he felt free of the red cloak of dust. The shampoo left a lingering tea tree scent.

——

Maria appeared in the empty dining room as soon as Dave appeared. She passed him a small square of card.

Menu

What you would like tonight is a linguini pasta, with squid and a hint of chilli and garlic. On the side a fresh green salad with tomatoes from my garden.

A glass of Montepulciano would complement it perfectly.

Dave tried to hide a smile as he studied the menu for as long as he could. "The pasta will be perfect, and the wine sounds even better." The smile escaped.

A starched white tablecloth covered the table. Maria had already laid out a crisp bruschetta with tomato and garlic, and a frosted wine bottle filled with chilled water.

The pad of bare feet across the polished floor behind him would have gone unnoticed, but for the enticing food smell wafting across the room with them. Dave turned to face Martha. Her ebony skin born from pure Waluwarra blood. She smiled with a whispered greeting as she carefully placed the food. "I am Maria's aunty, her father's sister. Maria would like to join you for dinner."

"Of course."

Maria came and sat down, and Martha brought her plate, then ghosted away. Dave leaned across to pour a wine. Maria talked, pausing only occasionally to see if Dave was engaged. She explained the long journey her mother had made as a broken-hearted twenty-three-year-old, running as far as she could from the man she had intended to marry. Her bitterness with her best friend who betrayed her. "Where is the farthest place away in the world?" her mother had asked the travel agent in Naples.

"Melbourne," he had suggested. The story wove in the familiar restaurant world in Lygon Street, where Maria had cooked in the kitchen for a distant cousin. Then the quiet afternoon in a Melbourne gallery, and the shy artist from way out somewhere in the outback. The looks of her family when she arrived for dinner with this gentle and wise black man. They arrived in Urandangi after two weeks of clattering in Jaco's battered Hilux. Jaco had introduced her to the country, his red billy tea matched with her pasta as they sat beside dry ghost gum billabongs. Under rich clear blue skies, they climbed the rock and looked down on the country, and Maria's mother could see the patterns of Jaco's paintings. She got to the soul of the country through the eyes of a master.

Dave felt at home in the gentle monologue. It touched common threads with his own father-in-law, Bapp. The old man quietly sitting under his namesake blue gum tree. At home with his country, his land. The land so much part of his history and his being. Dave's mind shifted back to the journey in the morning. Maria sensed the shift and moved into a listening silence.

"Wonderful country, I will miss it," Dave finished. "Thank you. Can I fix you up tonight? I want to get on the road early."

Maria reached across and touched his arm. "You go in peace - this is a small gift from the people of Urandangi. They thank you for looking after their country. And the door here is always open for you."

Dave stood. Maria embraced him with a warm familiarity, then quickly stood back with her deep welcoming smile. "Go in peace." Dave held her eyes and felt her peace; it laid the first thin layer over his pain.

———

Sleep came instantly and, in the dream, Dave saw Simone storming into the cottage, furious at the world. She fired first at Bruno. Bruno always surrounded himself with kitchen chaos as he prepared meals.

"Clean up this mess!" she yelled. "You always leave a rubbish tip for the women to clean up!"

Bruno shrugged. Simone stormed up the stairs to her bedroom. Dave heard the sounds from the back of the cottage, and went looking for Akeyo. She had an extraordinary patience and calmness which allowed her to defuse Simone's rages. She worked layer by layer to the root cause, often a long and painful journey.

Today the cause was much clearer. Simone had embroiled herself in a messy affair with one of the Professeurs at the Institute. The cottage had been woken late in the night with the Professeur's wife screaming for Simone to come out. The wife, drunk and distraught, then burst into high-pitched sobs. Akeyo gently led the woman into the house. Akeyo sat with her arms around her until she had calmed. Finally, Akeyo asked Bruno to drive her home. She rode sobbing in Akeyo's arms in the back seat. Dave followed in her own car. At least a roadside fatality had been averted.

The three had arrived home at three am, the two men convinced that Simone had to leave the cottage. Only Akeyo's conviction in providing resolution held her place. Both Bruno and Dave had distanced themselves and left the problem with Akeyo, with a two-week deadline.

Akeyo pulled out her bicycle from the old barn. Her face set, her heart pounding. She had an anger, deep anger, directed at Professeur Dupont, but burning from somewhere deeper. The ten kilometres to the Campus passed in a blur. Both she and Dave shared the same course with the Professeur, and the Professeur held the chair of the Overseas Scholarships Review Panel. A potentially powerful enemy. His office was empty, but the Faculty Administrator directed her to Lecture Theatre 3A.

The door to the theatre creaked open. Akeyo stood spotlighted in front of perhaps one hundred and fifty under-graduates, and the Professeur paused in mid-sentence, "Oui?" he snapped.

"J'apporte un message important pour vous, Professeur."

The Professeur strode to the door, ushering Akeyo out.

"Oui?" he snapped again.

Akeyo spoke directly and clearly, telling the Professeur he must stop his affair with Simone immediately. She explained that his wife had already visited the cottage in a highly distressed state and that she had threatened some dire actions. The Professeur refused to meet her eyes and gave no response. She took two steps over the line she had drawn in her rehearsal on the bike. She altered the edge to her voice and mentioned the other women in the class who were receiving his attentions, public knowledge to all in the class but in a deliberate blind spot for Simone. The final warning was more direct, to take the issue to the Faculty Head if she did not get an immediate response.

Finally, he nodded abruptly and curtly returned to his class.

Akeyo felt terrified. She ran to the toilet block, gagging at the wash basin, then washed her face repeatedly until her tee shirt was saturated. At least she had the bike to blame for her appearance. She rode back along the familiar quiet lanes, but her head screamed of a myriad of consequences.

The church spire and the tall headstones in the little walled graveyard signalled her return to the village. Red poppies lined the stone wall. She stopped and took them in, breathing deeply; the head noise subsided.

At the top of the long lane to the cottage she saw an unfamiliar car, grey and sleek. Dave was alongside, and Bruno came striding towards the car. Dave gestured, but it was too far for words to carry. The familiar figure of the Professeur unfolded itself from the car *like a snake uncoiling* she thought.

Dave's hand rested on the Professeur's chest, with enough pressure to seat him back in the car. Both Bruno and Dave were pointing down towards the village. The car started and reversed at speed down the narrow drive towards Akeyo.

She whipped her bike off the road and stepped into the wheat field, losing her footing and falling gracefully backwards into the tall wheat stems. They folded around her, only the blue sky above, one small puffy cloud and a wall of wheat.

Akeyo lay back and a calm came over her. She knew Dave had at much as stake as she did. She had a complicit ally. She stood and smiled at the two indentations in the wheat, the bike-shaped one still complete with bike.

Bruno took the initiative to face Simone and told her of the risk both Akeyo and Dave had taken. He left her with a question, "Did she deserve such friends?"

Her answer was simple, "Non."

But Simone changed. Her shock in realising that people she had regarded as house-sharers cared for her. They had cared so much to put themselves at risk on her behalf. The cottage changed. Bruno took on the challenge of halting Simone's shifts in mood, forcing reluctant laughter then genuine unsuppressed fun. Rituals started, like the Saturday picnics in surrounding villages, the long Sunday lunches at the chateau next door. Dave bantered with Simone about her pristine dress standards for every occasion, and she surprised everyone by borrowing one of his old work shirts to wear to lunch. It became a ritual. Friendship grew.

———

Dave awoke with the vision of Simone wearing his shirt. He rubbed his eyes and looked at the long shards of pink light penetrating the blinds.

The road east gathered the momentum of approaching civilisation. Nobody waved anymore. The smoke of burnt sugar cane hung in the air. He headed for Ayr, south of Townsville, heart of sugar country and flat cropping land. The truck was due for a service; sixty thousand kilometres in less than nine months - a lot of road.

Dave did not recognise the girl in service reception. Her long blonde hair hid her face, eyes looking down to her phone. Dave said "Hi." She looked up briefly. Dave spotted a small coffee machine in the corner. He left his keys and logbook on the counter and pressed the button labelled "Latte." He sat down and picked up a four-wheel Drive magazine. One thing he had now was time.

'Maddie', as her label announced, was shaken by his apparent disinterest. "Can I help you?"

"These Desert Rat tyres look interesting."

"Are you after tyres?"

"No."

Maddie now cast a worried look through the glass into Tom's office. Tom came from a tough background, old school, hard as nails and owner of the business. He could hear the conversation and started developing his "what the hell is going on" look.

Maddie slipped her cell phone into her bag, and put on her most efficient stride-to-the-counter manner. She picked up Dave's log book looking for clues. "Ah - your thirty thousand service is due."

"Missed that."

Dave glanced over and could see Tom now hovering in his office doorway. He had spent hundreds of thousands of dollars with Tom over the years.

Maddie knew Tom's flash points intimately and desperately reached for defuse mode. Dave decided to let her off the hook. As he stood up, Tom rushed across to the counter, literally brushing Maddie aside. "Dave, how the hell are you me old mate?"

"Good Tom, good. Long drive in, ready for a beer."

"What can we do for you – apart from the beer? Maddie, a beer for one of our best customers." Maddie took her terrified smile rapidly towards the fridge.

"A full service thanks Tom, got a few miles to do."

"Any specific issues?"

"A/C joints are a bit wobbly, front drive has a bit of a rumble and a little bit too much bounce in the rear suspension, swag on the back is a bit uncomfortable."

Tom chuckled. "No worries." He scribbled a quick list. "She's a bit vacant sometimes, but nice tits." Tom nodded his head backwards towards Maddie.

"As long as she can change a tyre."

"She actually races dirt bikes, and bloody good she is too."

Dave finished his beer and a passed a few more pleasantries before escaping to the street in the bustling little Queensland town. He had a weekend to kill before the truck would be finished, and that was the limit of his immediate future plans.

———

36

The pub in Ayr had a quiet country band, a female vocalist with a good voice and two guitars backing. The music flowed, and Dave caught himself humming half-remembered lyrics. The pub began to fill. The 'Sugar Town Country' were obviously a local favourite. Animated laughter suddenly caught Dave's attention. Three attractive women had entered the bar: two elegant dark-haired ladies and a slightly shorter blonde, hair neatly swept back in a pony-tail. All wore checked western-style shirts and short tasselled skirts. Girls' night out.

Dave resumed eating with quiet humming to the renditions of a John Denver classic between mouthfuls. A whiff of French perfume reached him before the gentle touch at his elbow. The blonde from the trio. Without her badge Maddie was less recognisable; she seemed transformed from a twenty-something vacant blonde to a cheery, attractive thirty- something. Laughter at the corners of her eyes.

"Maddie!" she shouted in his ear. "From the workshop. We have a quiet booth over there. Would you like to join us?" As they reached the booth, the female vocalist announced a short break, and the noise level briefly dropped in the bar.

"Sorry about this arvo, I was trying to organise the kids for tonight. Meet my mates, Trish and Sue."

The name 'Sue' sent a brief jar, but this Sue was bursting with good time fun and determined to enjoy every moment. The fun was infectious. "We're celebrating Mad's win in the Birdsville Bash last week, first woman to take an overall win," she said.

Surprisingly, Maddie's face blushed. "Awesome effort girl," Trish chimed. She hugged her friend and left a perfect lipstick imprint on her cheek.

"This calls for cocktails, ladies."

"With umbrellas please."

Dave got up and leaned across the bar. The music had restarted and the order needed direct ear contact to deliver. "Cocktails with umbrellas please."

The young Irish barman touched his nose knowingly and gave him the thumbs up. The cocktails danced in their aluminium shakers for five minutes or more, traversing the space around and behind the young man's back, each acrobatic manoeuvre adding to the final price tag. A fifty-dollar bill turned into a few coins.

The friends squealed in delight as Dave reappeared with the cocktails. "To the fastest lady with a bike between her legs!" Again, Maddie blushed slightly, but Dave saw a new fierce pride in her eyes.

The cocktails were unfinished as Trish and Sue took to the dance floor. "Dance." Maddie gave him no choice with a surprisingly powerful pull off the leather seat. She danced with a strong rhythmical grace, guiding his less co-ordinated body with firm control. Gradually he relaxed, feeling her movement and following her lead. He laughed for the first time in months.

Song by song they twirled around the dance floor, Dave apologising for the odd passing foot trample. Trish and Sue jived past, both with exaggerated winks. The music slowed; Maddie slipped her arm around his waist, head against his chest. Smells of her French perfume and her hair.

They sat down only as the band began packing their gear. Trish and Sue were animatedly talking to two younger surfie- looking types. Fun banter with clear boundaries, which the boys were trying to test. The bravado quickly dropped as the girlfriends emerged from the toilets.

Dave turned to Maddie; her eyes were alive and happy. "Thank you," he said. She reached up to put her hand around his neck, and kissed his lips. "Likewise," he said.

Dave and Maddie stood hand in hand outside the pub. Trish and Sue had issued their generous hugs and said goodnight and disappeared in a taxi. "They live a way out of town," Maddie explained. "Where are you staying?"

Dave stumbled a little. "I don't mean this to sound..." he trailed off, "but I haven't got anywhere sorted yet."

"I don't do one-night stands, but you are welcome to sleep in one of the kids' beds. It's only a short walk." The clarity of ground rules immediately relaxed Dave; the slight gnawing conflict of the evening could be put aside. Dave remembered the plastic bag of breakfast food he had left behind the bar. "Be back in a minute."

They walked hand in hand to a small brick house a few blocks away. Maddie welcomed him to her house with a relaxed cheer that seemed so out of sync with the initial impression in the workshop office that morning. In the kitchen she walked up to him and hugged him, with another warm moist kiss. "Goodnight, I would love to see you again – once you have sorted whatever you need to sort."

Dave wondered at her perceptiveness. He thought there had been no inkling of past leaked in the evening. Again, it rocked his view of this woman he had so recently met.

———

Dave awoke to the unbaffled staccato clatter of a race-modified two stroke motor. Blearily he looked out the window. Maddie in pink, grease-splattered overalls, blonde hair crushed under a back-turned cap, was adjusting a bike engine on a stand. *The neighbours must love her on a Saturday morning* he thought. A neighbour's motor mower joined the chorus, followed slightly further away by the rattle of a chainsaw. It was nine o'clock in suburban Ayr.

Dave showered and dressed. Opening the fridge, he reached for his plastic bag with bacon, eggs, tomatoes and avocado. He scrambled through the neatly laid out cupboards and quickly filled the kitchen with the tantalising smell of bacon. He went to the back door, to be blasted by the cacophony of sound, his hand signals eventually raising a thumbs up and five-minute signal from the bike mechanic.

She emerged fifteen minutes later in a warm steamy cloud from the bathroom. Hair in towel and dressed in shorts and tee shirt. Her physical beauty in that moment made

Dave leave his carefully tended bacon, walk across the room and hug her. He kissed her damp forehead, then rather awkwardly said, "I hope you like bacon."

"I had a moment's hope for something better than bacon," she said cheekily. "I'm ravenous."

"Listen, the boys are staying at Mum's until tonight. Let's take the bikes and go for a picnic somewhere down the coast. Oh – can you ride?"

"Sounds great. Yes, I've been on stock bikes since I was about ten, but I have broken a lot of them."

Dave followed her out of the small town to open straight tarmac. They reached a twisting beach track, and Dave slipped behind. He saw the grace and balance of a master rider disappear into the dust ahead. At the end of the track a single line split a tall sand dune. The track disappeared over the ridge. Dave throttled his bike and attempted to follow. The bike slewed and snaked and the rear wheel dug a deep hole. After three attempts he left the bike and followed the track up the deep sand onto a small tussock plateau. Maddie's bike had been propped against a small stunted bush. She had already shed her bike gear and had stripped to shorts and tee shirt, feet bare. "Where've you been?" she laughed.

"Too good for me."

"Race you to the beach."

They rolled and tumbled down the last dune which revealed a small sandy cove. A glassy sea lapped small waves at the shoreline.

"It's one of the few places which doesn't really get stingers this time of year."

They sat on the sand face to face and talked, fingers and eyes often touching. There was room only for truth. Maddie's voice hardened as she talked of the boy's father. He wasn't a bad guy, he worked in West Australian offshore oil rigs to earn money to "set themselves up." He often arrived home broke after spending his cash on "the best deal" he had ever seen. Eventually as Maddie started to probe, he became defensive, then violent. She walked out the day he lashed out at their eldest son Peter, who was only five. Children were sacrosanct. She had spent the next few years simply earning whatever she could to support the boys. Her widowed mother had moved down to be near her grandsons, and it was she who insisted Maddie have time for herself. The dirt bike passion came from a secondary school camp. She chose the dirt bike training as a dare with a friend. The instructor took one look at her

riding the course and declared her a natural. He spent a
week with her, with patient one-on-one training, even
making her dis-assemble the bike and try to put it back
together. She remembered the day she tracked him down
in a Rockhampton Rest Home to hand him her first major
race trophy. His eyes told her that she had given him a
precious gift.

Dave started easily, recalling life on the outback station as
a kid. The shock of moving to secondary school in
Melbourne, the wild university days, then France, the total
culture shock. A struggle with language which turned out
to be one of his passions and loves. Three years' study in
the middle of beautiful French countryside. The friends in
the stone cottage in the woods. Then Sue. He knew the
story had to reach Sue. He started falteringly and looked
up at Maddie. Maddie had tears in her eyes. "It's too early,
it can wait 'til next time," she said. "But now it is swim and
lunch time".

They arrived back at the house late afternoon. Maddie
said, "I don't want to push you off, but I don't want the
boys to see a man at the house. They will jump to all the
wrong conclusions."

Dave felt the kiss lingering on his lips as he checked into a
motel an hour later.

On Monday afternoon, Dave had butterflies in his stomach as he walked the short kilometre from his motel to the workshop. The office was empty. He rang the bell and Tom bustled to the counter. "Here's the paperwork mate, most is covered by the standard service, but a couple of cracked leaf springs needed replacement. We've repacked them all."

Dave cleared his throat. "Where's Maddie today?"

"Delivery to a farmer up the road, new wagon."

Dave cut in. "She's an asset, Tom. You will want someone you can trust to run the business when you decide fishing needs to take higher priority. How long has that boat been stuck in your garage now? I met someone who knows her bloody well, and he doesn't give recommendations lightly, nor do I for that matter."

Tom looked up, rather startled. "Never thought about it mate, but I'm not getting any younger. Thanks for that, I'll give it some thought."

"And could you give her this please." The small post-office box gave no clue of its contents.

In the cab of the truck, he opened the logbook to check the service record. A small pink envelope was tucked inside. It contained a note that simply said, "Dave, would love to talk again. Maddie." And her contact details.

Chapter Four – Melbourne

Melbourne's morning bustle registered with the clang of a tram bell. Bruno instantly woke, eager to join the bustle below. He loved this little central core of the city he now called home. A leisurely morning ramble through the park, familiar faces on the way. The morning banter with namesake Bruno, Italian Bruno in his corner café. It was almost a ritual now.

"Bongiorno Bruno."

"Bonjour Bruno."

"Usual this morning, mate?"

"Something better than yesterday my friend, the expresso was verging on Wagga Wagga bakery diesel fuel."

"You bloody foreigners are impossible to please. I work hard for my wife and fourteen children. I keep my finest beans for my best customers and still I get this shit every day!"

Today also promised a date with the girl with the hat. The girl with the hat had fascinated Bruno from their first meeting. She served coffee in a small alleyway patisserie, but immediately buried herself deep in a pile of books as soon as the immediate needs of any customer were met. She possessed an innate sixth sense of the next customer demand, and ghosted to their elbows with immaculate timing. Her black floppy hat covered one of her eyes. A partial dress code demanded flowing floral clothing to match. Instead she always wore plain elegant calf-length single-coloured dresses, usually red, always with elbow length sleeves.

Bruno's coffee cup clanked down. A jarring realisation that his mind-song mirrored his mother's ruthless fashion assessments. Assessments that always used to annoy him intently. Assessments that reduced innocents to untouchables in seconds, equally elevating empty-headed prats to worthies. Her parisienne fashion scales were righteous and arrogant.

"Merde!" he said aloud.

Morning papers rustled around him, exposing questioning faces.

Bruno gazed vacantly at the coffee in his cup. What was the flash of substance he had seen in the woman? Was it her intelligent quips, not the polished routine said-a-thousand-times-daily quips, but sharp, often with edge but somehow without impoliteness? What did she detect in him so quickly to extend the boundaries of those quips?

Bruno glanced at his watch – enough time to reach the office before the morning routine stream of demands started. Pete's phone call promptly relegated office routine to the background. Pete and Bruno jointly owned a four-wheel drive. The pride and joy of them both. They relished the space and adventure that the harshest outback tracks could bring.

Pete cut straight to the point. "Ivanhoe this weekend, mate. There is a great track around the back of Mungo National Park, and I want to test the new self-inflators. Pizza night at Ivanhoe pub Saturday night."

"That's a long-haul Pete - might need a day off work."

"OK, see you Friday night."

"Pete, is Donna free? I might bring someone else along if things work out tonight."

"Good as gold, mate – see ya."

The conversation took less than a minute, but Bruno had already switched to planning mode. The jump to suggesting that the girl with the hat might be interested in his weekend world had slipped out unexpectedly.

Bruno smiled as he pictured Donna in her nurse's uniform. Always effervescent and cheery. He winced as he remembered the last female friend he had asked Donna to chaperone. An accounts administrator from the hospital. She had refused to budge from Birdsville after a harrowing descent of the Big Red sand hill on the Simpson Desert track. She arrived back a week later, still in a cold fury.

First priority on the planning list was food, always Bruno's domain. Next came logistics and fuel stops. An hour's internet research put a few dots on the map. Bruno cleared appointments for Monday and Tuesday. Tuesday looked like a necessary contingency, especially after a Pizza night at Ivanhoe Pub.

The day passed quickly, living in images of the Mungo National Park, an area with an ancient history of human occupation. Late in the afternoon Bruno booked a table for two at a bistro in Brunswick Street. Low key, but with excellent food and usually quiet enough to talk. Instinct told him that the bohemian style of Brunswick Street might appeal to the girl with the hat.

The warm water cascaded from the shower. Bruno suddenly registered he had no timetable or meeting point for his date. The only common contact point was the patisserie. *Did the place open in the evening?* He dressed hastily, feeling suddenly unprepared and out of control. He strode quickly down Little Collins and across the bustle of post-work Swanston Street. An alarming number of daytime coffee haunts had closed doors. The pace of his walk raised a sweat, making him feel more ruffled and uncomfortable.

Restaurants in the familiar alleyway were not yet open for evening trade. People passed, heads down striding towards Flinders Station. A light from the kitchen dimly illuminated chairs stacked on tables through the patisserie window.

"Hi, looking for someone?" The voice was behind him. The girl with the hat was sitting in the open frontage of the restaurant opposite, face in deep shadow under the hat, books open on the table. "Your date organisation skills leave a little to be desired."

"Sorry, thank you for waiting," Bruno spurted, the rehearsed silky opening lines deserting him. He moved quickly across to the table, hoping to catch the title of a book to give a clue to conversation starters. The books were already packed into a beautifully-embroidered hessian bag.

"I'm Julia." She extended her hand.

"Bruno." He took the hand in a decidedly sweaty one of his own; the hand felt cool.

He sat down opposite her and found himself without words and feeling uncomfortable.

"You need a water." She stood and disappeared into the back of the restaurant, taking the hessian bag with her. Tonight, she wore a red dress, but the shoulders were bare. Bruno noticed an elegant tattoo on the right shoulder. Was it a snake?

The water took a few minutes to arrive, but Bruno was grateful for the space. Julia smiled. "I am glad you showed, I was only going to give you until six."

"It was dumb. If there is a next time, I will do it better."

"If I had known the offer was for real, I would have done it better myself. I gave you sixty-forty against showing."

The smile relaxed Bruno, and he unconsciously slipped from his usual heavily French-accented patter. "I was quite flustered - I had been quite looking forward to this, and I realised I had nearly stuffed it up at square one."

The girl with the hat stood, and said "Hi, I'm Julia, would you like to go dinner somewhere?"

"Do you like Brunswick Street?"

"Sounds great."

So, the evening restarted. The conversation skimmed lightly over topics and Bruno found Julia quick-witted and fun. He was mildly shocked to find she was two years older than him. He asked about the hat and the snake tattoo. "The hat is my identity prop," she told him. "People recognise a familiar prop better than a name or a face. The snake is a long story, but not a first-time story." He forgot to ask about the books.

She insisted on paying half of the bill and as they stood outside he asked, "My second date suggestion is Ivanhoe Pizza night on Saturday night, but it does include some rough four-wheel driving."

"Where the hell is Ivanhoe?"

Bruno explained, and she pulled out a small pocket diary, checked it, then handed it to him with a pen. "Make sure the details for this one are a little more precise."

Julia exchanged a three-cheek kiss. "You are French?" "Oui."

Bruno saw her to a tram on Johnston Street and she disappeared. He took a long stroll home through his favourite parks. It was nearly two am when he arrived back at his familiar "Little" street.

———

Friday evening Bruno arrived at Southern Cross Station, early for him. They had agreed to meet at four pm for the four-twenty-five to Bendigo. The hat quickly gave Julia away in the crowded Collins Street Concourse. He spotted her waiting at the Information Desk as they had arranged. He took stock of her as he approached. Her shorts and tee shirt were complemented by a woollen jerkin hanging artistically off one shoulder. Her bare legs disappeared into dusty desert boots. She carried a small pack over one shoulder. She immediately handed him some cash. "My fare." Bruno refused. "No, you shout the pizzas and beers at Ivanhoe, and I promise we will do a tally up at the end."

On the train Bruno excitedly described the country around Mungo National Park. He explained that Mungo provided some ancient interest with twenty thousand-to-forty-thousand-year-old relics appearing in the sand dunes. Foot prints preserved for centuries in the layers revealed by drifting sands. He described the "Walls of China", site of the earliest human remains outside Africa. The cremated remains of Mungo Man and Woman had huge cultural significance, and dated some forty-two thousand years old.

Julia smiled; engaged by his enthusiasm. "Hey, I'm the Aussie here, and I feel totally ignorant of my own country."

"It's big enough to hide a few secrets for foreigners like me."

——

Pete and Donna sat on the platform at Epsom station; it was six thirty. Donna paced the platform, grumpy. Pete had omitted the detail about Bruno's companion for the trip until they arrived at the station. "Another bloody stiletto tottering damsel you expect me to nursemaid the whole bloody way. You need to learn to say no to Bruno's bits of fluff!" she huffed.

When the train arrived, Donna scanned the disembarking passengers for city girl types in high heeled shoes. She completely missed Bruno, who embraced her in a huge hug from behind. She turned and kissed him.

"Which one is she?" she whispered in Bruno's ear, still eyeing the most likely-looking city girl on the platform.

Bruno pointed at an aging damsel, stark-faced, with makeup, elegant in black and matching Dior handbag. He was foiled immediately by the cluster of children running towards her. "Granny!" they yelled.

Donna gave Bruno a sharp elbow to the ribs.

"Hi, I'm Julia, and you must be Donna and Pete."

Donna looked approvingly at the boots, then worked upwards to the warm friendly face. *Maybe Bruno has finally got his shit together,* she thought.

"Love the hat – welcome to Bendigo."

Pete had already shouldered the large cooler filled with Bruno's food selection, and became engaged with Bruno on details of the new auto-inflation system for the "Beast."

Donna took Julia's arm and started her well-worn briefing on what to expect over the next few days. "The nights can get really chilly, but we have a good spare swag." Julia listened carefully, asking sensible practical questions, and Donna warmed to her.

Bruno suggested that they have a quick meal and get a head start on the long journey ahead.

"Already onto it, mate, all fuelled up, and Donna has a roast chicken ready to scoff."

Donna looked approvingly over Julia's choice of clothing and gear as they loaded everything into the four-wheel drive. *Less nurse-maiding required for this one* she thought.

Julia watched fascinated as Bruno explored technicalities with Pete. She observed the ease and closeness of the pair as they emerged for the tenth time from underneath the wagon. Surgeon and mechanic, an unlikely mix.

The road out of town blazed in light a kilometre or more ahead as Bruno switched on the powerful spot beams. The road reflectors flashed brightly past. "OK for roos until after Kerang, mate, they've had a bit of a cull", Pete grunted.

Julia chatted comfortably with Donna in the rear seats. Donna probed beyond the comfortable level Bruno had reached on their first date. She liked the honesty of this woman, and found only a few quiet spots on her radar. Clearly Bruno didn't know what he had stumbled on here. They kept their voices low so the conversation was not shared with the men.

They drove for a little under four hours, and before eleven they pulled into campsite a few hundred metres off the road. Pete disappeared with an axe and returned with a bundle of firewood. Soon the blaze started sending red sparks high into a clear night sky.

"Night cap time. I hope the Frenchman delivers something decent this trip."

Bruno emerged from the back of the truck with a bottle of Chinon Rouge. "I couldn't find anything rough enough, so I threw this in."

They sat in a small circle on the camp chairs. Bruno reached and touched Julia's arm. "Look at the space in the sky. No light pollution. Look - there's the Southern Cross, and off to the side the two pointers. Draw an imaginary line from the two pointers to the long axis of the cross and that's due south."

Julia looked up and observed the clean space above. She looked at the face of the Frenchman engrossed in the limitless view. She smiled at her shift in view of this man, who until a few days ago she had regarded as the smooth Frenchman, slightly too smooth and oh so self-centred.

The fire died slowly to warm flickering embers. Donna appeared from the darkness with her head torch pointing. "Long drop right over there Julia, a composting job so not too bad on the nose. Good night everyone."

The four swags lay like spokes radiating from the fire. Julia found hers comfortable, but kept the insect net open so she could see the sky as she quickly drifted off to sleep.

———

The morning chill merged into a strange dream for Julia. Something was eating her face, and trickles, yes, trickles of blood running across it. She tried to lash out, hands bound in the swag. The trickles on her face were real. She got her hands free, slapped her face hard. The bodies of several ants stuck in her palm. In the pink dawn light, she saw a trail of big red ants filing across her unused insect net. *Outback lesson one*, she thought dozily. She quickly extracted herself from the ant-riddled swag and stumbled across the campsite to the long-drop.

She emerged to a rich golden glow, warbling magpies and screeching galahs, white-trunked gums reflecting the light glow. She sat in the chill on her swag, watching the colour changing and brightening. She sat with a peace she had not felt since... since... she couldn't remember when.

Impossibly, Pete slept until Bruno had the breakfast fire delivering omelettes, and croissants lightly toasted on the embers. The sun quickly took the chill off the morning air. Julia cheerfully followed the simple morning routine and helped Bruno with the food. She wandered with a billy to fetch water from the creek, but found nothing but sand and rocks, her only mistake as a camp novice.

———

The distance between homesteads began to lengthen. The road had turned to dirt, still fast dirt, and Bruno expertly kept the speed to cover the ground. Dust billowed behind. Pete traced his finger over the map. "About ten ks ahead, the track should turn off to the right, immediately after a bore and cattle yards."

Neither the bore nor the cattle yards were marked on the map, but Pete's internal GPS mapped memories of outback track descriptions from old records to real locations. Bruno had given up checking Pete's navigation on the real GPS many trips before. The bore and cattle yards arrived as the trip metre turned over nine point six kilometres.

"You're four hundred metres short, Pete. Bloody hopeless! How do you expect me to drive with shoddy navigation like that?"

"I said after the bore, mate – see about three hundred and fifty metres ahead on your right. Turn right and shut up."

Bruno grinned.

Julia sat at the back window watching the country unfold. The stories of endless unchanging outback desert she had grown up with seemed far from the truth. Subtle changes in soil, residual changes in moisture in old creek beds, salt pans, grazed country and raw bush changed the complexion of the vegetation minute by minute - some small, some creating a completely new vista out her window. She wondered about the people in the remote stations they passed. *What was it like to live seven hours' drive from your nearest shop?*

The track started forgivingly, Bruno easing only slightly from the gravel road speed. Then the going got rough, with lumps of rock littering the track at first.

"I'm dropping the tyres by ten PSI all round, so you don't shake us all to bits."

The clattering jolting ride immediately became slightly more forgiving.

"Sand, Pete!" yelled Bruno. "Drop a few more!"

Pete fiddled with his new toy, happy. His hours of patient plumbing and careful calibration were actually delivering a significant difference to the driving response. Bruno turned to him, "Great job, mate, it's working perfectly. Take them up a bit for this rocky section, I don't want to chop a side-wall."

In spite of the jolting ride, the wild adventure enthralled Julia. She was fascinated by the changing rock formations, and vegetation. She recognised salt bush, only by jogging memories from one of her primary school reading books. Pete explained there were over one thousand species of eucalypts.

"So much native country heritage, somehow missing from my education", she mused.

Pete had chosen one of the few permanent water holes for their lunch stop. Perhaps the only water for one hundred kilometres. A huge overhanging rocky outcrop created a cool shaded oasis; tall eucalypts guarded a small pool, with green spongy edges. Birdlife filled the surrounding trees. Lunch consisted of ham, cheese and tomato sandwiches, bread still fresh from the cooler. Pete boiled a billy for tea. The tea tasted as raw and fresh as the surrounds.

Julia walked over to the rock Bruno was sitting on, head laid back watching the birds. "Thank you, a wonderful date so far."

"These spots make it all worthwhile," Donna said to no one in particular.

———

Ivanhoe appeared in the late afternoon. Julia could not believe a town could be so small. It looked like the classic outback cartoon in the ancient illustrated "Post" magazines her grandfather kept in his office. Their camp would be the small and dusty enclosure directly over the road from the hotel. The big hand-painted sign "Pizza night – this Saturday" looked as if it had seen a few Saturdays.

Donna and Julia headed to the small shower block. Bruno and Pete lovingly conducted an inch-by-inch inspection of their vehicle.

As the women emerged fresh and soap-scented from the shower block, a battered and Toyota Hilux pulled into the camp in a cloud of red dust. Two equally dusty female farm hands emerged from the cab, "Gidday!" they chorused, one with a heavy Irish accent.

Donna and Julia brushed the red dust from their fresh clothes.

"We need another shower", muttered Donna. "You could have slowed down coming in."

"Sorry, mate", said the busty Irish one, her small dusty mate looking sheepishly at her boots.

Julia and Donna looked at each other and agreed an immediate beer was necessary.

 "Meet us in the pub. We need a cool calming beer before we take Busty and Dusty apart", Donna yelled to the two men.

———

Ivanhoe pub began to fill as more dust-coated farm vehicles pulled to a stop outside. Pete and Bruno arrived with Busty and Dusty. The farm girls, freshly showered, were giggly and talkative. Donna and Julia sipped their beers across the other side of the room. It took a few minutes for the men to be served. The landlady stood on the bar to announce that their new pizza oven had been delivered to Ivanhoe near Heidelburg in Melbourne. "Useless bloody couriers. Pizzas will be a bit slow off the barbeque so get your orders in quick", she yelled.

With beer in hand, Pete spotted Donna and Julia across the crowd and made his way across. Bruno stayed engaged with Busty and Dusty at the bar. Julia watched as Bruno's well-practised patter enrolled the girls. Lots of head-back laughter and touchy giggling. Julia found herself in an ambivalent space. She relaxed in the rough friendly atmosphere. Donna began to seethe; her eyes kept darting across the room. She gave Bruno fifteen minutes before whispering in Pete's ear, "Get that Frenchman away from those tarts, and get his arse over here."

Bruno arrived and looked at Julia, testing her reaction. He got none. He felt the tension more in Donna and Pete. Bruno looked around the group and said something that surprised even himself. His usual cavalier bluster deflated, contrition in an instant recognition of how he was behaving.

"Sorry all. This is a far better group to join. Hopefully I can leave that idiot in me behind."

"Here's to good company and a new experience for me," said Julia, raising her glass. Donna relaxed.

———

In the early morning light, Julia made her way across the campground, past the heaving, grunting swags of Dusty and Busty, clothes strewn across the ground. Julia smiled.

Chapter Five – Melbourne

Dave registered the sudden realisation he had no plan and no idea of what to do next. He braked abruptly in the driveway of his son's house in Williamstown. He had to leave - Ryan and his wife Bridget lived at a frenetic pace. In the two months or so there had only been brief quiet moments. Their combined world of high-paced IT business and legal wrangling often left him exhausted in a mystery of acronyms. *But where to next?*

The drive down from Ayr he found peaceful. An unhurried wander down the inland highway, then out to the coast stopping wherever took his fancy. Most nights he had emailed Maddie. Her replies deepened his appreciation of the person. The first phone call started falteringly, almost formally, then relaxed into over two hours of rambling through respective lives, until his cell phone battery died.

On the waterfront in Williamstown, perhaps two hundred metres down the street, Dave parked the truck and wandered into a little café. He closed his eyes. His mind wandered back twenty years to the student cottage in Thure.

———

The group had a bottle of Chinon Rouge open on the huge
wooden table, door open, with the wheat fields rippling
across to the village church steeple. Akeyo, those big dark
beautiful eyes across the table, water in her glass. Bruno
holding court with some wild adventurous plan. Simone
engaged in her constant phone battle with her mother.
The thick stone walls created a cool space in the summer
heat. The French oaks outside, Simone's red Peugeot and
Bruno's battered green and white Citroen haphazardly
parked on the grass…

———

Dave snapped out of his reverie - Bruno! Bruno had
appeared unexpectedly at the funeral. Amongst the throng
of half-remembered relatives, Bruno had talked for a few
minutes, then disappeared. Bruno worked somewhere in
Melbourne; was it St Vincent's hospital?

Dave brought the directory up on his phone and picked
the most likely-looking number. The phone rang, and he
skipped through the layers of automated voices until he
found a voice on the end of the line. "Could I speak to
Bruno Lappriere please?"

"Bruno who?" Dave spelt the name.

"Which department please?"

"He is in a lab, microbiology I think."

The phone rang again. The call progressed.

"I'm sorry but Bruno is on leave until Wednesday morning. Can I help you?"

"Listen, I'm an old friend of Bruno's. You don't happen to know his cell phone number do you?"

"It's against department policy, but if you tell me his home town and worst habits I can probably help."

"Poitiers, red wine and dizzy bimbos equal first."

The chuckle was followed by Bruno's cell phone number.

A female voice answered his second call. "Hi, Bruno's phone, Julia speaking." The call had the echo and buzz of a familiar outback connection.

"Dave Lang here. I'm a friend of Bruno's from way back. I'm in Melbourne and hoping to catch up with him."

Julia repeated the name, and Dave could hear Bruno's voice cut in and out over the roar of an engine.

"Tell him... make himself at home... next door Mrs...parking...code for ..."

Julia repeated the directions, filling in the gaps, and the line went dead.

———

It took Dave over two hours to reach Little Collins. Dave eased the truck into the car park entrance, sandwiched between two up-market clothing shops. The security code took him three attempts before the door opened into the foyer and lifts.

On the second floor he found Mrs McLeod. Bruno's neighbour greeted him like an old friend. She had an air of elegance in spite of her ninety odd years.

"Come in, come in, I've just made a pot of tea. Bruno said he's known you for twenty years. That's lovely - not many of my old friends are left now. And please call me Anne - 'Mrs McLeod' makes me sound like an elderly school teacher!"

Dave looked around the room, filled with graceful wooden furniture, photographs packed the wall space. A tapestry with a boldly-stitched inscription caught his attention.

Dave read and re-read the words as he waited for Anne McLeod to return with the tea tray.

Next to the tapestry hung a black and white print. A strikingly tall, beautiful woman runner stood in the centre. At a glance, it was clear the group of male runners surrounding her were not comfortable with the female in their midst.

"That was about 1955, I was thirty-two. I loved running, but there were no women's distance races at the time. I used to sneak into the pack after the start. They tolerated it until I started to beat a few, then the ranks quickly closed. One man even dragged me down a bank in a cross-country race but I still beat the nasty little fellow. Mind you, the blunt end of a stick in the gonads does slow any man down a little. Another scone?"

Dave smiled, enjoying the conversation flow with this feisty woman. Sue would have loved her - the same irreverence and willingness to tackle things outside the boundaries. He momentarily lost the thread of Anne McLeod's conversation.

"Sorry, I missed that, Anne."

"Tai Chi dear, every Monday in the park, I really must fly. I'll get you the key."

71

Bruno's apartment made a stark contrast to that of his neighbour. The clean, uncluttered space had light streaming in from a large skylight. A scattering of canvas-board prints of classic Monet garden and Rembrandt haystack impressions broke the clean wall lines. Dark grey polished slate benches slashed the light wood tones of the kitchen/lounge area. One photo stood alone on a coffee table. Dave picked up the heavy oak frame. It held an image of the Thure cottage, four friends on the steps.

Dave recalled the day instantly. A Sunday, mid-May, sun starting to warm up for summer. They would shortly wander through the forest to the chateau next door for lunch. Bruno on the bottom step, pointing at Havane, the huge mastiff from next door. Havane had arrived as the "signale d'invitation" for Sunday lunch, usually lasting until a late afternoon swim in the cool pool. Only the tip of Havane's tail was visible, but Dave could remember him clearly.

Next Akeyo's eyes caught his attention, as they always had. That deep serene pool of a soul at peace. She had her hand on Dave's arm and he could feel it now. Simone stood on the other side of Dave, hand on his shoulder. One of the days when Simone had her guard down. Free from the social pressure of her pretentious circle of acquaintances. Dave still remembered her genuine warmth from such days. They balanced the haughty public snubs she occasionally iced him with. Simone, so complex, with a perpetually tortured soul, usually hidden behind elegance and well-practised grace.

On the bottom step sat Bruno, eyes alive with mischief and fun. He would have arrived home late from some party, but the eyes gave no hint of a hangover. His Sunday morning ritual was to make Simone laugh; once she laughed she relaxed for the day. Dave had admired the subtlety of Bruno's Sunday approach to Simone - always incredibly sensitive to her flashpoints and almost always successful. Dave treasured those relaxed Sundays with Simone and wished she could have seen through the trappings which consumed her most of the time. *I hope you have found peace my friend*, he thought. It had always surprised him that day on the platform in Poitiers. Simone's shaking silent sobs as she hugged him, public emotion so unexpected but touching. Her defiant mascara-streaked face held up as he waved from the window. There was a different Simone again in those last moments. "Je t'aime toujours, mon ami."

Dave held the photograph for a few moments longer, eyes glazed with fond memories.

———

The clink of bottles outside the door announced Bruno's arrival. Dave leapt from the couch to reach the door. Bruno slipped the kit bag from his shoulder and stepped over the cluster of plastic bags at his feet. He hugged Dave warmly. "Tonight I cook Lapin au Moutard, we drink red wine, but first I have about a centimetre of red dust to scrape from my body."

Steam billowed from under the bathroom door as Dave ferried the shopping bags to the slate benchtop. He couldn't resist looking inside the bag that clinked. "Mon dieu! Mon Lapin – where on earth did you find that in Melbourne?" he yelled.

Bruno poked his head out from the bathroom in a waft of steam. "Pardon?"

Dave repeated the question. Bruno grinned, touched his nose and retreated back to the steam. Dave had discovered Mon Lapin in the Chatellerault market, a cheap local wine. It had become their Sunday lunch tradition. Bruno and Simone would feint elaborate disdain, then promptly down their first glass. Simone would screw up her face and ask in her best Australian accent, "Urine de kangaroo?" It was so un-Simone the group never failed to chuckle.

74

Mon Lapin proved very palatable. They had left a small mountain of bottles in the woodshed as testament. Lapin au Moutard was a favourite of Dave's which Simone cooked on special occasions, so Bruno had expertly set the scene for a night of warm reminiscence. Bruno began turning his immaculate kitchen into a chaotic mess of used instruments, bowls and rabbit bones.

"Before you ask, the rabbit is road kill from the bull bars of the four-wheel drive."

"Mon Lapin can sanitise anything - Simone can vouch for that."

"The look on his face will be with me forever."

It had been late in the afternoon after Sunday lunch. Jean-Pierre, a prim elegant little man, a pretender in Simone's mother's circle of old-world nobility, had arrived unexpectedly at the chateau. The group were on Mon Lapin bottle number three. Simone wore an old work shirt of Dave's and equally old jeans cut off at the knees.

Jean-Pierre greeted both their hosts formally and acknowledged a neighbouring family also at the table, but had pointedly ignored the four flatmates. He had urgent changes to plans for a wedding to be held at the chateau which he wished to discuss with their host, Jean. He immediately butted in with the unwelcome discussion, oblivious to the impact on the group, his hand anchoring Jean's arm to the table.

Jean had stood up abruptly, brushing the hand aside. "Jean-Pierre, I wish to introduce you to some very good neighbours and friends of mine. You of course know Simone, Dave is from Australia, Akeyo is from Sudan and I think you also know Bruno."

Jean-Pierre nodded a token "Bonjour" and with suicidal stupidity had looked at Simone and said, "Your mother would be ashamed of your presentation. You need to dress to honour your family traditions."

Simone stood calmly, a deadly smile on her lips, Mon Lapin bottle in hand, "Jean-Pierre, have some wine." Jean-Pierre's other mistake on that day had been to wear a very expensive cream- coloured suit. The Mon Lapin streaks were artistically highlighted against the light colours, long streaks of comb-over hair dropping listless drops of Mon Lapin down the front of his face and onto his silk tie. Simone wasted an entire bottle of their day's supply.

Jean promptly sat down, choking back the laughter. "Au revoir Jean-Pierre. There are many other wedding venues in the valley."

The wine-streaked figure of Jean-Pierre had not reached the safety of his car before the laughter broke fully at the table.

The stories kept unfolding as the night progressed. Bruno's cooking proved excellent and the wine had the bonus of nostalgic reminder. Close to midnight a few moments' silence allowed Bruno to gently probe, "And how are you inside, Dave? What is it, fourteen months?"

"Sometimes fourteen months, sometimes yesterday, sometimes it never happened, then I wake with a fresh knife in my belly."

"Time, I guess. Remember what Akeyo used to say: 'Layers of time are like bandages; they hide the wound deeper and deeper. The wound is there forever but time allows good to come from the wound."

"We were young, silly twenty-year olds and she had the head of a philosopher. Perhaps the amount of living and number of wounds she already carried. I loved that woman."

"She had a special kind of peace. Any signs of daylight for you?"

Dave hesitated, "Well I did meet someone briefly on the way down. A hint that there may be life after, but still a little early yet."

"You have been lucky, Dave. Sue was special, but if there is even a hint of someone else, give it a shot. God knows I have wasted a lifetime of frivolous relationships, going nowhere, not caring I guess, not committing…" Julia was on Bruno's mind. They had kissed at the train station. Julia had said thank you almost formally, with no hint of what she thought about him or the weekend. The parting left him in limbo for the millionth time in his life. He didn't even have a phone number.

Unexpectedly, Bruno found himself saying, "Tomorrow night I would like you to meet someone. I trust you like no one else, and I need a second opinion. Favourite restaurant, good food, and hopefully good company (*if I can find her*)."

Dave welcomed the shift and offered to clean up the bomb site in the kitchen. It took another hour, by which time he could hear Bruno gently snoring.

———

Bruno left early, gently closing Dave's bedroom door so as not to disturb him. He altered his route to work, heading across the city to Julia's patisserie. He hoped the owner, Maria, would be there, as he knew the baking started early. He arrived at the alley slightly out of breath, so sat down under one of the umbrellas before knocking on the front door. There was no response but he could hear and smell the baking. He banged louder.

The third knock brought Maria to the door, arms white with flour, silicon-gloved hands on hips. "Have you got the drinks delivery?"

Dave knew his window was short; behind Maria on one of the tables he spotted a familiar pile of books. "No, but even better, I can make one of your staff very happy. Julia asked me to collect her books for her this morning."

Maria opened the door and Bruno reached for the books. How to ask for a phone number now was going to be difficult. Bruno flipped the cover of the top book "Cognitive Behaviour Therapy." Inside in neat italic hand writing was Julia's name and phone number. Luck was on his side today.

Bruno had almost reached the corner of the alley on Little Collins, when from behind he heard a voice.

"Stealing my books, are we? That's all the thanks I get for digging you out of the sand all weekend?"

"I didn't get your phone number. And I had to stop the investigation before it discovered my sordid past."

Julia grinned. "I had the same thoughts. Fourteen years of behavioural studies and I can't even get a phone number for the suspect."

"Time for a coffee?"

This morning something shifted. An ease and sense of relief. Julia started the conversation. "I'm sorry, I didn't really tell you how much I loved the trip. It was like a childhood dream come true. Real outback, I loved it. And…" she hesitated. "Well, I thought I would be fighting you off all weekend, but you were simply doing your thing. It was good to watch, and good fun. Donna and Pete were great people, and Donna had my back straight away. So, thanks, apart from the layers of dust in every bloody thing."

"The girls in Ivanhoe bar, I'm sorry for that. Old habits. And I totally misjudged you – thought you were someone arty, maybe into philosophy, something different. A psychologist? I don't think I have ever met a psychologist. I put you in the wrong box completely."

"Ex- psychologist. I'm doing a Masters in machine learning applied to psychology, study leave no pay, hence the waitress jobs."

They talked for over an hour, finishing with Bruno's invitation to dinner:

"I know it's a bit strange asking someone to meet a friend on a second date, but Dave's recently lost his wife, so I am not happy to leave him at home alone."

"Well I met your friend Busty on the last date, so Dave will be a welcome change." There was no hook in the comment so they both could laugh.

Julia's hand slid across the table and their fingers touched.

———

Dave came home from the dinner feeling a little uneasy. He wasn't sure exactly where his unease came from, more a gut instinct. He could see Bruno, alive and alight, plunging into infatuation. Julia had been intelligent and witty but there was an edge. A moment's look in her eyes when Bruno left the table, a shift, a slight pause when asked questions about her past. Maybe it was something of his old protective instinct, those days of worrying over Bruno madly in love with some society flitter-bug, all over a week later. Dave felt he had talked to the woman all night and got no closer to knowing the person behind the words.

When they parted ways, he said, "Take it slowly my friend. Time is on your side, let it mature like a good red."

Chapter Six – Ayr

Maddie fiddled with the papers in her hands. She had reworked the words perhaps a dozen times, and still the pages were scrawled with last minute ball-point. She felt Dave's hand on her arm. "Just look at me and talk to Grant," he whispered.

The undertaker introduced her. She gripped the lectern, looked at the sheaf of paper then lifted her eyes to the packed church. The tears came from her belly, the papers shook. She looked at Dave and folded the pages to blank squares.

"I have known Grant since he ran a course at my Year Nine school camp. He has been my inspiration, my mentor and my friend ever since. He and Mary gave me a purpose and a passion. He taught me everything he knew about bikes, how to set them up, how to tune them, how to fix them. He also taught me how to ride and get the best out of a bike. How to fix anything in the middle of a race."

"I spent hours in his shed at number thirty-four. Mum would arrive with a plate of scones to check up on us and Mary would do the same. The three of them became my number one support team, every race. I am just so grateful for that incredible support."

"Some of you know Grant had been a promising Super Bike rider on the Honda team until he nearly lost his leg in a crash. He then worked his way up to head the engineering team, but eventually the transient life on the race circuit lost its appeal. He and Joe founded a youth adventure camp which is where my connection started. I know Grant gained a great deal of satisfaction in shifting something in the lives of young people like me."

"Grant gave me my first bike, my best ever birthday present. When Mary died, I know Grant's worldly anchor had been slashed. My Mum and I also miss Mary deeply. "

"It was thanks to him that I won the State Championship. But the greater joy for me was seeing his eyes light up when I gave him the trophy. We both won. Grant I will love you always."

Just before she sat down, Maddie saw Brad at the back of the church. For the first time she felt nothing. She saw a person she had once been married to, an absent father to the boys. A ghost from the past.

Chapter Seven – Melbourne

Few people even glanced at the non-descript building lurking under the Westgate freeway behind South Bank. A square concrete box, the door an imperceptible dent in the side wall, accessed from a shaded alley. A stainless-steel hood guarded the keypad underneath. The woman approached the door and swiped her access card. A small foyer was briefly exposed before the door slid silently shut. The foyer had a reinforced glass window, manned by two suited security officers. The woman identified herself at the desk before proceeding through a metal detector to a wall rack of small lockers. She placed her cell phone in locker eighteen, locked the door and pocketed the key.

The next door had both a swipe card scanner and a thumb imprint detector. The identity card had to be swiped in less than eighteen seconds after the thumb print had been verified. The door opened. A flashing blue light announced her arrival and her security clearance. After thirty seconds the blue light stopped flashing. The room she entered had a number of partitioned work stations; each station had a curtain behind the occupant to protect casual views of their computer screens.

She sat down at a cubicle under the window darkened by screens preventing imprest radiation from her workstation from being monitored. She pulled out her notebook and began typing her weekly report. She had allowed forty minutes to enter the report before it would be transmitted up the hall to her controller and for her to follow fifteen minutes later for verbal briefing. She really had only one subject for the verbal, and that was not within the contents of her report.

She finished the report quickly, hardly needing to refer to her notebook. She had identified two important links in the network. The controller would be happy: he lived in the technical realm of intelligence, and these were significant links. In contrast the human side drove the woman. The tragedy averted, the innocent protected and the lives saved. In this job the distinction was not so clear. Her two years in the drug world had had their share of filthy villains, lost soul street kids, and life cheapened almost to insignificance with the greed. Only the possibility of one life being changed sustained her through the squalor of life in the underworld. In the new world of financial-crime she had become bored. It struck her in that moment - she really wanted her own life back.

Her controller excitedly pencilled the new links on a huge chart that filled one wall of his office. He didn't turn as she entered. He began his briefing still facing the chart. She sat on a chair and made a few notes. Then he paused, a gap she knew was her signal to leave the office. She cleared her throat. For the first time in five minutes, he turned to face her, irritated, "Yes?"

She made her request.

He looked back at the chart on the wall. "No, we must stick to strict protocol at this stage." She had been dismissed; she knew the man was not capable of rational compassion.

As she collected her cell phone from locker eighteen the older of the two security guards in the glass box called, "Your hat, ma'am."

Chapter Eight – Nairobi

Martin shifted uncomfortably on the couch which had been his bed for nearly a month. His torn and battered back pack served as his pillow. Today he had resolved to break his tie with the back-pack. Far too shabby a reminder of a past that deserved a better memorial.

Martin's old friend from the Ministry had insisted Martin stay with his family. They lived in a small fibro government bungalow on the verges of the suburb of Karen. Twenty or more identical houses tightly clustered in a small compound. The women kept the grounds as neat as they could, but plastic bags festooned the trees and security fence. A small play area in the centre also served as a soccer field. Youths were kicking a ball around this morning. The tall trees screened the settlement from some of the noise of the nearby road and market.

He sat up on the couch, picking up the backpack, and began idly searching through the pockets. The rear flap contained a small clear plastic bag with their passports.

Martin stared at the cover of Akeyo's passport for a long time before daring to open it. Her eyes caught him with a sharp stab in the chest. He sat until he could be at peace with the photograph; it wouldn't come. He turned slowly through the pages. The visas to countries, mostly for conferences, each one having a memory she would excitedly share with him on return. New possibilities, new hopes.

The last page opened, and two folded papers slipped to the floor between his legs. The first one he opened contained a photograph. He recognised the group instantly, although he had never met them. It was Akeyo's friends from university in France. The paper protecting the photo had email addresses for them all.

The second paper was yellowing and crumpled. A certificate of some kind, in French. He could not decipher anything other than the words "Societé Nationale d'Insurance." A second slip of new crisp paper was enclosed inside the first, again in French. It was dated only a few months ago, and acknowledged a payment of fifty euros. The figure of two hundred and fifty-four thousand Euros caught his attention. A fortune. What was this secret of Akeyo's?

Martin fought the rising excitement. His pension and payments outstanding had taken months to process. He had been living poor, relying on friends and a small emergency payment his head of department had managed to extract from the system. He washed and left the house before his host family stirred for their normal noisy weekday ritual. The matatu into the city filled with the tinny beat of rap music. Bodies pressed tightly on the torn bench seats. He arrived in the city at seven thirty am, far too early to find or talk to anyone. He found a street stall and sat down on a red plastic chair to eat some breakfast.

He slowed down, beginning to process the possibility. It needed to be handled with care by people he could trust. Someone with the knowledge to firstly confirm, then help him in the process. But who? Martin flicked through the hundred or so names on his mobile phone. Nobody.

Then he recalled the visas from Akeyo's passport for Ghana. He had spent a week at the Ghanaian Consulate trying to get that visa. He had been saved by the Vice-Consul, a rotund, cheerful woman who had seemingly no patience with the endless corrupt demands of her staff. She had only recently been appointed and Martin had been able to connect her to some key officials. He had met her many times since and they had established a mutual respect. Two rare straight dealers in a world of corruption. Akeyo had been a little more cynical, suggesting the Consul's principles may have wavered without the wealth of her husband's mining interests. Today, Martin took comfort in his belief that his friend would not be overawed or swayed by the possible wealth in the slip of paper in his hands.

———

Martin left the Ghanaian Consulate in a daze. His friend the Vice-Consul had unravelled Akeyo's secret provision in a rapid series of phone calls. Yes, the life insurance policy had been quietly accumulating since her university days. Yes, the value was payable to her immediate family in the event of death. Yes, the current value was over two hundred and fifty thousand euros. The only catch required that proof of identity, along with all the other documentation, needed to be presented by the claimant in person at any branch of Societé Nationale d'Insurance. Nearest branch, Marseilles.

His friend had hugged him close, and spoken with genuine feeling as she saw the magnitude of the windfall glazing Martin's eyes, "You see, my dear friend, your loved ones have reached out even after death to give you a great gift."

———

Martin spent the rest of the week chasing his back payments and pension from the Ministry. Once he had seen the deposit into his bank account, he submitted his final resignation. His total payment from thirty-two years' service came to less than two thousand US dollars.

He gave his friend and his family a generous two hundred US dollars for his month on the lumpy couch. He bought a small airline carry on suitcase, and transferred his life's possessions from the tattered back-pack. He made his way to a small market internet stall, pulled out the first slip of paper from Akeyo's passport and started an email using Akeyo's email account:

My Dear Friends,

I call you friends although we have never met. You were always in the heart of my beloved wife, Akeyo. I know she loved you and thought of you often.

It is with great sadness that I now have to tell you she is no longer with us. She died with our beautiful daughter in the desert. She was a victim of the violent unrest we suffer from time to time in our country. She died peacefully in a place of great beauty.

You will be always welcome in my life, should our paths ever cross. I know that would be the wish of my beloved wife.

I comfort you in the sorrow I know you will feel.

With great love from Akeyo.

Martin

He re-read the email several times before eventually pressing the send button. He then started a second email:

Dear Simone,

Following my last email, I have one request for help. Dear Akeyo (unbeknown to me) had been saving money in a French Life Insurance scheme for our family's future. In order to make this claim I am required to travel to France, and I am greatly in need of some French-speaking assistance.

I have attached a file containing both Akeyo's and my own passport photo (to assure you that you are in fact dealing with old friends).

If you are able to assist me with this, I would be deeply indebted.

Kindest and warm regards

Martin

———

Few passengers boarded the matatu Martin took from the market. He relaxed in the rare space of the entire back seat as the matatu bounced and rattled through the potholes towards the guesthouse. He had often stayed at the government guesthouse, which he always found clean and quiet. He had booked there for a week. The housekeeper welcomed him with friendly familiarity and led him to a large room at the rear of the complex. Martin laid back on the clean bed and closed his eyes.

Sleep arrived surreptitiously; there were misty figures in a hot desert haze. The old man leading his donkey, dissolving into the sun. Pools of water shimmering, always slightly beyond reach. A scarf fluttering on a thorn bush. A voice, faint, so faint, then gone. Consciousness fought to the surface, trying to escape the sound that would come next. The baby's cry, the soul lost before her life had begun, merged with a wail from the old women from his childhood village. A toothless, endless monotone churning into a spiralling dust storm, sucking life up from the desert floor.

———

Simone's four-page email arrived next morning. It took Martin nearly an hour to digest it. It shifted from deeply emotional in one sentence to a rambling memory in the next. Martin sensed the love from raw outpouring in the composition. Simone had composed herself for the last paragraph:

My dear Martin, excuse me, my own emotion is less important. I must feel also for you. Your loss is the greatest. You are not alone in the world with this. Akeyo was a dear friend who touched me in a way no other person has ever done. She knew me deeply beyond my outward personality. So, for you, anything I can help with at any time, I can do. Simply send details of your flight. I live close outside Paris and can meet you at Charles de Gaulle Airport within one hour. My mobile number is below.

With love and great sadness at your loss which I share in my heart.

Simone

———

Within another hour Martin had booked his flights and responded to Simone with the details. Now something shifted in him, a feeling entirely new: the possibility of a future beyond ghosts.

Chapter Nine – Ayr

My daughter, so elegant and professional, that red blouse flashing defiance. Maureen Jacobs pulled her battered Toyota to the kerb outside the workshop. Through the glass doors she watched her daughter for perhaps five minutes.

Maureen's thoughts were racing. She remembered the time Maddie had been invited to join an outback endurance race to Cape York. The boys were tiny, perhaps two and four. Maddie thrilled at the prospect but Brad said no, flatly and curtly, in his view Maddie's sole role was as mother.

Maureen had watched the shift in Maddie's eyes. She almost cheered aloud. It was child becoming a woman in an instant.

Now it was nearly eight years later, and Maddie was Manager of the largest workshop in town. *Her dear father would be proud*, thought Maureen.

———

Maddie looked up at her mother's car for the third time. *Mum has been sitting there for an age*, she thought. The outside heat hit her as she left the air-conditioned office.

"You alright Mum?" she asked anxiously as she arrived at the car door.

"You have to do it love. It's a once in a lifetime opportunity. The boys can take the school holidays with their father, and I can deal with the rest."

"But Tom - I only started the new job last month…"

"Tom's already your number one sponsor. I talked to him last night."

The invitation had been sitting on the kitchen table for nearly a month. It had gone from the impossible dream to a real possibility. An enduro race the length of Africa, Cairo to Cape Town. It seemed exotic, dangerous and incredibly exciting. Two months of hell on wheels, ten countries, the whole of Africa. Independent Broadcasting (IBC) wanted a woman rider, and she was one of the best.

———

Maureen added gently, "Do it for Grant and Mary."

Maddie looked at her mother, eyes brimming with tears. "Shit."

Excitement overtook fear and Maddie sprang into action. First, she hit the team in the workshop. She swept into their afternoon tea room. "I'm going to race a dirt bike across Africa. What the hell do I need to keep a bike going for twelve thousand kilometres of the toughest territory on earth?"

The boys were filled with excitement and arguments, firing lists of 'must haves' and 'must dos'.

"Shocks - you are going to kill heaps of shocks. I read Ewen McGregor's book about his ride - he blew shocks all the way up."

"No – tyres: tyres are the key. You are going to have every kind of surface from sand to rock - even the tarmac is chewed up."

"Fuel filter system, you are going to have all sorts of crap fuel supplies."

Afternoon tea drifted into late afternoon. Maddie's list quickly grew to two A4 pages long.

———

The next three weeks blurred for Maddie. Her spreadsheet list grew daily. She emailed her acceptance to IBC, and immediately received a deluge of paperwork and contracts.

Her lawyer friend Sue took all the paperwork. "You worry about the important things, Mads. I will tell you if there are any hooks in this lot."

Her other friend Trish, a nurse, took on the vaccination list. "Don't worry Babe, it's nearly every travel vaccination there is. We'll start tomorrow with the hep twinrix, that has the longest lead time. You'll be a pin cushion by the time I have finished."

The IBC film team arrived in Ayr to film a pre-race interview. The clutter of microphones and cameras crowded the reception area of the workshop. The mechanics made lots of trips to the counter to check on client details. Maddie got lots of digs and encouragement: "Her best side is her backside."

Tom arrived, squeezed into his best suit, sweating profusely, looking for a prominent position on the side of the test shot. "We are also a major sponsor, and provider of all the mechanical support for setting up the bike," he loudly informed the producer.

"Let's get a sound-bite of that."

Tom beamed.

Maddie immediately connected with her interviewer, Rachel Steenkamp. Something appealed with her slim lively appearance and her direct no-nonsense manner. She introduced herself to Maddie with a slight South African accent:

"I grew up in Zimbabwe, my parents lost their farm, they moved here when I was ten. I am going to go with you the whole way, along with a couple of cameramen and a sound person. I'm really looking forward to working with you."

Rachel expertly and gently prepared Maddie for the interview. "Ignore the camera, chat to me."

Maddie's excitement and passion for racing bubbled out naturally during the interview. The producer did have to make surreptitious wrap-up signals to Rachel during a long technical discourse on the bike preparation. The workshop crew broke into applause at the end.

———

The phone in Maddie's house rang at eight thirty. Nine-year old Peter ran to the phone. "Mummy, it's that man again."

Dave had been idly channel-surfing on Bruno's huge flat screen TV, and noticed a familiar building flash onto IBC news; then there was Maddie, eyes alive and talking excitedly to the screen.

"What a great interview! That sounds incredibly exciting."

They talked for over an hour. Maddie talked; Dave listened. He felt a strange sense of wonder; he felt her strength and determination in spite of her few moments of nervous terror. "You are an inspiration."

It struck Dave then, that he wanted to be part of this inspiration.

Chapter Ten – Cairo

Maddie stared out the hotel window. Fear knotted in her belly. The fourteen-hour flight into Dubai had been the longest she had every flown, but the crazy pace of Cairo had totally freaked her. Traffic chaos and Arabic curses, donkey carts vying with buses. The prospect of getting on her bike on these streets terrified her. Worst of all, she already missed the routine of home and the lesser chaos of the two boys. The IBC crew had their flight delayed, so for now she was the lone member of her team.

Although the room was large and comfortable she had reservations about sharing with Rachel Steenkamp, a virtual stranger. She re-read the filming schedule Rachel had emailed. It would hamper her usual race routines. *At least Wrighty from the Ayr workshop is one familiar face.* But even he would not arrive until at least the next day.

Maddie wandered down to the restaurant. The wall clock signalled late afternoon but her body clock was telling her breakfast was due. The first table in the restaurant had a huddle of crisp white and blue uniforms of the German BMW crew. Maddie had spent her hours on the plane researching every rider and recognised Ralf Hettingen, winner of the Paris-Dakar on two occasions. The team huddled around the table, deeply engrossed in conversation and no one looked up. Maddie picked her way along the buffet line. On reaching the end she looked at her choices; the appetite had gone. She sat down at a table by the window.

As she sat, Ralf Hettingen stood and made his way to the water cooler beside her table, and caught her eye.

"You are with the race?" The German accent was only slight.

"Yes, the IBC team from Australia."

"You are crew?"

"No, I am their rider."

"This race will be hard for women."

"I think it will be about the same for everyone." Maddie felt the edge in her voice, and shut down the conversation by starting her food. She glared at the retreating white shirt.

———

Maddie woke early. Alert and eager. She spent an hour with maps and GPS working out her route from the start.

She had to tackle the Cairo roads and put her fear to rest, or at least in proportion. She intended riding the route until clear of the city, then re-ride until she memorised every turn. Fuel for the bikes had been left in drums in front of the hotel. The drums were guarded by a large man in a grey uniform. He lounged on the first drum smoking a drooping cigarette with matching moustache. His machine gun barrel dangled, pointing at the danger sign on the drum. Maddie grinned.

She quickly fuelled the bike. She noticed a few teams emerging from the hotel, including the pristine white and blues of the BMW team. The bike started first kick. Maddie spent a couple of minutes setting her GPS. She had fashioned a velcro cushion on top of her tank. Today it had the GPS and her boldly penned route notes, sheathed in a plastic cover. She felt ready.

The bike revs surged, perfectly weighted to lift the front wheel. Maddie expertly and gracefully rode the length of the hotel entrance on her rear wheel, and with a subtle shift of balance merged into the chaotic stream of Giza traffic between a large old truck and a donkey cart.

Ralf Hettingen grunted to the mechanic beside him, "Anyone can ride cheap tricks." But somewhere inside it registered that he couldn't have ridden with the same level of control himself.

In the traffic Maddie felt the familiarity of the bike, and her fear dissipated with the challenge of quick manoeuvres through the brief gaps. The route followed a wide boulevard, a median strip of palm trees separating the traffic flow. Above the buildings on the left, glimpses of the tops of the Pyramids, pink in the dawn light. The excitement hit the pit of her belly. The sense of history thrilled her.

She saw the entrance to the Pyramids on the opposite side of the road, but it took a few hundred metres before she could get across to the middle lane. She lifted the front wheel onto the median strip, feeling the wheels slew in the sandy surface as she laid a U turn. It took the same few hundred metres to slalom back through the traffic, leaving a small window of time to make the turning.

The road climbed steeply to two large parking terraces, fronted by a block row of office buildings. The gate to the Pyramids appeared on the left, cluttered with camels and their handlers waiting to ply their daily tourist trade.

Maddie paused in the car park on the top terrace. She took off her helmet.

A tall, well-dressed man appeared at her side, twirling the end of an impressive moustache. "You must be Madeline Jacobs, rider for the IBC team in the Africa Odyssey Race – welcome to the Pyramids of Giza."

Maddie was impressed. "Thank you, yes. I am hoping to check out the start."

"Of course, preparation is key. Follow me."

The tall figure swept into the crowd at the gate, creating a swathe through the camels and touts. A brief word at the gate house, and the guard directed Maddie through with a sweeping arm gesture. Maddie rode slowly, cautious of the stream of camels making their way to their daily trade.

She rode past the east wall of one of the Pyramids a few metres on her left. Maddie stopped the bike, and looked up, each giant block crisply outlined in the morning sun, sky still pink above. She felt a shiver and a brief sob. This was special. The phone message with the photo to her mother simply said:

"Can't believe where I am, love to the boys".

The access road curved around an arch to the right, then ended at a wide parking area with a sweeping view of the three Pyramids. A flock of pigeons swept low over the dunes. Maddie sat on the bike and drank in the atmosphere. This is where the race would start in three short days.

———

Maddie rode the route out into the eastern desert four times. By the third trip she recognised buildings or mosques at key intersections. On the fourth ride she headed further out into the desert, opening the bike up, revelling in the blast. By the time she arrived back at the hotel she had covered over three hundred kilometres. She felt relieved that the Cairo traffic no longer held the dreaded fear in the pit of her stomach. The cool water of the shower felt good; Maddie felt both at peace and in control.

———

Dave received her text late in his Melbourne night.

"Can't believe I am here in this story-book history. Felt really emotional under the Pyramids today, wished I could have shared it with you. Traffic is not so bad once you are amongst it, so that is a relief. Feeling ready and excited. With Love Mads."

107

———

Rachel Steenkamp swept into the hotel room in the middle of the afternoon. Maddie was impressed with her two small back-packs. She travelled light. They hugged with a warm familiarity.

"Sweetheart, I need your passport for the Sudanese Embassy. We have a car waiting." Passport in hand, she walked out the door.

The rest of the IBC team drifted into Maddie's room. Steven Wright arrived first, and immediately he asked, "How's the bike going?"

Maddie looked at the two cameramen. Steven Reid still retained his Kiwi vowel inflections despite twenty-five years' residence in Australia. The voice drawled softly,

"Hi, I am the other better-looking Steve."

Richard Wills didn't introduce himself. He mumbled in a distinctly English public-school accent to no-one in particular:

"The damn hostess has ruined these trousers. How someone so clumsy can get a job as an air hostess is beyond me. What a hell hole this is, so bloody hot and the

108

traffic! Never have I seen such a disorganised shambles, why do they even bother to have lanes marked?" Both Stevens rolled their eyes.

The sound tech Nat Papadopoulis bounced into the hotel suite.

"Anyone for a beer?" Without waiting for an answer he dropped his bag and headed straight back out.

Steven Reid sighed, "It's the Greek genes, he is impossible to stop, the original energiser bunny."

Nat arrived back shortly carrying cans of Australian beer for the group. They were on their third can of beer by the time Rachel arrived back from the Sudanese Embassy. Rachel introduced Abdul, their local fixer, driver, mechanic and the final member of the team. Abdul spoke fluent English, Arabic, Ampharic and several other African languages. He described himself as a tolerant Muslim and immediately opened a can of beer with an exaggerated wink at the group.

"Before you all get too pissed – we need to take a quick shot of our leading lady and her pre-race thoughts," Rachel announced.

"I just got off twenty-six hours of plane flights," grumbled Richard.

"No worries, I'll get this one," and Steven strode off to get his camera, closely followed by Nat.

"Imagine yourself talking with your Mum. Simply tell her what it feels like today," Rachel advised Maddie as the guys arrived back with their equipment.

Maddie felt relaxed and happy with her day's preparation.

"I was scared, really scared of the Cairo traffic," Maddie started. She caught Abdul's dark smiling eyes, and he nodded enthusiastically. Maddie started talking directly to him:

"But actually, getting out there today on the bike felt great. You have to be more alert and react to grab the gaps, but I had fun. The Pyramids caught me by surprise, the emotion choked me a little. I'm not sure what it was. The size, the history, being there beside them…it really choked me. It felt sort of like a living dream, me here. I think checking out the route was good therapy - it is good to know where I will be heading, where to turn, what it looks like. It was really only me and the bike, same old feeling, different, incredibly different place…."

Abdul clapped. Rachel smiled with a thumbs-up. "OK guys that's great. Time for a girl shower before dinner, breakfast, whatever it is."

———

Over the next two days, while Rachel led a preparation whirlwind, Maddie and Steven Wright were left to their own devices. Meticulous bike preparation, checks and rechecks, long rides out to check and re-check the route. A few of the other riders began to become familiar: Kim from Denmark, Nikki from Japan, Henry from Holland and Dennis from Germany. The factory team riders remained largely aloof and apart, always buried in deep technical discussions with their large support crews. "Steven Wright" became morphed to "Righty Ho", a distinction from cameraman Steve and acknowledgment of his own most over-used expression.

Race day dawned on Maddie's bedside clock: three-fifty-three am. By four am she had finished her shower and began quietly laying out her race kit. The pit of her belly was knotted. From the next room Rachel sleepily asked what the time was.

———

Beautiful pink sky. More donkeys this morning. That little girl looks familiar - I'm sure she was on the back of the same cart yesterday. Such dark eyes. The Pyramids again, what are they - three thousand, four thousand years old? That must be the back of one the sphinxs against the city lights. Huge city. So much noise so early. Lots of cars in the carpark today. Satellite dishes, from all around the world. Big flash start banner. Bikes, that noise, a few two strokes, love that rattle. Nikki there, helmet off, bit late for adjustments now, mate.

Officials, lines of them. Big men, big moustaches. Big black cars. BMW white looks good so far, wait for the dust, not a good colour guys. Try Uluru red. Wonder if Dave is awake. Where's Rachel? I can't see the truck. What do I say? I feel good, the bike feels good, but now doesn't count, it's one thousand ks out when it matters. Two thousand, ten thousand. Shit, it's a long way. Speeches. Minister of Tourism or was he the Mayor? Let's hit the road. Could do with a pee, nowhere. Rachel, really don't want to talk. More speeches. Find a spot on the outside of the start. What's the start protocol, a single gun? Wave to the camera for Rachel. Bloody Ralf Hettingen bully, bulldozing in front of little Nikki. Arrogant bastard.

What was that? Shit! Start your engines. Here we go, girl.

The gun blast lifted a flock of birds from the desert dunes as the bike noise rose to a crescendo. Ahead, blue lights of

Police bikes flashed a pathway. Ralf Hettingen started with a flashy loose wheelie, putting a few metres in front of the pack, then he was quickly swallowed again. Elbows touched in the pack.

Cairo Police had cleared the lane on the street, save for the odd insistent taxi and a stream of donkey carts. Beyond the first intersection the road closure lost the battle against the streams of traffic. By the third intersection a few riders were already on the wrong roads. Maddie slipped down a gear and eased into a gap between a bus and truck, gunning to the outside of the lane. She anticipated opportunities to weave and dodge. Big grey mosque coming up, hang a right here. She became aware of someone on her wheel, a glance in the mirror showed the distinct white and blue BMW colours. Word had spread of her meticulous preparation, and Ralf was taking advantage.

Maddie kept her line until the last moment, then with a weight shift and burst of power she slipped between two large trucks. The simultaneous horn blasts rattled both riders, but Ralf was left stranded outside the trucks, while Maddie started invisibly creeping ahead inside the big traffic. She looked behind as she made a turn at the next intersection and grinned as she saw a flash of blue and white miss the turn.

Long race, she thought, and eased back into a graceful weave out towards the great Sahara, relaxed enough to return the enthusiastic waves from children on the roadside. Smaller and smaller settlements dotted the landscape as the sand rolled in with limitless horizon. Maddie let out a yell of joy, grateful in afterthought for her earpieces inside the helmet.

Maddie glanced in her mirror. Perhaps a kilometre behind, a white van sped up the centre of the road. She checked her speedo – it showed one hundred and thirty kilometres per hour, and the van was catching fast. She felt the pressure wave as the van reached her and pulled alongside, the beaming face of Abdul at the wheel. How on earth had he managed that? As if anticipating her question Abdul raised a finger skyward. Allah had been kind.

Both Stevens and Rachel were in the van, with Steven's camera out an open rear window. Rachel held up four fingers - presumably she was fourth on the road. Maddie waved as they passed and the camera trailed her for a few minutes down the road until she floated above the road in the heat haze.

The blue flashing Police lights warned of the checkpoint, a cluster of vehicles, donkeys, onlookers and a race banner. Kim the Danish rider pulled out with a wave as Maddie pulled in. "Righty Ho" Steve had started lowering tyre pressure on the bike. Abdul engaged in an animated discussion with one of the Police Officers. He returned with the story. One of the leading riders had paid the race officials to turn a blind eye as he continued down the highway, bypassing four hundred kilometres of tough off-road sand.

"It's just not cricket," said Abdul in his clipped English accent. " Bastard!" said both Steves in unison.

Maddie began eating the sandwiches Rachel handed her. As she ate, Rachel began replenishing her water supply. Maddie turned her attention to the deep tyre tracks leading off from the highway. Soft, soft sand.

———

The birds above the desert soared in disjointed flight; they were swallowed in heat haze, then reappeared again.

Chapter Eleven – Sudan

Maddie sprawled, exhausted, on the back seat of the truck. She awoke, still drowsy when they stopped at the Sudan border. Within minutes she restarted the bike. Stretched ahead, the shimmering space of the vast desert. Great emptiness. A brief stop, and a small boy and his donkey appeared from nowhere. The sand flew beneath her wheels, she was grinning. In her element.

———

On the Sudan map a heavy black line extended from Wadi Halfir and curled out west into the desert, then joined the twisting path of the Nile at Dongola. Dave traced the line with his finger; he said the name – "Dongola" – and wondered what Maddie was doing in that strange town on the Nile. Resting a little, he hoped.

The phone call had been surprisingly clear. Maddie's voice sounded buoyed.

"I made it through most of the lead riders today. Second place! Still about two and a half hours behind the BMW team. You remember the Korean rider disqualified on the first day? Well his GPS track clearly showed him missing the compulsory off-road section; he had also been seen in Bahariya Oasis – way off track. He arrived at Abu Minqar check point an impossible four hours ahead of other riders and still had the cheek to say his GPS transponder was faulty. Bloody little cheat!"

Dave laughed.

———

The following day at Abu Simbel, Maddie arrived at the hotel check point. Across the courtyard the Korean rider staggered drunkenly. A half-empty bottle of whisky was raised to his lips. He wiped his mouth then swore loudly. The diminutive Korean team boss appeared from a doorway. She marched directly up to him and stood hands on hips confronting him. He swung the whisky bottle at her. Maddie stared incredulously as the team boss leapt horizontally towards him, legs scissoring. One heel had crunched sickeningly under the patella of his right leg as the other boot simultaneously hit the back of the same knee. He squealed and hit the ground clutching his knee. The boss pointed to the car and he began a painful crawl towards it. Drunken bravado completely obliterated. His race was over.

The next morning Maddie noticed a different figure on the Korean team bike. *Gutsy lady* - Maddie's highest accolade.

The race followed old camel train tracks, sometimes right on the banks of the Nile, sometimes wending far inland, with nothing but sand and sky. The sand gradually worked its way into every component of the bike. Into bearings, into chain links, into filters and intakes. Steve worked tirelessly on the bike from the instant Maddie stopped for a break. Together they had worked out a routine of maintenance which kept the bike running. The factory teams were swapping out engines and components daily. Mechanics swearing in the backs of bouncing vehicles as they tried to work on components.

Maddie had also taken to drinking Coke. She caught herself choking on the first can, remembering her schoolmistress-like lesson to the boys, carefully measuring out the sugar content from the container on the kitchen bench.

"That's how much sugar is in every can, so what's that going to do to your teeth and bodies?" she had scolded.

The ramshackle stores along the way offered no other safe drinking choice. The desert riding also created a clear space in her head. She reflected on her life and she looked ahead. She longed for conversation with Dave. How had they grown so close so fast and with so little? She searched for the answers. He listened with respect. *Oh, how different from Brad.*

———

In Dongola she had broken the ice with Rachel. After their daily interview they had wandered down to the market. Rachel surprised Maddie with a smattering of Arabic in a small café. Soon Rachel started telling Maddie's race story to the owner and a small gathering outside the open entrance. There were smiles and thumbs up from the small boys at the front.

Sudan felt so different from Egypt. Here, shopkeepers meticulously counted back the correct change. Egypt's inflated prices had grated with her rules of fairness. Here in Sudan, she got the sense of being somewhere different and enjoying the experience beyond the routine on the bike.

The shop keeper had called as they left: "We have more pyramids than Egypt – you must come back to see us longer next time!"

"That's true," Rachel had said. "They are still uncovering more on the outskirts of town."

Dave had listened patiently as she had rattled through her morning. When she had finished, he quietly said,

"Send me a photo, I really want to see you as you are today."

———

The stop in Dongola lasted eleven hours in total. The race gap had extended out. Steve had stripped the bike and replaced the drive chain. It gleamed in the small hotel courtyard. Steve rolled back in the dust, grease-splattered and exhausted.

"I want you to keep it clean this time."

"Sure boss."

The other truck had long departed to start the leapfrog to the next checkpoint ahead of Maddie's unrelenting pace.

———

Dave sat for a long time staring at the map, thinking of Maddie. He had flown back to Townsville and spent weekends with her, meeting her mother Maureen. Those were relaxed weekends – beach walks and bike ride picnics, talking and laughing. On the last trip Maddie finally introduced him to her two boys, Peter and David. Peter had assumed the big brother protective nine-year-old huff, eyes saying more than his words, but Maddie had snapped at him for a couple of mumbled nasties.

Younger David appeared very like Maddie both in looks and personality. Dave sat down beside him with his new electrical circuit set. Dave used his bush wiring skills and the pair quickly emptied the box. Within an hour they had built a circuit that flashed and buzzed. Just as quickly, their creation burnt out the batteries.

On the way to the shop to buy replacements, David had asked,

"You will be careful with my mum?" With the serious stuff confirmed, David could concentrate on coercing Dave into adding an ice cream to the shopping list.

Maureen Jacobs had approached Dave with rapid fire questioning, unafraid even of some of the areas Maddie had hesitated probing. It was an unexpected question about Sue that changed their relationship. Sitting at the breakfast table, Dave was simply unable to answer. He turned to the window to hide the tears. Maureen had instantly stood and hugged him from behind the chair, and she whispered, "Sorry, Dave – still too early for that one".

Maureen quickly changed tack. "When I get to the pearly gates, there will be so many bods waiting to clobber me, St Peter won't even need a casting vote. I will need to pack plenty of gin to breathe fire into the flames." Dave laughed and the tension eased.

———

The chime from his phone broke Dave's reverie. Maddie's picture had arrived. A scarf draped around her shoulders held her hair off her face. Her smile held his eyes. He could see all the excitement and wonder he had heard on their call.

Africa had held a fascination for Dave since boyhood. The yellowing National Geographic magazines in his grandfather's book shelf were filled with exotic pictures. Plains impossibly crowded with wildlife, acacia tree sunsets, lions stalking prey, hippos wallowing and tall Masai tribesmen holding sheaths of thin spears. Maddie's Dongola presented a different Africa again. He flipped open his laptop and Googled 'Dongola'.

The shop keeper was correct - more pyramids than Egypt. Safari suit-clad archaeologists digging around a field of small triangles, tips of pyramids buried by thousands of years of sand shift. Dave flicked through the images and blogs of travellers: long flowing robes, chickens strung up above charcoal roasts, minarets, donkey carts laden high. There, surely - the animal-less zoo across the road from Maddie's hotel, bright painted fences and green grass. The Nile snaking under ancient bridges, neat square mud-brick houses painted in pastel shades.

Dave had been drifting around the Google labyrinth for nearly an hour when Bruno arrived home. He dumped his usual supply of food market bags on the kitchen bench with an exasperated sigh. "Women! I thought I found something special with this one. But always too busy, too much study, no time for romance. Mon dieu!"

"I gather you have seen Julia again?"

"Seen yes, but she tries hard to not be seen."

"Pour us some of your special medicine, and I will show you where Maddie is today."

By the time Bruno sat down beside Dave to look at the race- tracking web page, the small blue dot labelled '**M Jacobs (IBC)**' had started to move.

———

The road out of Dongola followed the Nile. Traffic clogged the road. Large trucks travelling eighty kilometres an hour scraping past donkey carts and tractors crawling alongside. Maddie felt refreshed and the bike sounded better after Steve's meticulous attention. She tried to push the pace, but the road narrowed. The gaps between the slow-moving carts and the trucks were too small to risk. She sat in convoy mode behind a lorry with a massive load of sugar cane.

The route would eventually arch out through off-road country to bypass the capital Khartoum. Rachel and the second vehicle needed to head into Khartoum to send some footage home and collect some supplies. For over nine hundred kilometres Maddie would be on her own. She hoped the first truck would be able to make its way through to the checkpoint ahead of her.

"Only worry about the things you can change", Rachel had constantly reminded her. "Focus on hauling in the race leaders."

A small rise in the road showed the narrow green belt of the Nile ending abruptly to her right. Swallowed in the desert. Traffic had thinned a little, and she had started a rhythm of overtaking the lumbering lorries. The mid-morning call to prayer abruptly eased the traffic, truck drivers jumping down from their cabs, prayer mats under their arms. Maddie could increase the pace.

Ahead loomed another compulsory off-road section, joining the road to Khartoum about one hundred kilometres after leaving the green pathway of the Nile. Maddie was looking forward to the peace of the desert and a respite from the concentration required on the road. Immediately before the checkpoint, Maddie spotted the bright signage of a roadside bar. She pulled the bike into the car park alongside a battered Toyota. A distinguished-looking man in immaculate white robe smiled and nodded. He was drinking mint tea. Maddie caught the aroma as she passed.

Maddie sat down at the table next to the Sudanese gentleman. Her own mint tea arrived soon after. She had also ordered some food. "Chicken," she had asked for, after a few pantomime gestures. A number of dishes began arriving at her table including chicken, rice, vegetable pickles and a spicy bread dip.

The man at the next table introduced himself and asked Maddie where she was heading.

"Cape Town," she answered. "I am riding in an international motor bike race."

"So far," he responded. He was on his way from Khartoum to his village for a funeral. "I trained in the UK, as a surveyor." He continued in impeccable English, "I currently work in the oil industry. Oil is a vital industry in Sudan. We have large oil reserves, especially in the south. In spite of the way the world sees us, northern Sudan is the most peaceful country in the world."

Maddie had to agree with that. She finished her meal and excused herself.

"Peace be with you and safe travels."

She glanced at the time as she reached the bike. She had taken thirty minutes out of the race schedule, but gained a bright little snippet of Sudan in her memory. A short distance down the road, Maddie spotted the flags for the off-road checkpoint. The cultivated strip extending from the Nile dwindled to harsh rocky and stony desert. Quickly she got into her stride, absorbed in concentration on lines and speed. This was her zone. She felt content and enriched from the brief lunch encounter.

The horizon stretched to infinity, the space gave a wild sense of freedom.

———

Dave and Bruno had opened a second bottle of wine by the time the blue dot started veering right away from the Nile. The conversation had grown reflective and meandering.

"I would love to see Africa," Dave began. "I started looking at the place Maddie stopped last night. Dongola. On the Nile. I've never heard of it before. More pyramids than Egypt, and they are still uncovering them from the sand. Real sense of mystery and adventure. I think Africa is one of the few real adventurous continents left to travel. No same-old same-old Hilton to Hilton bus trip."

"We must do it my friend. We will drag Pete along. He has never been out of Australia. Get a truck and explore."

The plans developed into an untidy pile of wild ideas as the level on the second bottle of red wine dropped.

"We could also make the reunion, the Famous Thure Cottage Four on Safari in Africa."

Dave moved to his computer and opened his email. "Bruno, you wouldn't believe this - incredible coincidence - there's an email from Akeyo."

Dave started to read. The silence grew too long. Bruno looked across the room at his friend. The shoulders were shaking, face clamped in his hands. Bruno jumped up and started to read over his friend's shaking shoulders.

"Mon dieu, mon dieu." he held his friend gently, arms around his neck. "Mon dieu. Non non non."

Dave's grief opened, starting at his gut, reaching his throat. Sue merged with Akeyo: Akeyo's eyes on the porch deep black to her soul; Sue's strong voice, warm gentle hands; Akeyo's gentle calm. A swirl of thoughts and memories. His mind drifted back to the student cottage in Thure.

———

The time for final exams shifted focus for everyone in the cottage. Bruno had months of uncompleted assignments to catch up on, feverishly working till two or three most mornings. Akeyo, with the biggest workload in papers, constantly studied late on Campus. Dave would take the Citroen to collect both her and her bike at midnight from the library, in spite of her insistence on riding. Hints of the old self-centred, snappy Simone resurfaced. Dishes piled up at the sink and the laundry basket stayed constantly overflowing.

Akeyo remained the calmest of the four. She had done the assignments and completed lab work; now she reviewed with a relentless refining process. Always in the back of her

128

mind were those who had shown faith in her to award the scholarship.

Dave felt the relief as he walked from the last of his three-hour examinations. He hadn't finished all the questions, but thought he had done well enough in the questions he did answer for a good pass. He wanted to celebrate but none of the others had finished. He sat down and ordered a coffee from the little campus café. He didn't hear the footsteps behind him. Akeyo stood close alongside.

"You have finished now. You need to celebrate with more than a coffee. I have two hours before the next one, time to buy you a wine to celebrate."

Dave started to protest, but she reached and took his right hand in both of hers. He looked at the hands and felt the warmth, it wasn't the touch - it was the care and thought that hit him. Akeyo pulled gently then led him quickly across the campus and down the street to the student local wine bar. His hand remained comfortably in hers.

"Red, I assume?" she smiled.

She returned with a carafe of red and two glasses, one with water. Once again, she took his hand in both of hers. Her face moved close, the brown eyes deep and soulful. Dave held the gaze for a long time. Akeyo broke the silence, but not the connection.

"What shall we toast? Our contribution to a better world?"

"Perfect – and to your success."

Dave drank his wine with his left hand, unwilling to break the touch on his right. A waiter arrived with a platter of fresh bread, ham, cheese and cherry tomatoes. The hands reluctantly parted.

Everyone had completed their exams. Bruno had disappeared to party with a dizzy blonde waitress he had met that afternoon. Dave and Simone had resumed their nightly runs, but the weeks of inactivity had Simone doubled with stitch after three kilometres. She waved Dave on.

"I'll be fine, I can walk back."

They had started later than usual, so by the time Dave arrived back a huge golden moon silhouetted the church spire. Akeyo waited on the steps of the cottage entrance. Dave sat down, unconsciously leaving a big gap on the step between them.

"Beautiful," Akeyo sighed. She slid across the gap on the step. He could feel her warmth against the damp of his running top. He put his arm around her shoulders; her head nestled into his neck. He turned his head and looked down, she lifted her face. Those deep warm eyes again. He bent to kiss her, then pulled back, but her hands were around his neck pulling him gently down.

———

Bruno rocked on his feet, swaying his friend in the tight grasp, eyes brimming, locked on the last sentence in the email:

"With great love from Akeyo."

Chapter Twelve – Sudan – Dinder Desert

Maddie lay for a moment feeling the heat in the sand. The haze above the surface shimmered. It had been an almost slow-motion fall, soft, painless. Ridiculous. The front wheel of the bike had disappeared completely into the sand. There were holes in the track, deep holes. Some of the holes alongside sprayed sand plumes from shovels. Back-breaking mining.

The children appeared silently beside her. They materialised from the desert. Three or four added their slender weight to help Maddie extract the bike. They smiled. One of the miners emerged from his hole, then another.

"Thank you," Maddie smiled to her cluster of helpers. Her words broke the silence. Little hands explored the bike as Maddie brushed the sand, checking for damage. One broken brake lever on the right, hanging from a tread of metal. She pulled it off and looked at the stub remaining. Not enough to grip.

One of the miners pointed at the lever in her hand and then towards the small compound perhaps a hundred metres off the track. The helpers began pushing the bike the towards the gate. Maddie felt a moment of concern. The smiles in the deep brown eyes reassured her. *Trust.* She trudged behind her bike towards the compound.

Thatched sheaves of grain stalk woven with twisted branches formed the village fence. Buckled and sagging. Pairs of round-thatched huts and small square cooking huts. All were built with rough mud walls. Outside the door of the first, an old woman continued grinding grain with a heavy stone mortar. She looked up and smiled "Salaam". Maddie returned her greeting with a smile. She stood for a minute transfixed by the bare simplicity inside the hut. A sleeping mat, one pot, a hoe and a bush broom. Nothing.

The miners gestured to a log seat in the centre of the huts. Three of the miners were clustered around the bike, talking animatedly. One disappeared into a hut, returning with a short length of thin pipe. The discussion around the bike continued.

Maddie caught the fragrant whiff of mint. A tall figure in immaculate white robes approached with a tray. "Good morning Madam, I am Chief of this village. Would you like mint tea and a biscuit and perhaps a cold drink?"

Maddie cleared the tight clod of emotion from the back of her throat.

"Thank you so much, this is wonderful Chief."

She laughed at the chief's joke - "You are lucky to be travelling in our winter, in the summer it gets really hot."

A tall young man in an immaculate white robe shyly approached. "Our children have a song for you if you would like to come to our school."

The whispered hubbub of the school children hushed as the teacher stooped under the entrance of a slightly bigger hut. A chalk board with a pitted surface distinguished the space from the other huts.

"We will sing you a traditional song of welcome."

Maddie engaged with dark eyes as the chorus gained momentum. The taller boys in the back row broke into a deep rhythmic harmony. She clapped as the sound trailed off:

"Shukraan – thank you, thank you".

The brake lever had been repaired. The pipe had been heated to fit over the stub then neatly bound with wire.

The loose end crimped and curled to a spiral. It felt firm to her grip. *What can I give back?* There was nothing useful on the bike.

Maddie turned to the circle of smiling faces. "Thank you so much."

The race seemed distant and insignificant. *Was it an hour, maybe two – who cares?*

Chapter Thirteen - Ethiopia

Rachel's anger seethed. She had had a long conversation from Khartoum with her Melbourne producer about Richard. His camera work was bloody awful and he didn't contribute anything outside his few minutes of required filming. The tension in the team escalated day by day. "Waste of space!" she had shouted. The producer had refused point blank to fly Richard home from Addis.

She looked at the road sign beside the vehicle. It said "Awala". She could see the scattered houses marking the border post between Sudan and Ethiopia. She knew that close to the Ethiopian border they would reach the small town of Metema.

The second camera posed no problem. Nat Papadopoulis, the sound man, had proved more than adequate on the camera for interviews. Steven Reid, the supposed number two camera, really worked hard to capture the essence of the country. He had walked for over an hour in the fifty-degree heat of the Dinder desert to position for Maddie's approach along an old disused railway line. The shot panned the twisted lines, dust raised by a goat herd, and then Maddie's small ball of dust expanding, growing then sweeping in a roar past the goat herd. A perfect capture of the feel of the desert and Maddie's pace through it.

Rachel had wanted Richard to capture some of the essence of the Sudanese people: the warmth and generosity from a base of poverty. The calm and peace in an incredibly harsh environment. Richard had no sense of cultural sensitivity or empathy with the people; he simply thrust his camera in their faces without any dialogue or permission. The man was an idiot. Rachel looked at the red face in the back of the car, eyes closed, shirt dark-stained with sweat, coupled with the body odour that filled the cab with a rancid stench.

Rachel turned away, taking a few long belly breaths, switching off her thoughts. Into the space drifted Maddie; she now felt she could count her as a genuine friend. They laughed a lot together. Rachel had developed a deep respect for Maddie's inner strength. She had watched other riders collapse off their bikes - big strong men, exhausted, short- tempered.

Maddie would always ensure mechanic Steve was briefed on every issue. Physically she must have been exhausted but she maintained a positive outlook. She had superb control, which she would maintain until Rachel had finished with the daily interview. Rachel also admired the way Maddie's initial obvious discomfort with the camera had grown into a professional confidence. Maddie always took time to reflect on the personal feelings of the ride, hints of the hardships and the roughness deflected with a laugh.

One day early in the Dinder desert, south of Khartoum, Maddie had suffered two punctures in quick succession, the second with a bad tyre tear. She had burnt her wrist quite badly on the hot exhaust, but still managed to complete a repair that Steven said was good enough to last the race. Rachel's mechanical knowledge rated zero, but she heard Steven speak in awe of Maddie's tuning ability.

"She can hear every component in the bike singing."

Maddie's account of that day highlighted the humbling experience that followed. At the end of the repair she had lain back exhausted and sore. When she opened her eyes, she had been surrounded by a group of women. They offered water, and one had removed her burning hot boots and started bathing her feet. Maddie had watched as they finally departed, each bearing a huge load of corn harvest on their heads. She had searched for some small token to repay them, but the small packet of broken biscuits simply wasn't worthy.

Perhaps the incident that earned her the most respect came at the checkpoint on that same day, a dusty spot close to the town of El Hawata on the edge of the southern Dinder desert. The BMW rider, Hettingen, had arrived about an hour before Maddie, but his bike had refused to start. His team had troubles with both of their vehicles, so he had no support. After tinkering for twenty minutes or so, he had resorted to swearing and kicking at the bike tyres.

Maddie had arrived and in her sweetest girly voice had offered to help. She then set about what even Rachel could see was a careful logical tracing of potential problems. Within minutes the big BMW started purring into life. For the first time in the race Ralf Hettingen offered a hint of humility.

"Thank you. I will give you one hour's start."

With that he promptly walked over to lay down in the shade of the huge spreading fig tree. That one hour, he would live to regret: Maddie would never release her hold on that lead.

The distant sound of a motor bike shook Rachel out of her reverie. She opened the truck door to where Richard was sleeping.

"You've got work to do my friend. We need to follow her all the way into the border post and through. I really want something that captures the difference between the two countries."

As it turned out, the difference screamed to a level that even Richard could register with his shots. From the quiet and peace of Sudan, the Ethiopian side clamoured, bars and brothels, children calling "Money, money, money", a transition to a louder, more demanding culture in the matter of a few hundred metres.

The other truck had already passed through the border, leaving Abdul at the Sudan side preparing the documentation for the rest of the team. They planned for a few hours' rest stop, to fuel Maddie and the bike and let her get some sleep. They had found a small rest house with most of the essentials, and Steven Wright and Nat were preparing some food. The host arrived with a large jug of water, "Very clean for drinking."

Steven and Nat looked at each other and the grey murky water.

"Have you got gas for cooking?"

In spite of boiling, the water became the prime suspect for the onset of stomach bugs for the team over the next few days. Richard, surprisingly, had no ill effects.

———

Maddie could see the imposing cliffs of the Ethiopian tablelands as she started the long climb of nearly three thousand vertical metres. The bike climbed a little sluggishly. Maddie suspected the fuel supply from Metema had been contaminated, or perhaps had been sitting for too long. She had managed perhaps two hours' sleep, and started the ride feeling relatively refreshed. Within an hour, the first pangs started to knot her stomach. She kept concentration on the road, trying to will the nausea away. Rachel had already succumbed to a bout of diarrhoea and had passed her a packet of Imodium tablets as she headed off:

"Let nature do its clean out thing a couple of times – then use the stoppers."

The road ascended steeply, and Maddie now began urgently looking for a place to stop. The wreck of a burnt-out petrol tanker lay across one side of the road; behind it a small track led off the road. She laid the bike down and leapt behind the inadequate cover of a small bush. As she crouched, paralyzed by convulsions, the tinkle of bells announced the arrival of a small goat herd. The tall bearded goat herder in long flowing robe smiled cheerfully and greeted her with a friendly, "Salaam."

Maddie tried to smile.

Back on the bike, feeling washed out and squeamish, Maddie found it hard to find a riding rhythm. The corners swept upwards with expansive views over towering lines of cliff face. The temperature cooled, Maddie zipped up her jacket. At the top of the climb, she stopped to take the Imodium tablets. She needed no distraction from the road.

The ride to Bahir Dar turned into a struggle. Maddie had not registered the dehydrating effects of diarrhoea, and had developed a pounding headache. She texted ahead to the team:

"Find a place with a good toilet."

Bahir Dar sat on the shores of Lake Tana and close to the Blue Nile Falls. Rachel had also described some of the ancient Christian monasteries around Lake Tana. They were decorated with Italian renaissance-style paintings, reputedly dating from the 16th century. The camera crew were going to film some of the sites that afternoon.

Maddie struggled to remember the conversation through blurred memory as she approached the town.

She fought to hold the bike into every corner. The tall rock pillar formations beside the road barely registered. The ride had covered a little over three hundred kilometres, but had taken Maddie nearly five hours. She knew the afternoon ride would have to wait.

On the outskirts of Bahir Dar, Maddie spotted Abdul waiting with the vehicle. At least now she could avoid the navigation into the bustling town. Maddie's ashen face had Abdul clucking with concern:

"You must rest. The race can wait."

Steven Wright immediately spotted Maddie's distress as he helped her off the bike. He ushered her into the hotel room they had taken.

"Stinking headache," Maddie mumbled.

Maddie lay down on one of the beds and fell asleep within a few minutes. As Steven and Abdul gently eased her helmet and boots off, Maddie opened her eyes.

"Hydration, drink this." Steven had mixed hydration salts in some bottled water along with some paracetamol. He held her head as she drank.

"Now you can sleep."

———

The Bahir Dar rest stop stretched to eighteen hours. Two of the other teams had passed in the night. Rachel had arrived in the other vehicle with Steven and Nat. The team all needed the break. Everyone had suffered some degree of stomach problems, apart from Abdul and Richard. Surprisingly Richard shook off some of his sullen malcontent and was cheerfully playing nurse to the team. Rachel noted he had even bought a new shirt in the Bahir Dar market, a rather garish orange-patterned business shirt, but thankfully missing the unwashed rancid body odour of his previous garb.

By mid-morning the following day the azithromycin antibiotics Maddie had taken were starting to win their battle with the microbes in her gut. She attempted a light meal, then declared herself ready to ride. Richard and Abdul, as the only fit members, were sent ahead on the race route; the others would rest a few more hours before following, sticking to the highway. Rachel packed the bike bag with extra fluids and hydration salts, along with some high-energy snacks.

"Take it easy, drink plenty and stop for snacks. You can't afford to run down to empty."

Then Maddie took off. In the traffic of Bahir Dar, the bike felt heavy, and her arms arched.

The ride today would reach its highest point at nearly three thousand metres, before plunging eighteen hundred metres into the Blue Nile Gorge. The temperature rose to over thirty degrees celsius as she reached the bottom. Clear of the traffic she opened out the bike into the rolling brown country of wheat fields and small herds of cattle. Squat roundel huts sat in clusters with stick fences. Off the road a farmer walked behind a wooden plough pulled by a single ox. Looking closer, Maddie could see that the plough consisted of a twisted and gnarly tree root. A sense of unreality, like an old sepia film, blurry at the edges. She struggled to maintain attention, her body wracked with pain.

Old castle ruins framed the slope of a hill. She slowed, feeling she was riding in some mysterious dream. Time for a break. As she stopped, a herd of goats and a young goatherd emerged from the ruins; she had slipped back into a pre-biblical time.

The sun sank low as she reached the Blue Nile Gorge. A golden shimmer with a silver snake swirling its way far below. She saw the road twisting downward and across the huge valley, the upward climb, another black snake. She stopped and took a long drink and a handful of dry biscuits. She tried to shake the aches and pain in her belly. She needed focus both on the descent and on the climb. A woman and small boy with a donkey passed, smiling.

The road started smoothly, a long lateral descent down the first cliff face. Above, craggy cliffs leant out over the valley, small huts clung to the sides of the slopes. The first hair-pin bend flowed; she shifted down and eased up the throttle. The next few turns flowed, and she worked her body weight instinctively. She leaned into the next turn and saw the twenty centimetre crack a second too late. The front wheel caught, wrenching her arms. The bike flicked to the side, with a flash of sparks as the foot pedal caressed the pavement. The back wheel slid. She flicked on a burst of power and righted the bike, then braked gently. She had it back, but directly ahead lay a line of rocks and a tree branch. Warning signs of a broken-down vehicle around the next corner, a huge old truck laden with heavy timber.

146

She laid the bike over into the opposite lane, then braked hard into a small clearing opposite the truck.

She sat, shaking and sweating, the nausea welled. She kicked the bike onto its stand and slumped down in the gravel. A trickle of water ran down the cliff face above. She pulled off her helmet and let the water drain down her head and neck. The shaking took a few minutes to ease, then she carefully inspected the bike. Thankfully no real damage. A few deep breaths, focus, shut out alarms, back on the bike.

By the time Maddie reached the sweeping bridge at the bottom of the rift, her bike rhythm had returned. She eased off the pace slightly, ready for the next obstacle. The fog in her head had cleared a little.

Above the far canyon rim, the sun became a huge golden orb. She paused for another snack, and looked up. An eagle soared over the canyon, wingtips catching the light on every turn.

The road changed to dirt and the dust clouds billowed orange. A bus headed towards her then enveloped her in dust. She rode blind for a hundred metres or so. Darkness descended and she followed the hole in the night created by her powerful halogen lamps. Cool air brushed her face and cleared her head.

Ahead she saw a flash of red. It was Kim, the Danish rider, pushing his bike. He smiled in his usual friendly fashion as she pulled alongside. He pointed to the lights on his bike, totally smashed. He had met the bus on a corner in a spray of gravel and stones and had been plunged into a terrifying dusty blackness.

"Luckily I chose the same direction as the road."

Maddie took his GPS position and agreed to contact his team as soon as she had coverage. He refused further help.

"Go, go safely, you are wasting valuable race time. And thank you for stopping, that BMW bastard rode straight past."

No moon shone in the sky above. Maddie looked back in her mirror. Kim was only visible from the intermittent flashing of his brake lights. He used the lights to warn other traffic of his presence. Maddie reached the small town of Fiche and checked her cell phone. She made the call to the Danish team. Their nearest vehicle was three hours ahead; Kim had a long push yet.

———

Richard had carefully cooked some plain pasta, trying to provide Maddie with safe energy. Maddie, although aware of the growing tension in the team, had not spent enough time with Richard to judge his behaviour. Her preoccupation with the race kept their relationship neutral. Tonight, she deeply appreciated his thoughtful preparation. She had ridden nearly seven hours and seven hundred kilometres, with one brief refuelling stop. She was shattered as she walked into the shabby Gogetti guest house room.

Richard had filled a water bucket and cleaned the area around a bed for her. Her sleeping bag was neatly laid out. He had also boiled drinking water and set out a water bottle and glass with her antibiotics beside. She smiled and thought, *He's a good mother today.* She gratefully sank onto the hard mattress, and was asleep in minutes.

Rachel and the second vehicle arrived as Maddie emerged from the guesthouse. They had had a nightmare journey - cameraman Steven and Rachel both had chronic diarrhoea, Nat and mechanic Steve were also suffering, but mostly from nausea. Nat and Steve had shared the driving, with multiple long stops for the other two. The sicker members both collapsed onto beds in the guest house, exhausted and grey.

Richard offered to do the morning interview from behind the camera. Rachel gratefully accepted and also headed for a sleep, pausing briefly to note the carefully prepared bed.

As Maddie started her bike maintenance ritual, the three others joined her around the bike.

"We have a bit of a problem," Richard started the conversation. "With half the team sick we are not going to be able to keep up with you. The old leap-frog is simply not working."

Maddie had had the issue churning in the back of her mind since breakfast.

"The big things are bike parts and support, help from Wrighty and fuel. Food means I will be mucking about finding stuff but not too much of an issue; sleep the same, I can stop at anything that looks like it has a bed. But one critical thing is the filming..."

"I think what we have is an issue of manpower. Of course we need man power without the weakness of soft European stomachs." Abdul was beaming. "An issue of manpower can be resolved simply with the addition of more men."

The response Abdul was expecting fell well short. Blank stares. "Number one manpower is a very good old friend of mine in Addis. He is a doctor and has a very good vehicle. Number two manpower is another very good friend of mine who lives in the town of Konso, not far from the Kenyan border. He also has a very good vehicle."

From there the plan quickly evolved. Abdul's friend from Konso would come down to meet Richard, Abdul and one vehicle carrying essential supplies. Richard would continue with the friend to support the next rough stage of the race starting back at Konso. Abdul would continue directly on to the border crossing into Kenya, to prepare for Rachel's arrival. Meanwhile Abdul's doctor friend would take the hour's drive to Gogetti from Addis. The doctor would then continue at a slower pace with the sickest, leaving Wrighty and Nat immediately free to chase the race. If no problems were reported from Maddie, they would pick up Richard and head into Kenya to set up a first stop camp.

Abdul was busy on his cell phone. The laughter at his end of the calls indicated long time friendships being happily re-established.

Richard quietly outlined the plan to Rachel, who was happy to fund the new members. At the end of the conversation Richard added quietly, "Apologies for my grumpiness. In Khartoum I found out my dear old mother had died in UK. It was impossible to get back in time for the funeral, but I rather took my angst out on the team. The old British stiff upper lip didn't really work." In spite of her discomfort Rachel felt touched. She reached for his hand and gave it a brief squeeze. She had forgiven.

Outside, feeling relieved, Maddie finished a few minor repairs on the bike while Steve quickly replaced the gouged and bent foot pedal. She came inside to check on her friend. Rachel was already in a deep sleep. Maddie gently brushed her cheek and headed back out to the bike. She had nearly five hundred kilometres before the route got really rough again and she intended to get to the off-road section as fast as she could.

Chapter Fourteen –Dida Galgalu

"You are number one, first to arrive here. You ride well."

Abdul's smiling face greeted Maddie at the Ethiopian border station at the Moyale crossing to Kenya.

There were large numbers of military milling around, a certain tenseness in peoples' faces. The Ethiopian border station was ominously quiet. Abdul had prepared all the exit documentation cards; all Maddie had to do was sign them and present her passport. She smiled as the officer recorded her exit in a huge ledger. She was eager to get back on the bike, to stretch her advantage.

Abdul handed her a bundle of Kenyan shillings and a large paper bag with food. "I must head back to check with my Doctor friend. We will catch you tonight. You will find best fuel on the Kenyan side."

With a wave, Maddie rode across the dusty no man's land into the Kenyan border station. She noticed the immediate change over the border. *British colonial*, she thought, looking at the fibro government buildings. The young girl at the shop with the petrol pump outside spoke perfect English.

"Welcome to Kenya, Madam. We have heard about the race. You are the Australian rider?"

Her smile showed perfect white teeth. Maddie relaxed a little as they chatted.

"How is the road south from Moyale?"

"Terrible Madam, it is very, very rough. Lots of sand. It is very hard to travel that road."

Maddie quickly changed the subject. "Do you have family here?"

"Yes, I have two boys, but my husband has gone to find work in Nairobi. I work here to feed my boys. My mother also is here, and she looks after my boys."

Maddie reassessed the girl's age - perhaps nineteen.

She told the girl she had two boys back home; her mind drifted to her boys' faces. She struggled for a moment to turn her attention back to the race.

With the tank filled, Maddie found shade outside a small café, where she bought a soft drink to go with her bag of sandwiches. She guessed she had two or three hours of daylight left; she wanted to make the most of it.

The ride out of Moyale started with a long sweeping downhill, rocky with ruts filled with sand. It took concentration on lines, but Maddie rode fast. The road flattened out to a sandy surface. She stepped up the revs, riding flowing lines. She was in the zone. Her bike instincts went into auto-pilot, focus about forty metres in front of her wheel. Anticipating, alert, feeling every movement of the bike.

—

Left hand side. Change in colour, soft. Switch sides, some smooth running on the verge. Rock, slide right, big rocks, find a path back across the middle. Tail out, ease back then gun it. Deep sand, ease the weight back, work it out. Nice.

The desert periphery framed the view, shimmering haze and purple hills in the distance. Thorns, wicked thorns, classic African acacias spreading, a small thicket. Dust ahead, bells? Surely not bells. A camel herd sauntered across the road, need to ease back, quickly. Disdainful stares through the long- lashed eyes. A few startled trots as she weaved through the herd. An old man and a white-smocked boy, both with long sticks, ended the procession. Friendly waves. Throttle eased up. Splats of camel dung.

A long line of road stretched a dividing line across the desert. Ahead on the right a tall tower, shimmering in the heat. Perhaps five kilometres away a pall of dust rolling behind a large vehicle. A truck or bus. Maddie watched the approach. The gap quickly closed. She could hear the cattle truck rattling, trying to keep momentum over the rock. She heard the tinny loud beat of music blaring. On the high wooden sides, perhaps a dozen people perched on top with more above the cab. Three hundred metres away, still holding its line in the middle of the road. Maddie looked left, a steep rocky drop away from the road, but enough of a lip to get a lift. She gunned the bike and lifted the front wheel over the lip. Almost perfect back wheel landing three metres below. Maddie's heart pounded.

The cacophony of sounds from the truck were punctuated by yells from the precarious perches. The dust cloud rolled above. The truck disappeared. Maddie still had a lot of speed, but the surface looked OK. It felt better than the road, a bit of scrub, but clearing further from the road. Maddie dropped a gear and decided to stick to her path. *This is better than the road*, she thought.

Then, a searing metallic crunch. The front forks bottomed out and transmitted a force upwards. Maddie's wrists were smashed simultaneously. The momentum and right twist of her forward fall dislocated her right shoulder. As she flew forward and over the front of the bike, she saw a bird high above in a brilliant blue sky. Then her boots obliterated her view. She floated into blue, then black.

Minutes perhaps hours. The air reeked of petrol, ants in the pool of blood from her nose. A loud click, click, click of hot metal cooling. *Move away from the petrol*, she registered. Screaming, someone was screaming far away. She closed her eyes against a brilliant white light.

———

High above the old vulture circled again. A day had passed. The figure on the ground had not moved. The sun had dried the blood to a black stain. The thorn bushes were black and charred. Tonight would be the time for the feast.

Darkness changed the desert. Cool now. Twigs breaking under padded feet, grunts and howls. A truck passed the lonely road, same tinny music beat blaring, headlights sweeping into the dust. A predator scurried into the thickened bush.

———

The donkey trod soundlessly. The old man in white followed. They had a meeting place, a tree, with a pile of rocks beneath. The donkey halted, and the woman appeared. She held her baby at her breast. Her face glowed in the moonlight. The old man silently celebrated her beauty. Tonight, there was another. A tall, lean desert man from far away. He carried a spear, his body painted in white markings. He spoke in soft tones. He dug some roots and handed them to the woman. She had gathered fibres from the bark of a tree. They crouched in a circle as she ground the roots with a stone, coating the fibres with the root paste. They bound a large bundle and tied it to the donkey's back.

The trio moved through the desert, led by the old man. They moved quickly, gliding across the rough ground, bare feet finding smooth rock in the darkness.

—

Maddie saw the faces in the darkness. Behind them were her two boys and her mother. Dave appeared, standing apart. He pleaded to her, but she couldn't hear the words. The boys were crying. She tried to reach out her hand but her hands no longer belonged. She saw the beauty of the woman comforting her, and she could see a familiar tall figure behind her. She knew him, from where? The hands were cool and soothing; she felt a white blanket of peace. Then there was nothing but the face of the moon.

———

The group moved through the desert. Two branches from the donkey's back supported the wooden structure, expertly stripped from thorn branches. A woven stretcher, the ends of the branches dragging in the desert sand. Two markers of the journey in the moonlight. The white face in the fibre cocoon reflected back at the moon. The breathing became shallow, tentative, drifting. It was nearly time.

———

Then the scream split the night, a long terrible wail. Maddie felt the pain; it gripped her chest, it burnt in her arms, it ripped at her with searing claws.

———

The old man spoke first. "Allah has already chosen; we must continue now."

The tall one shook his head. "She fights hard. She has chosen. We have not reached the sacred place; she has time yet."

He looked into the desert, waiting for the woman to speak. He could see far away Wandjina Spirits dancing in the moonlight. The woman looked into the eyes of the infant, communication of deep wordless love. The infant chose life. She smiled at the other two. "We must give life a chance. We must find a place to give her that chance."

"I know such a place," said the old man, and he turned the donkey south.

A pinkish glow lit the eastern sky as Sister Evelina dragged the heavy gates of the Presbytery open. In recent months they had locked the gate with a heavy chain and padlock. Morning service would start soon, although the congregation had been dwindling. Many people had fled to their home villages because of the continued troubles. She pulled the gate wide and looked out. Something in the shadows caught her eye. She jumped nervously and stared. Nothing moved. She took a few steps closer.

"Devil worshippers," she muttered. Then she heard the moan, a soft whimpering sigh. She pulled out her phone and lit up the white face in the strange cocoon. Blood was dried at the corners of the mouth.

"Agnes!" she yelled.

Mother Madeline stood at the back of the group of Sisters clustered around the cocoon. Something about the neatly-woven fibre sent a shiver up her spine. Sister Agnes worked efficiently, stripping the cocoon from the body with a large pair of scissors. She gently tutted as more white flesh marred with deep black bruising emerged. The woman only wore one item of clothing - a scarf tied neatly over the wound on her forehead.

"Gently, everyone - we need to get a sheet underneath."

"Now lift together, on three."

"Somebody please get hot water and disinfectant, and fetch my medical kit."

Agnes's fingers gently probed the entire body, following as the two nursing sisters successively cleaned the wounds. She could feel the bone fragments in the arms.

"Mother, could you find something to write a list on please. I will need to talk to my friend Doctor Ramish in Nairobi."

Agnes' voice remained calm and steady, but she knew the injuries were well beyond both her skills and the facilities at the Presbytery.

"And everyone else, we need some space and some prayers please."

Madeline returned with her notepad and pen and Sister Agnes began listing the injuries and her suspicions of other damage. Madeline turned the second page, then the third.

"We will start with some fluids and something for the pain."

Madeline looked Agnes directly in the eye. Two old friends with a straight question, unspoken.

Agnes's response was direct: "Prayer and hope is about all we can provide. And we can try to keep any infection at bay. How the wounds have stayed so clean is a mystery; they are at least three days old. Maybe bush medicine in those bindings."

"You ring your doctor friend. I will try to find some way of getting her to hospital, and try to find out who she is," responded Madeline as she walked briskly outside, passing the pile of fibrous bindings still littering the pathway. A tiny flash caught her eye, something shining underneath the layers. It was a plastic card with an emergency medical number, BMI Insurance. Madeline reached for her phone.

Chapter Fifteen - Paris

Charles De Gaulle Airport disgorged thousands into the long connecting walkways. Martin followed the signs with the baggage picture, feeling tired and lost. His small carry-on clicked its wheels across the travellator. The pit of his stomach knotted tightly. Uganda, twenty-two hours in the small airport immigration office. Questions, threats, yelling and the constant menace of live weapons prodded in his back. The fear came rushing back.

The French immigration officer remained talking to his neighbour as Martin approached. He continued the conversation after a brief look up to check that Martin matched his passport image. He gave a brief nod, and Martin passed safely onto official French soil. Martin waited a minute, unsure if the process was complete. His fear cheated but his heart still raced. An armed security guard waved him through the exit. Martin hastily followed the pointed finger. With no luggage he quickly found himself on the concourse to Terminal 2C and D. He had agreed to meet Simone at the information centre to the TGV, a short walk away. He took a few minutes to compose himself.

Simone stood tall and elegant, unmistakeable in the crowd. A new emotion gripped Martin. This woman had loved Akeyo like a sister, shared every secret and dream. He felt fondness and connection. He approached, right arm extended to shake her hand. She ignored the hand and pulled him into a warm embrace, brushing his cheeks with her lips. Martin felt her warmth and smelt the scent of her perfume. They stood, green eyes into black, tears brimming both. Martin felt a shiver pass through his body and felt the reflection in Simone's. They held each other in silence, until Simone finally spoke.

"Welcome to France, my dear friend."

Martin fell into a safe place of peace in the welcome; the welcome exuded love. The demons were left behind.

———

They turned into Avenue Sully, Chaville. Old trees hid the frontage of Simone's apartment, as the Audi glided under the electric door. Martin awoke with a start. Smells of new leather and Simone's perfume in the car were replaced by a rich smell of something cooking.

"Your bedroom is on top, your own space, make yourself at home."

Simone swept up the polished wooden stairway to a huge room, with a large bed, an old wooden desk and an equally spacious adjoining bathroom. Martin's small carry-on looked tiny in the space. Simone continued the tour:

"Cupboard, hangers, bath robe, slippers, towels here, plenty of soap and shampoo in the bathroom cabinet."

The comfort and space overawed Martin a little. He ran his fingers over the smooth polished oak of the dresser. His mind slipped back to the rough covered couch in his friend's house; the gulf yawed.

"I must check on the food. Come down when you are ready. Maybe something light to eat then some proper sleep."

Simone disappeared back down the stairs, shutting the heavy wooden door behind her. Martin walked around the room. He had stayed in many big hotels, but this space had warmth and comfort. Flowers on the dresser were fresh, with pungent sweetness.

Martin took a long shower. The strong flow massaged his shoulders and back. He stepped out to touch the soft towels. He felt refreshed and awake. From the small pile of clothes in his case he chose a white tee shirt and jeans. Both new from the market, the jeans stiff and crisp. He kept the slippers Simone had offered on his feet. His hand slid smoothly down the polished banister. Through the open door to Simone's small office he could read the details of his flight on the laptop screen. Alongside on the desk stood a photo, the same photo as the battered copy from Akeyo's passport. This copy was bright and uncreased, housed in a thick wooden frame as it held pride of place on the desk. Martin stood at the doorway for a few minutes, savouring the connection.

The table at the bottom of the stairs reminded Martin of the glossy culinary photographs in the airline magazines he had endlessly flicked through on the flight. There were prawns with the hint of chilly and garlic he had smelt from the car, lush green salad, thick pink slices of ham, crisp bread sticks, wooden platters with snake-like coils of saucisson and cheeses, a frosted water jug with attendant glasses and two bottles of wine.

Simone appeared in the kitchen, hair tied back with a comb, apart from one curling strand down a cheek, with a small drip of perspiration gathering at the tip. She smiled, "Feeling better?"

"One hundred percent, and a lot cleaner. This looks better than airline food, but I am not sure of my appetite."

Simone arrived at the table with the last two dishes - a small bowl of cherry tomatoes and another of small round boiled potatoes.

 "Sit, eat as little or much as you like, relax."

The tastes were light and fresh, and to his surprise Martin found himself reaching for more and more food. Simone offered a wine and the silky red joined the rich saltiness of a slice of ham with crisp bread.

Simone talked, creating an easy flow of food, wine and a little laughter. At one point she reached over and placed her hand on his forearm. She looked down at the whiteness of her fingers against the ebony of his arm. She smiled, recalling the little mantra she had always shared with Akeyo: *"Ebony and Ivory."* A counter to those who misunderstood their closeness, those who could only see the differences. Simone felt the choke of emotion in her throat, tears welled, a sob lifting her shoulders.

Martin placed his other hand over hers.

"You know Martin, I called her my younger sister, but she also had the wisdom my mother never had or never shared. She saved me so many times from myself."

The conversation shifted. Simone reminisced, with stories of those three years, stories sometimes familiar to Martin, sometimes new. Martin shared his pride in Akeyo's ambitious projects, her fearless grinding through the bureaucracy and corruption. Both saw the common love and respect. Laughter returned. The red wine bottle emptied. They moved to the comfortable leather seats in the adjoining lounge.

"Coffee?" Simone asked, but by the time she returned from the kitchen, Martin's eyes were closed.

———

Strong sunlight radiated heat from the heavy drapes as Martin woke. Reluctant to leave the soft supportive bed. He stretched, unsuccessfully willing sleep to return. He repeated the long hot shower, although the process didn't have the same refreshing effect as the previous night. He still felt groggy and sleepy.

He padded down the stairs in bare feet, a small creak alerting Simone as he reached the first-floor landing. She swivelled in her office chair, with a wide smile, cell phone cupped in her hand.

"I suppose you would like that coffee now?"

Martin nodded and continued down the stairs. Once again, the table displayed a welcoming array of food. The frosty jug of fruit juice caught his eye. His mouth was dry. After a few minutes Simone finished her call and walked past his chair. Her hand brushed gently across the back of his shoulders. A light welcoming touch.

"Would you like a fresh ham croissant?"

"Croissant?"

Simone explained and set about preparing some crisp delights with tomato, cheese and ham.

Simone sat cross-legged on a chair across the table, as Martin savoured the flavour of the croissant.

"It is already past twelve; today I think you should rest. I take a walk with my friend in the woods at one thirty. You are welcome to join us."

Martin nodded, wiping a small drip of tomato from the corner of his fully-engaged mouth.

———

The running shoes Simone had found for him to wear felt springy and light. Martin couldn't resist a bounce, reaching for the leafy overhanging tree outside the house. Simone smiled and caught his arm. Martin's wardrobe had been quadrupled with a pile of left-over garments from a string of ex-lovers and partners. "Take whatever fits," she had insisted.

Simone's friend Florence stood under the park entrance, tall arching wrought iron gates dwarfing her small frame. She had a rounded cheerful face, dark curly hair and a huge smile. She bubbled with enthusiasm and curiosity. Martin had to lean to reach her welcoming kisses. She had the smell of fresh scented soap. Simone translated her heavily accented English, question after question. Martin felt the warmth and attention, struggling to keep up with the barrage of questions. Eventually Florence turned to her friend and began a rapid fire catch-up. The French conversation gave Martin a chance to take in the deep greens, the majestic old leafy trees and the space of the park dotted with bright wildflowers. The laughter of the two women embraced Martin; it gave the warmth of a family outing; an experience Martin hadn't shared in a long time.

"This is our favourite spot; we always spend a few minutes here. Peace and reflections," Simone announced. They had reached a small pond, where the forest rose at the back, sunlight dappled through green branches, reflecting off the pond, and lilies decorated the water surface with whites and mauves.

The trio sat down on a bench beside the pond, in silence. Martin looked at the reflections glinting off the pond. He could feel the two women beside him, their warmth and the rhythm of their breathing. The brown of the water stirred; Something under the surface. A face. He stiffened and stared. A scarf swirled around a lily. Akeyo smiled, she stood and spread her arms around the space, and Martin's eyes followed. He saw the deep greens and the beauty, he saw the safe place of Akeyo's dreams, her anchor. When he looked back to the pond she had gone.

The two women felt the shudder beside them. Simone knew instantly. She reached her arms around his waist, head on his shoulder. Florence reacted with instinct, arms around both. Martin felt their warmth, their love. Still, it took a long time to clear the image.

A mother wheeling a pram passed the bench, a toddler clinging to one handle of the pram. He let go, walked close to the huddled trio and stared. The mother was also fascinated, but hissed gently to her son, "Allez."

Martin eventually turned to Simone's side and kissed her on the forehead.

171

"Thank you."

He turned to Florence. Her brown eyes showed concern, brown eyes of depth and soul. He touched his lips to her forehead.

"Merci, a passing ghost. I'm sorry."

Sensing the moment, Florence leapt to her feet, clapping her hands.

"Trois glaces, mes enfants, allez!"

She strode off down the path towards a small kiosk. Simone paused a moment, rubbing a hand up Martin's back.

"Looks like ice-cream time, my friend."

By the time Martin and Simone had reached the kiosk, Florence was walking back with three huge multi-coloured cones. She handed Martin a cone, and he bit into the real fruit flavour of strawberry. The mood lightened with the race against the sun and dripping ice-cream. Both Florence and Martin laughed and pointed at the inelegant strawberry blob on Simone's nose. She responded with a flick of ice-cream landing squarely above Florence's right eye. The ice-cream melee quickly escalated, along with the laughter.

Crazy moments of fun ending with all three splattered in ice-cream.

Still laughing they gathered around a water fountain. Florence produced a small box of tissues from a shoulder bag and they took turns at cleaning each other. Simone's pristine white blouse and shorts had fared the worst. Florence tried to turn the strawberry blobs into artistic rose patterns. Both were giggling so much the drawings spread randomly, ending with one breast clustered in a red swirl and the other an orange spiral.

Simone held up her hands in mock defeat, and they sat down on the grass to try to dry their clothes. Florence began posting a photograph of Simone from her phone, still giggling uncontrollably.

"You cannot post that. It will ruin my reputation for ever!"

 But for once Simone did not actually care -the nonsense had been a tonic and a release, a deflection from her normal control and distance. Martin smiled; he could remember a time in the village on the way home from school when he and a friend had had a mud fight. Both covered in mud and laughing, they had spent an hour under the village pump trying to clean their school uniforms to avoid the inevitable beating. He couldn't recall anything since with such a childish sense of fun.

———

Simone sat in her office, clean and refreshed after a shower. She enlarged the photo Florence had posted from the park. Her own face but somehow a different person. A person she could like, unlike the bitch she usually saw in herself, the cold uncaring woman she hated. Florence had celebrated before her friend had even recognised the shift; she had whispered as they parted,

"Let the fun in always – it lights you up."

It wasn't only the fun. She had noticed the shift since first receiving Martin's email. She treasured her memories of Akeyo in a way she had never felt before. Her attention shifted from her own demons to simply *What can I do to help this man?* Being that helper left no room for the selfishness or the scheming and manoeuvring which drove her normal frenetic life. The driving whip of her mother's expectations was peacefully absent.

The reflection left Simone in a clarity of space. She was free to create a new way of living. She also realised that she needed a different type of people in her life, and she needed to act fast.

———

The Societe Nationale d'Insurance building towered with stone archways over the entrance. '1853' said the bronze plaque. Martin's head craned upward, full of fascination with the age and beauty of the building. Under his arm he held the folder of documents he had assembled in Nairobi, all carefully recopied by Simone that morning. Simone waited patiently, enjoying the view through new eyes and new perspectives that Martin's curiosity created.

Simone navigated the labyrinth of offices until she found what appeared to be the Claims Office. Towering walls housed huge portraits of a succession of Society Presidents, austere, unhappy gentlemen. Arched wooden counters framing a glass partition separated the claimants from their potential benefactors, a disinterested cluster of uniformly dressed clerical staff. None seemed aware of their presence at the counter.

Martin calmly adopted his usual Nairobi-bureaucracy-waiting mode. Simone had a little less patience.

"Excusez-moi." She tapped the glass.

The first respondent seemed also to be the junior, young but with a shaved head and John Lennon glasses which blurred his age range. He immediately shuffled Simone's request to the next up the chain. "Louisa" appeared next, a portly mid-forties woman. Perhaps she had another name, but her large right breast was labelled 'Louisa'. Her grasp of the process seemed better informed, but after hearing the same request she walked away to engage in a long discussion with a middle-aged man with a bow tie. He repeatedly looked over the top of small bifocals at the two intruders at the counter. Eventually Louisa returned with a large form. She rapidly showed Simone the portions required, boldly marking sections with her ball pen as she went.

It took Martin and Simone forty minutes to complete the form. By this stage a small queue had built up at Louisa's window. She seemed the only person of the dozen or so behind the glass willing or able to deal with real people on the outside of their aquarium. The rest were deeply engaged with phone conversations or clicking pens as they re-read complex documents, folded around favourite magazines. Simone felt certain she could see a social media webpage reflected in the bifocals of the master.

As they reached the counter window for the second time, Simone decided it had reached the point of unleashing her bureaucracy whip. She laid the documents along with the business card of her uncle on the counter. Her uncle served on the executive of the Society, an extremely powerful man.

"My uncle wishes to be kept informed of the progress of this application", she added.

Louisa responded instantly with a rapid word to the bifocal master, who in turn trotted to the counter, beaming:

"We will afford the highest priority; however, we do need to sight the originals of all documentation".

He glanced at his watch: *Lunch time, less than an hour away.*

Fortunately, Martin had included the originals in his folder, and he passed them through the window. To his credit the bifocal master barely relaxed his smile with the bad news on his lunch date. Louisa would have to wait.

As they left the office Simone and Martin exchanged a smile. Martin asked how long the process would take.

"Two weeks with priority – normally one month for such a large claim," Simone translated.

"In Nairobi it would take a bundle of notes to even get past step one. It pays to have contacts in high places. Thank you. I will find somewhere cheap to stay for the two weeks. I do not wish to impose on your hospitality for that long."

"Absolutely not. I enjoy your company. Two weeks is nothing. What would you like to see in Paris?"

Simone guided them to a small café for lunch. As they sat Martin mulled over the question Simone had asked. At his school he always remembered a book, torn and dirty. It had few words so the teachers had discarded it. He recalled the title, "French Impressionists". The book had only a few pages left and perhaps five or six pictures of the paintings, some half torn. The style had fascinated him. He had tried to emulate the style, daubing dots on newspaper from the four colour pots at the back of the classroom.

"I would love to see some original impressionist masters, maybe Monet, Manet, Gaugin, even Renoir, anything."

The request took Simone a minute to assimilate; she realised how little she knew about the man. "Tell me why," she asked gently.

The story left Simone humbled. She felt the gulf between their backgrounds - her own privileged, wealthy, spoilt, unlimited opportunities, so many of which she had squandered. It struck her also that she had never seen any of the masters herself, in her own city. Her mother would know where best to go.

———

Madame LeLievre heard the difference in her daughter's voice. For once the telephone call did not descend into a bitter argument over some triviality. She had asked if she could accompany her daughter and the interesting African gentleman to Musée D'Orsay. Simone had heard the request, saddened by the formality her mother felt necessary to use for the request, saddened also by the obvious expectation that the request would be declined. She surprised herself when she finished the conversation with: "Je t'aime Maman." She could not remember saying that since she was a child. She would have been touched by the tears in the old woman's eyes as she put down the telephone.

Her mother stood at the Musée entrance hall, tall, white-haired and distinguished. She held passes for the three of them. Despite living less than thirty kilometres apart, Simone had not seen her mother in over three years. Simone immediately noticed the age those three years had added.

Lost years! the new voice in her head shouted.

Simone introduced Martin, and her mother attached herself to his arm, full of charm and with a wealth of knowledge on the Impressionists. Simone walked alongside, helping her mother's English translation as she occasionally searched for a word. She saw her mother's white hair close to Martin's black and thought: *Ebony and Ivory*, this time without the sadness. There was a joy and pride in her mother's enhancement of Martin's long time wish. Her mother listened with respect to Martin's questions, answering with brief precision where she could. She sensed the significance this connection had for Martin and deftly avoided any diversions from his focus.

"I remember this one from the book."

Martin sat on a bench in front of Charles Monet's *The Argenteuil Bridge*. He said, "Look at the light on the water." Martin's voice was dreamy.

The joy in his face touched mother and daughter. Simone hugged her mother. The trio sat in silence for a long time in front of the painting. Eventually Martin stood up, walking close to the painting, taking in the detailed brush strokes. He then walked backwards until the cumulative effect of those strokes merged. He repeated the process for various segments of the canvas, enthralled.

Sensing when Martin was finally satisfied, Madame LeLievre stood up and announced,

"I would love for you to join me for lunch, if you are not too busy."

Martin looked at Simone and they both nodded.

Madame LeLievre pulled out her cell phone.

"I have a Bla Bla car waiting –we can go immediately."

Simone smiled. She had no idea that her mother had even heard of Bla Bla Car, let alone being a competent user. Extraordinary for a woman in her late eighties.

They arrived at the restaurant on Ile de la Cité, close to the Notre Dame. White linen tablecloths and old-world silverware; waiters in their seventies greeted Simone's mother with fondness and respect. The Senne drifted below the window at their table, through the red and white curtains. Martin was entranced. Beautiful food began a procession to the table, the wine glasses were filled.

Simone's mother pushed back her chair, wine glass in hand.

"It is wonderful to have you both. Today I celebrate ninety years…"

Simone felt the hot flush of shame hit her cheeks, along with a choke of emotion at her throat. Alongside her, Martin sensed her distress. He reached out his hand, finding hers and squeezing gently; she gripped tightly back. Her mother continued:

"My darling, we have shunned each other for too long. I know we have forgotten the anniversaries. Let's celebrate that chance made this one possible."

Simone pushed back her chair and met her mother in an embrace, tears streaming down her face. Martin slipped down the stairs, table napkin still tucked in his trousers.

Martin returned with a large bunch of flowers.

"Now we know we can celebrate. Happy birthday, Madame."

Simone smiled through her tears and raised her glass:

"Maman, je t'aime".

———

Martin woke in the late morning. He pulled back the curtains to streaming sun, his eyes screwed shut. As he started towards the shower, he noticed a large brown paper bag on the desk. On the bag were the words:

"I have missed too many birthdays. Here is your birthday gift in advance (for whenever it is). Love Simone."

The bag contained a box of paints, a sheath of beautiful camel hair brushes and a book of painting paper. There was also the full catalogue of the Musée D'Orsay Impressionist collection in beautiful colour photos.

Chapter Sixteen - Ethiopia

Sporadic gun fire could be heard as Rachel pulled up in the Doctor's car. Army trucks clogged the roads around the Ethiopian border township. Soldiers were lingering or sleeping as only soldiers know how. Both of the IBC vehicles were parked across the road. Steven Wright walked over to her car window. He explained that they had arrived at the border to find that Richard had lost his bag and passport. The delay searching for the bag meant that they were stranded by the border closure. The news had come through that terrorists or rebels were on the Kenyan side of the border.

"Well, I know where Richard's bag is." Rachel opened the boot of the Doctor's car and pulled out the missing bag. "We wondered who that bag belonged to. Where are Maddie and Richard now?"

After a moment's silence, Abdul finally spoke up.

"Maddie is safely across the border, maybe three or four hours ago. Richard is in the pub over the road there."

"Oh my God, the girl is on her own, in terrorist territory!" Rachel's hands went to her face in horror. "I need to have a talk with Richard."

Rachel strode across the road, the entire team following. She squinted as she entered the dark of the bar; shafts of light shone through holes in the roof iron. Blue and red lights lit up the bar fridge. The only two patrons, Richard and a bulky figure dressed in full safari uniform, sat perched on bar stools, a bottle of whisky between them. Rachel stopped at the doorway. Richard was talking loudly, with a drunken slur:

"...and I told the stuck-up Afrikaans *bissh* that my dear old Mum had died. She took it straight down hook, line and sinker. Perfect sympathy card!"

The two laughed uproariously.

Rachel turned in the doorway and marched through the group who had followed, back to the bag she had left on the road beside the Doctor's aging Mercedes.

"My vote is that from here, Richard is on his own, same as Maddie is. Does anyone disagree?" Silence.

Rachel walked back across the road and hefted the bag onto the bar beside Richard.

"Consider this your termination package. You are on your own, the same position you have left Maddie in."

Back outside, Rachel politely thanked the Doctor for his services and passed him a small bundle of US dollars.

"I shall stay with you to see if there is any assistance I can provide with your current catastrophe."

Rachel cringed at the word, but gladly accepted the local knowledge this well-educated man could bring.

"OK, we need to find somewhere we can sit down and plan. Anyone have any suggestions?"

The Doctor had a friend with a "very clean" rest-house a short distance down the road.

The group pulled a string of wicker tables together on the front porch of the guest house. Rachel fought to keep her mind off Maddie. Maddie's best support now would be from those who could make rational decisions, well-informed decisions. She would ask Abdul and the doctor to find the local commander, to try to assess how long the border might be closed. Nat suggested the other teams might have better contacts over the border; none had yet arrived. Maddie, being such an exceptional racer, had left everyone well behind.

The doctor cleared his throat:

"There is an old route about one hundred kilometres west of here; it is without the formalities of border crossing. An old camel trade route an uncle of mine used to ply with…" He cleared his throat again: "with certain goods".

Rachel resolved to try anything once other options had been exhausted. At the moment, as far as they knew, Maddie remained alive and mobile, with barely enough fuel to reach Marsabit. Her desert speed would allow her to out-race rebel vehicles as long as she had some warning….

Rachel grabbed the satellite phone, waited for the Iridium satellites to connect and pressed Maddie's number. Failed call. She tried again and again. Then she remembered the race tracker. She called the number for race control, who were still tracking from Addis. Simon answered immediately – yes, Maddie had tracked out of Moyale after about half an hour's stop. Bit of a signal loss but started tracking again about one hundred kilometres south-west. Then she appears to have stopped, probably for a rest. No signal since about four thirty pm.

Rachel relaxed and relayed the news.

"Looks like our girl is having a bit of a rest about one hundred and twenty kilometres south of Moyale."

The Doctor glanced at Abdul, who returned a look of concern. Both knew that the country one hundred and twenty kilometres south of Moyale was a harsh choice of resting place.

———

Rachel awoke at four thirty am, her stomach still suffering. She returned from the small pungent toilet and paced the room, checking her watch. Abdul and the Doctor had returned from the border with little news. The Commander knew little. He had been warned of a threat at the border and had ordered a sizable detachment to deploy. He had no intelligence about the group on the other side. All the Kenyan border staff had fled their posts. He would try to get someone over the border during the night to report the situation in Moyale.

On the dot of six am, Rachel called race control in their hotel in Addis. Rather slowly and sleepily Simon answered, "Just a minute." There were keyboard tappings in the background. After about five minutes he came back on the line:

"Still no signal since four thirty yesterday. But we lost about half the field at the same time. The satellites are in a low position on the horizon at the moment. I wouldn't worry. She will have cell coverage outside Marsabit; probably by about midday you should hear from her. By the way, the boss is considering what to do with the race. Most of the teams will have reached the border by midday today, so everyone gets neutralised by the border closure, apart from Maddie of course. She will be on a roll."

Again, Rachel relaxed; she had the news she wanted to hear - her friend was safe. She tried Maddie's sat phone again. Nothing, probably the same problem with the satellites.

———

The four men in the vehicle had followed the faint desert trail for over twenty kilometres. They had reached an old deserted well, broken rope wound around a primitive winch, the well filled with sand. Only a few hardy desert plants gave hint that water may have once been present. Steven Wright scanned the GPS. He had managed to download satellite imagery of the area overnight and now tried to match the white line in the desert to their current position.

The Doctor squinted into the surrounds, trying to register something through the mist of fifty years. He shook his head:

"I remember a small village, the track between two small hills…"

Steven Wright scaled up the satellite image. There were some faint regular shapes in a cluster that looked to be perhaps thirty kilometres west of their current position on a parallel track.

"I suggest we head back and try to find this village - maybe somebody will remember."

It took them nearly an hour to backtrack down the rough track and along to the point where the village should have been. They were surrounded by small rounded hills, rocky and barren. Steven and the Doctor climbed the nearest hill. The view greeted them with endless sameness, small rounded hills disappearing into a shimmering heat haze. Then the Doctor turned south; two hills stirred a memory. He pointed them out to Steven, and they could both see the line of a goat track heading back towards them.

———

Nat had the Landcruiser grinding along in low ratio four-wheel drive. Progress was painfully slow. Frequently the track closed to a rocky, impassable gap between two hills which they would then have to circumnavigate to re-join the track. Steven calculated the distance between their

190

current position and Maddie's last location. It worked out at over three hundred kilometres, seventeen hours' travelling at their current pace. Beyond their fuel range. A small tight knot settled in his belly.

The village consisted of a cluster of roundel huts surrounded by a straggling fence of wooden stakes, partially woven with saplings. A small herd of goats raised puffs of dust inside the compound. As the vehicle stopped, perhaps a dozen children materialised. Shyly standing around the vehicle, silently staring.

A tall, elderly man emerged from the central hut, white robe flowing as he approached Abdul and the Doctor. The men had a short conversation, then Abdul turned and motioned the other two men towards them. The children crowded around Nat and Steven, all inquisitive, many reaching to touch the white skin.

The men sat under the shade of the single spreading acacia in the compound, Abdul and the Doctor cross-legged on the ground, Nat and Steven perching on rocks. The entire village encircled the group - men in white, women in long colourful dresses. Mint tea appeared, along with a precious packet of biscuits.

The conversation eventually drifted into the practical options. Yes, a trail across the border still existed, infrequently used by a camel trader from Mega. Usually taking two weeks' journey across to the Kenyan side. The only option would be travel by camel, and the only camels were in Mega, another one hundred kilometres back into Ethiopia.

Steven found some sweets and snacks in the truck for the children. The discussions ended and Nat started the slow grind out. Village children shouted and clutched at the doors for perhaps two kilometres. Once they got back to the road Nat stopped the vehicle. Steven summed up the situation succinctly:

"The camel option is no good. We will arrive too late, illegally across the border with no transport. We need to find another plan."

———

It was late afternoon when the truck arrived back at the guest house. The streets were filled with race support vehicles, and it was clear the little town was under assault from the unexpected influx. Tents were pitched in side streets, with guest houses packed. Crews were standing in shady patches in grumpy huddles. Rachel called for another meeting on the guesthouse porch. There had been a number of offers of help from other teams.

"If the alternate route can be tackled on a dirt bike, Kim and a couple of the other riders have offered to ride through."

Steven had been considering the alternatives on the way back. He had no doubt a dirt bike could get through the route, but it would be at the extreme end of fuel range, and would likely result in more missing riders.

There had been no movement on the race tracker for Maddie, although now other riders were being tracked. In another hour Maddie should have reached Marsabit, even at her slowest race pace. The scales were tipping. Rachel had also received a call from the race organiser. The pressure was now on him, with the risk of losing major sponsors unless television and film schedules could be maintained. He had set a twenty-four-hour limit for the border to reopen, after which he would have no choice but to abandon the race.

Once again, the Doctor cleared his throat:

"We have really two possibilities. One, that Maddie is alive and well and still riding across Kenya, in which case at some time she will be able to make contact. Secondly, that something has happened to her and she is stuck somewhere before Marsabit. In either of these scenarios she would be best supported by someone on the Kenyan side. I must travel back to Addis tonight and I suggest someone travel back with me to take the first flight to Nairobi."

The team nodded their assent and Rachel asked for a volunteer. Steven Reid immediately offered, "I have a good friend in Nairobi who will be able to help."

Darkness was closing in as the old Mercedes raised billows of golden dust down the road from the guesthouse. Steven Reid settled into the large, comfortable leather seat. The Doctor squinted over the top of his bifocals. They waved to some of the other crews as they reached the main road. On the CD player, gentle classical violin matched the old-world charm of the vehicle. *Like a big old cruise ship* thought Steven as they picked up speed heading out of town.

Rachel busied herself with a raft of chores and phone calls. Still no answer on Maddie's sat phone. The gnawing in the pit of her stomach had grown. Steven Wright sensed her feelings and gave her an awkward hug. "Maddie's a tough lady – she will be fine."

The remains of the team sat down to a meal. Nat had found some pasta in their dry food stocks and concocted a tasty sauce with some doubtful looking local vegetables, disguised with a heavy helping of dried garlic from the stores. Rachel quietly celebrated the return of some of her appetite. After the meal she announced her plan:

"OK, we wait for the twenty-four hours. If the border opens we go like crazy to catch up. I'll take up Kim's offer for riders to chase. They will be faster and we can support them. Border doesn't open, we high-tail it to Addis, dump the vehicles and fly to Nairobi to back up Steven. Any other thoughts?"

"No, that sounds like the best plan." Steven summed up the thoughts of the team.

After the meal Steven and Rachel took a quiet stroll down the dusty track to the main road. The Danish team were camped outside another small guest house down the road, the team manager claiming the only room and the rest of the team in a cluster of tents. Kim looked up. "Any news?"

"Nothing yet." Rachel tried to keep a positive and steady tone to her voice.

"Anything I can do to help, anything, just ask."

Rachel outlined the plan she had discussed with the team.

"I have already talked to Nikki from Japan and Henry the Dutchman. We are ready as soon as you give the word. Bugger the race - that is a good lady out there."

They continued down the road. The BMW team had taken over one of the bigger bars on the main road. The entire team were camped out on the bar floor. Ralf Hettingen saw the pair approach and came down the stairs to meet them.

"I hope everything is going to turn out well. Can I help in any way?"

Again, Rachel outlined the plan, and Ralf shuffled his feet as he said:

"Actually, the team has already decided to pull out and head to the Scandinavian Classic. It will be tight but we have a well- drilled team. The Classic is a real race and properly organised to international…"

But Rachel and Steven didn't catch the end of the sentence. Empty offers they didn't need. They were already walking away.

One of the soldiers emerged from the darkness. "Good evening Sir and Madam. Do you have any cigarette?"

Neither of them did, but Steven offered a packet of chewing gum from his pocket.

"We think the border may be closed for weeks. The rebels have camped down in Moyale and taken over all the government buildings, and they control the road south. Many, many dead bodies."

Rachel's stomach churned and the deep knot tightened further. She turned to Steven, catching him wiping the corner of his eye.

"We don't give up on her that easily."

Then one of the soldiers gave Rachel the glimmer of hope she was so desperately hoping for.

"The scout also talked to some travellers coming from the south. They saw a motorbike, riding fast, very close to Marsabit."

——

Steven Reid sat back in the seat of the old Mercedes. Eyes closed. There was a screech of brakes. Steven's eyes opened. The Doctor was flying backward in his seat, glasses arcing with flashes of light, suspended above his face. The wind screen was an opaque bulging glare of light, meteors of glass exploding backwards. The tinny music was drowned out by the screeching of metal. The floor of the Mercedes started to lift his feet, then blackness.

Chapter Seventeen – Geelong

Pam Wong looked over her small business empire with some pride. Her mezzanine office overlooked the five call rooms. Two big rooms were dedicated to insurance clients. A small medical emergency specialist room was dedicated to BMI Insurance, her number one client. Pam had secured the Asia-Pacific call centre work for nearly eighty thousand policy holders for this international giant.

She had not minded the early morning call. It gave her a sense of urgency and ownership to fill in the odd shift. It also gave her the opportunity to keep in touch with the staff on the floor. Time permitting, she also had work to do on a new proposal for another telco.

This morning had been exceptionally quiet, with only half a dozen active calls. She turned her attention to the telco proposal.

———

Charmaine Watkins eagerly anticipated tonight's drinks with the girls. She added some sparkles to her cheeks, and deepened the black eye liner. *Bogun*, she thought. Her black dress matched the inky dye in her shoulder-length hair which sharply framed her face. *Pity the new job cuts so deeply into social time,* she thought idly.

The pre-mixes clinked in her shoulder bag as she boarded the 60 bus at Pontalington. The driver frowned and pointed: "No alcohol to be drunk on the bus – look at the sign."

Charmaine ignored him and sat across two seats by the back door, staring out the window. The bus lurched back onto Route 60. She met the girls in the dark gloomy interior of Gallows café. The poor lighting helped hide the pre-mixes everyone brought here to load for the late-night clubs. Hidden at least well enough for the staff to claim ignorance. Not that anyone really gave a damn.

The girls already had food on the table - a big basket of chips. The tomato sauce had been generously splayed over. They tasted good. Charmaine had also ordered a hot dog. It was going to be a long night so she needed fuel, and a drink. The others were already two or three ahead. Kat was already well- fuelled, and teary as usual.

"You OK, Doll?" Charmaine had a mouth full of chips, and the munched sentence was lost. Kat continued to stare at the empty glass in her hand, listlessly swirling the ice cubes in the bottom, eyes red. Charmaine took a long swill from her can and tried again, this time touching the thin cold hands around the glass. "Tell Charms everything Doll."

The red eyes focused somewhere between Charmaine and the old bar. "It's David - he doesn't want to go out anymore. There must be someone else…" The thin voice trailed off.

"David's a waster. A beautiful lady like you can have the pick of the bunch. Leave him behind, Baby Doll. Let's start tonight - go and dry those eyes."

"You think so?"

"Absolutely."

As Kat headed off to the Ladies, Charmaine rolled her eyes at the remainder of the group. "OK ladies, the programme for tonight is fun! Any other defectors?"

The group signalled their intent with respective long swills from their cans. Charmaine led the banter, with her big back-country laugh rasping at the edges with cigarette-toasted vocals. "Jules, you are man-scout tonight - good butts, great movers, any other criteria ladies?"

———

The Dance Club was heaving. Christmas parties spilling from offices, indiscretions developing. The girls claimed a corner. Charmaine checked on Kat. She had attached herself to a suit from one of the office parties. Mid-forties, married, and clearly not going to last the distance. Kat was safe. Maybe worth a few free rounds for the girls.

Charmaine swung past Julie on the dancefloor. She moved with easy rhythm, hands briefly clasping her friend behind her neck, and then flowed past towards the entrance. She needed a ciggy. Rex the bouncer was at the door. Big Boy Rex. Charmaine was a familiar face, and he smiled. Charmaine lit a cigarette and offered it. It disappeared into a huge tattooed hand.

"She's humming tonight. Any trouble?"

"Only the usual incoherent slobs."

Rex talked with a deep but quiet voice. Charmain had to lean close to hear. Wafts of after-shave.

A group of three office workers arrived. The two on the outside were supporting a legless middleman, grinning stupidly but eyes clearly in orbit. Rex passed Charmaine the cigarette, and stepped forward.

"Your mate needs a taxi home."

"Come on, mate, it's our big night out."

The wingman on the right propped his glasses back up his nose with his spare hand.

"Look after your mate, then you two are welcome back."

The warning delivered softly but with an unspoken edge. The two wingmen looked at each other, then turned towards the taxi rank.

"Easy job," smiled Charmaine, offering the cigarette again. Rex declined.

"The P-heads are the bad ones, there's no boundaries there, no reason, no sense. They are only good when they are unconscious."

A massive fist cracked into the palm of the other hand.

Charmaine shivered; she felt a sense of cold physical power in the man next to her. She headed inside. "I need a drink."

Kat's friend had conveniently lined up a row of shooters on the table. His eyes were drooping, tie askew, hands exploring the deep vee in the back of Kat's dress. *Ten minutes max*, thought Charmaine. It took nearly an hour.

Kat's dress strap dangled from her shoulder and the hand was needing constant redirection. He suddenly lurched towards the toilet and was not seen again.

The shooter tasted sweet and rich, and the kick immediately flushed in Charmaine's cheeks. She looked at her cell phone - one thirty, only an hour and a half till work. She needed coffee and a sleep.

———

The cool of the street felt good on her face. On the short walk to work she had rung Loretta to open the door. She didn't want her swipe card recorded yet. Loretta was a delicate and nervous little Indian who shared the same booth in the main call room. She had a strong mug of coffee waiting in the lunch room.

Charmaine slumped in the chair.

The tap on her shoulder startled her. She slapped at Loretta's hand. Loretta whispered urgently, "The boss has arrived! One of the morning shift supervisors called in sick."

Charmaine's throat was raw and dry. Her head thick. She rubbed her eyes and checked her cell phone. Five minutes. "Thanks Doll," she croaked.

She pulled her work tee shirt from her bag and headed to the washroom. The cool water on her face didn't help much. She cleaned her teeth, then stuffed three menthol mints in her mouth. Her head throbbed. She spat the mints into a tissue and replaced them with Panadol tablets. Loretta swiped her out and she "officially" swiped in at two fifty-nine am.

———

Charmaine struggled at her desk. The headset felt uncomfortable on her ears. She took it off and felt no better. She had promised Loretta to run through some pronunciation lessons, but her voice wasn't quite up to the task. Sleep nagged; the bright light in the supervisor's office above forced her to keep awake. The Solitaire game on her screen beeped warnings for repeated wrong moves.

Almost on the dot of four am, the console on her screen lit up. Travellers arriving in Asia with bags missing and a raft of missed connections. Charmaine held off picking up for as long as she dared, but there were now thirty calls for eighteen operators.

"Good morning BMI Insurance global helpline. How can we help?" Charmaine's voice sounded like her grandmother's.

The voice on the other end could also have been Grandma. "Hello Dear. I am in a bit of a tither. I am on my way to my grandson David's wedding in Essex and I have missed my plane. It's a different booking and the airline can't help, so I am stuck here with no bags and the flight has already gone."

"OK ma'am, a few things first. Could I have your name and policy number please?"

"Oh, sorry dear. Enid Russell. Do you have a cold? I seem to have a little bit of a throat myself after that dreadful long flight. Sorry what else did you ask?"

"Your policy number ma'am. It's the big number at the top of your green insurance card."

"Card, yes, that's in my purse with my passport and things. Just a minute dear...no that's the bank card... just a minute..."

After a long rustling pause in the call, Enid came back.

"The number, I think it's zero, zero, six, two...or is that a seven? Please hold on a minute, where are my glasses?"

Charmaine's head ached, and she had forgotten the client's surname. She reached for her glass of water. It had only an unsatisfactory, warm half mouthful left.

The call lasted forty-five minutes. Charmaine was dying for a pee. The board still had three outstanding calls, but Charmaine logged out. She stayed in the washroom for as long as she dared, then filled her glass at the water cooler. To her relief, by the time she sat back down the console showed no waiting calls.

The next lull lasted nearly an hour. Charmaine caught her head dropping several times. The Solitaire game had timed out.

———

Pam Wong closed the spreadsheet with her costings for the telco proposal. She thought she could get away with five new staff if the call volumes didn't exceed the projections. Maybe she could squeeze five more into the main call room. She turned to the main BMI call console. It was lit up again. Pam flicked up the operator stats; most operators had only handled three or four calls in the shift, cleared at an average of six point five minutes. Only one call for the Watkins girl, but forty-five minutes' resolution - could have been a complex claim. To cover all eventualities, she activated a review alert on Charmaine's profile.

———

Charmaine waited for the call board to almost completely fill before picking up a call. A very faint voice crackled and echoed down the line.

Oh my god, why me, thought Charmaine. She asked for the policy number three times, until the connection was lost. Charmaine waited. Procedure required a call back after thirty seconds. Charmaine waited nearly three minutes. She checked the country code for the call. *Africa, land of spammers.* She dialled reluctantly.

The call connected instantly, and the line was clear. Somehow the disconnection had gone unnoticed for the person at the Africa end. Charmaine interrupted, "Ma'am, can I please have your policy number from the card?"

The BMI console in Pam Wong's office gave an audible beep. The active call for the Watkins girl was both a priority corporate policy and a medical emergency. Pam grabbed the head phones and switched to the call channel. She heard Watkin's voice, clearly with a very bad cold, "..but ma'am you can't be unconscious now if you are talking to me."

The voice on the other end, although echoing a little and sounding tinny, spoke clearly and patiently, "As I said, the card belongs to somebody else. She has been unconscious since her arrival. Excuse me, my cell phone is about to lose power. Please act quickly - I need to inform someone who knows this person."

"*Get the location!*" Pam screamed mentally at Watkins.

"I need your name or the name of…" Charmaine started.

Pam slammed down the interrupt button, "Please give us your location and another number we can call you on."

"Marsa…" and the line went dead.

Pam swore loudly. Heads turned in the cubicles below. Watkins could wait. She grabbed a pen and scrawled "*Masa?*" with her left hand as she started downloading the policy details. On a second screen she flicked to the call number and looked up the country code. The scrawled note became "*Masa? Kenya?*" The policy details came down - IBC International Travel. Who was it?

Pam flicked the coms switch to Watkins.

"You sit there and ring that number every ten to fifteen minutes. They may be able to recharge it."

The ice in the voice cut through Charmaine's pending hangover.

The policy details included the name of the broker, Tim Williams, and a mobile number. Pam dialled and a sleepy voice answered,

"It's five thirty in the bloody morning. Who is this?"

Pam quickly explained. Tim jumped instantly out of bed and powered up his laptop. In a few minutes he responded:

"We have two teams from IBC - one filming wildlife in the Serengeti, and the other is following a trans-Africa motor cycle race, but they are still in Ethiopia as far as I know. The Serengeti is close to the Kenyan border so it's more likely to be those guys. I will email you the list then try to contact everyone".

Tim's email arrived less than ten minutes later. All three of the Serengeti team were accounted for, but one had lost his wallet in Nairobi. It contained his card. Tim concluded: "That accounts for a spam call from Kenya - someone has obviously found the card".

———

Charlotte lounged back in the seat on the 60. Morning sun glinted off the sea. The big mocha and cream bun at the station take-away helped revive her. She mentally high-fived her narrow escape. She had avoided ringing the number back in case it brought more trouble. To play it safe she had misdialled a few calls. Under the desk she had texted friends discreetly, phone on silent. She quickly turned her focus. *Big party at Sam's tonight, twenty first. That hot guy from the pizza shop will be there. Better doll up good.*

———

Monday morning, something still nagged Pam about the call from Kenya. Something half lost in subconscious. She pulled up the policy details for the team in the Serengeti. The clients listed included: Morris Hawkston, aged forty-five, Jim Williams, fifty-two and James Wright thirty-seven. Then it registered - they were all males!

Pam scrolled through the Friday call log and found the voice log. She skipped through the call and then, near the end she found it: "...card belongs to somebody else. **She** has been unconscious since her arrival."

Pam felt sick; the woman had been in a critical condition and three days had lapsed. She grabbed the phone to call Tim the broker.

Pam raced through the urgent follow-up procedures until there was nothing more she could do. She sat back in her chair and felt the cold fury directed at the Watkins girl consuming all rational thought.

Chapter Eighteen –Melbourne

Dave and Bruno had established a comfortable routine in the apartment. Dave had insisted on paying Bruno some rent which went largely into their food allowance. Cheese boards, acceptable in any restaurant. Cordon bleu dishes.

To compensate Dave had started a routine of jogging along the banks of the Yarra. He always finished at the same wooden bench beside the Swan Street Bridge. Time for a few stretches. Time also to watch the morning activity. Rowing skiffs gliding beneath the pillars of the bridges; the big tourist river boats shuffling into position for the day's tours. The scene gave a sense of familiarity and peace.

Today, as every day, his thoughts returned to the race. He felt proud for Maddie. The texts and emails arrived in sudden bursts as she reached a town. *So bloody hot today. Fell down a mine-hole. Incredible generosity from the poorest people. Makes you wonder about all the stuff we surround ourselves with. Does it really make us happy?*

Maddie's touch of philosophy stayed in his mind until he arrived back at the apartment. Anne McLeod greeted him in the foyer. She had assumed a closeness which demanded a hug and light kiss. Dave relaxed in her motherly fondness.

"Just off to Tai Chi Dear. How's that lovely girl of yours doing in Africa?"

"Great, she was in the lead last call. Bit quiet at the moment." *When did that last message arrive? It has been a few days now, but she is in a remote part of Northern Kenya.*

At that point the phone started ringing inside the apartment. Dave excused himself and struggled to find his key. Anne McLeod disappeared behind the lift door. By the time Dave had opened the door the phone had stopped ringing. No message. Dave headed for the shower. As he stepped into the glorious hot stream, the phone started ringing again…

Dave held the receiver in his hand; the dial tone buzzed. There was a dark damp patch on the carpet where he had stood. The peace of the morning had shattered into long shards of fear and uncertainty. Steam billowed from the bathroom.

Dave wrenched the mixer to a full blast of cold. The icy shock started to shift the daze; action lists started to form.

Shit, what was he going to tell Maureen? That one could wait - mother-daughter anguish would not help. He needed more information first. *What was IBC doing? Did Rachel know? Where was she?* The questions flooded in.

The call to IBC took a twenty-minute cycle of recordings and diversions to get to an operator in the Producer's Department. All Dave knew about Rachel's producer was that his name was Bill.

"Can you find me the producer for the IBC Team following the Africa Odyssey motorbike race, this is urgent. No - critical. His name is Bill."

"I will put you through to the PA for Overseas Productions."

"That will be Bill Struthers. He's on the phone at the moment. I will pop down to his office. One minute."

Bill Struthers picked up the phone. He had an abrupt tone and was clearly used to total control. "The team are waiting for the border to reopen and are planning the best approach to get through and support the rider…"

He didn't even remember Maddie's name. Dave exploded.

"I had a call from the emergency insurance line five minutes ago. Maddie is critically injured, unconscious in a Kenyan town, probably Marsabit. Were you aware of that?"

"No, but the insurance…"

Dave cut him off again and continued.

"The northern Kenya area is officially a war zone, so a medivac flight is not possible. I need to know Rachel's satellite phone number. I also need to know what support IBC can offer to a rescue mission. I am heading to Kenya as soon as possible."

Bill Struthers' assurances deteriorated into flustered waffle. Dave terminated the conversation with:

"Let me know as soon as you have something concrete and call me back."

He would get more help from Bruno. He quickly dialled his work number. Bruno was in.

"OK - we need a good team. I will ring Pete and Donna. Donna's a top-notch emergency nurse, and Pete is vital to keep vehicles going anywhere." Bruno was in familiar territory. "We will need two or three good four-wheel drive vehicles. By the way, how are we going to fund this?"

"The mining company that bought the station left an embarrassing stack of dollars in my bank account. Don't worry about finance."

Dave checked the time difference to Moyale before calling Rachel's sat phone. It would be four in the afternoon - perfect. The line had a distant hollow echo. Rachel's voice drifted in and out as Dave explained.

Rachel gasped, "Oh my God, Mads…"

Dave was surprised at the sudden level of emotion in her voice. Clearly Maddie had become more than a mere documentary job to Rachel. After a brief silence she gathered herself, then moved with Dave into practical steps. She would pull the team back to Addis and catch a flight to Nairobi to provide any ground support they could.

"Anything, absolutely anything we can do, please call."

Dave opened his laptop and started scrolling through his emails to find the last message from Maddie. On the same page was the message from Akeyo's Martin. A local, he knew the area and spoke the language, and he would also have a local bank account for the necessary funds. Dave hastily outlined the situation and emailed Martin for help.

The phone rang. This time it was Bruno's friend Pete.

"I'm sorry, mate, I would love to help, but I have a business to run. I can't afford to simply bugger off for weeks."

"Pete, I sold my farm, the woman I love is stuck in some hole in Africa, I don't give a damn what it costs. Is there any way I can help with the business? I'll cover the costs. If it takes longer I'll cover that as well."

In spite of initial protests from Pete, Dave could tell that the lure of adventure would hook Pete. In the seriousness of it all, Dave needed a team who could stand up to anything.

"OK, Donna and I are in."

Dave had started a list on his laptop. It had reached two pages. He knew he was putting off the next call. Maureen Jacobs deserved as much of the truth as she could bear.

"Hi Dave." Maureen's voice had a gentleness which reflected the fondness she felt for this man. She had seen the love the couple shared.

"Bad news I'm afraid, Maureen. Maddie's had a bit of an accident."

"How bad?"

"We don't exactly know how bad. She's unconscious, but she is in a local hospital being cared for by trained nurses."

Dave flinched inwardly at the lie, and quickly outlined the details of his plan for the rescue mission.

"Give her our love, especially from the boys." Maureen's voice quavered.

"Don't worry, everyone will be doing everything possible for a quick and safe return."

———

Bruno was focused. He called Pete first, and they rapidly explored the vehicle and logistical requirements.

"I'll ask Donna what we will need from the medical side," was Pete's last comment.

Bruno knocked on his manager's door. He explained the situation briefly and asked for leave without pay for at least a month.

"Starting when?"

"Now, today."

"Impossible. We have no provision for replacement resource, and a whole program of projects for which you are directly responsible. It's a ridiculous request - you should know better."

Bruno sat for a moment feeling strangely calm. "Then you can have my resignation, also effective immediately."

Bruno felt like the dove released from its coop, free and flying into a blue sky. It did feel ridiculously liberating.

"Excellent bluff. But still no way."

"No bluff." Bruno handed the hastily-typed resignation and left the office.

He spent the next hour preparing a hand-over list for his assistant, and a further two hours' research on the internet. The office printer delivered a folder full of documents and web-pages. He had also downloaded a full set of GPS topo maps for Kenya.

Bruno strode home purposefully, his small sports bag crammed with paper and bits from his office. Passing the café end of Bourke Street, he spotted a hat under an umbrella. Not Julia's usual turf but it was her. Bruno hesitated. His head was focused on Kenya already. Julia would be a difficult distraction. Maybe he could pretend he hadn't seen her.

"Bonjour Bruno," she waved cheerfully.

Strange, she seemed to have made every effort to avoid him in the last few weeks. She motioned to the seat beside her.

"Sorry, I have been buried with final exams and studies. I think I see a light at the end of the tunnel. Not a train I hope!" She laughed and reached across to touch his arm. "Great to see you."

Bruno's resistance melted a little. His mind still bubbled with plans for Kenya – so he shared his news: quitting his job, organising the trip with Dave, Pete and Donna.

Julia was entranced. This was the outback Bruno adventurer. She also sensed a finality in this move, something that didn't include her. She felt a sense of regret, something slipping away. She knew the wall she had built had nothing to do with her feelings. The lies were necessary to protect her other life.

221

Bruno described his resignation and the sense of liberation it gave him. Julia got it completely. She leant across and kissed Bruno firmly on the lips.

"I know you have heaps to do. Can I ring you tonight? Seven o'clock?"

Bruno floated away from the encounter feeling light and free. What had transpired with Julia - so unexpected, so electric, and so mysterious?

———

At the apartment, Dave was engrossed in a conversation with Bill Struthers from IBC. A very different Bill Struthers from the morning, apologetic and generous.

"Our insurers are well set up to cover the international emergencies, but if you can provide support on the ground that will be most welcome. We are happy to contribute to that. I will also send Rachel and the crew into Kenya to help in any way they can."

Dave cautioned: "Our first priority is Maddie. I don't want this turned into an IBC drama, unless Maddie is safe and happy to talk."

———

Dave turned to Bruno.

"That was IBC. They are putting twenty grand up front and providing any help with visas we need, even diplomatic ones if necessary. Their insurers will take the lead to support us."

The two men started on Dave's list. Bruno's afternoon research had already wiped half a page from page three. A few calls flew between Pete and Donna as Donna's medical list arrived, along with Pete's vehicle and equipment list. Normal meals were forgotten. Bruno took a jug of fruit juice from the fridge; a packet of nuts lay empty on the bench.

For the tenth time Dave answered the phone at first ring. His eyebrows shot up and he turned to Bruno mouthing "Julia." Bruno glanced at his watch. It was exactly seven pm. He walked across the room and sat on the large leather sofa. "Hi Julia."

There was a long pause before Julia began,

"Hi Bruno. Actually, it's Grace, Grace Satori. Same face, different name. I have a lot of explaining to do." The voice was shaky and nervous.

Now it was Bruno's eyebrows that raised. "I'm listening."

Fifteen minutes passed. Dave looked across the room. Bruno was having an uncharacteristically one-sided conversation. His face looked puzzled. It took another twenty minutes before Bruno finally spoke.

"Hello Grace, lovely to meet you."

Dave would have to wait for the phone call to end to get the full meaning.

Bruno listened as Julia/Grace had concluded her carefully rehearsed revelation. She continued.

"Bruno," she said softly, "I looked at you today and realised what I wanted was simply to be the real me. In the drug world I sustained myself with the thought that by keeping one kid away from the dealers, one kid away from death, it was worth it. Now I only want my own life. I want a chance with you without the constant drain of deception. I won't be untainted by my past, and the current stuff is still classified – but at least I can talk about most of it."

Bruno wiped his brow. Dave remained silent.

Julia continued, breathless. "I don't expect anything from you. I know this is a huge shock. But I am free to change my life. And I want to help. What can I do for you – for your Kenya trip?"

"That would be wonderful. We have a long list and an equally long night ahead. Oh, and we are both hungry if you could possibly pick something up on the way."

Bruno was smiling; the myriad of little mysteries and doubts had been cleared. Now all he had to do was remember the new name. He turned to Dave, who still had a quizzical look on his face. "Long story."

Bruno walked back across the room with phone in hand when it rang again. Bruno's face lit up and he spoke in rapid-fire French. Dave was struggling to translate with his rusty vocab.

"Who, Who, Who?"

Eventually Bruno handed over the phone. Simone's soft accent caught Dave off-guard. The emotions of the day filled his eyes and choked his throat. Simone reflected that emotion with sudden little sobs. Bruno held his friend around the shoulders. Dave wiped his eyes fiercely with his sleeve.

"Simone! This is perfect timing. It's so great to hear your voice. It's been a hell of a day."

"Mon Cherie, je comprend. Martin and I read your email together today. He is here chez moi, at this very moment. We are coming to help in Kenya. When are you flying?"

Dave had a momentary vision of the elegant Simone in tall stilettos tottering around in the Kenyan bush.

Dave had flicked the speaker phone on so Bruno caught the "…when are you flying?" Bruno held up two fingers. Dave nodded, looked at the list, gulped and said, "Two days, Wednesday our time".

"Martin asks what do you need immediately from him?"

"His bank account number and swift code so we can transfer funds, any contacts he has for buying vehicles, and any contacts he has who may be able to help us travel into the war zone."

"Martin has already contacted an old friend who coordinates with NGOs. For a small fee we can use Red Cross trucks, as long as we replace them with new vehicles. How many do we need?"

Bruno held up three fingers.

"Three and if one can be kitted as an ambulance that would be even better."

"Team Francais already has this in hand."

Dave and Bruno returned to their laptops. Emails flew. Eventually they were interrupted by the buzz of the intercom. Julia/Grace announced, "Dinner delivery."

Bruno opened the door. Dave looked up. Julia appeared transformed. She wore an ankle length black dress, elegant but casual, her hair somehow different. She started nervously, and looking first at Dave said,

"Hi Dave, I guess we need to start at square one. I'm Grace. I really have been hoping to meet you honestly, I mean as the real me...."

Dave broke the awkwardness by striding across the room to hug her, crinkling through the bundles of plastic bags hanging from both her hands. He stepped back and relieved her of the bags, so Bruno could also greet her. Bruno's hug lingered, he lightly kissed her lips and whispered, "Welcome Grace, goodbye Julia."

She smiled. "The white bag is sushi and sashimi from my favourite Japanese, the blue bag is my own Moroccan meat balls and noodles, the red bag is caramel crème deserts and the yellow bag is Chinese, to hedge my bets."

Dave laid some plates and cutlery on the table. "Sashimi followed by meat-balls sounds like me."

"Wine?" Bruno asked.

"Maybe a glass, we have a lot of work to do. I am also dying to hear the Julia/Grace story."

Grace turned to Dave.

"Dave, given what has happened, I'll stick to the short version. I operate undercover, at least until this afternoon I did. Julia was my cover name for a big organised crime operation. I was a spook. Today I got my own life back. I simply feel relief, it is so good not to have to lie day after day. Especially to you. I will fill in the real me when we have time."

The Chinese bag remained unopened. The spicy sauce on the meatballs won the accolades. Grace declined on the crème caramels and started to clear the table.

"OK guys, point me at the first job on my list."

"Probably air fares and bookings for Nairobi. We decided to push for Wednesday kick-off. Please check with Pete and Donna, and you will need their passport details. Take my credit card. If you max it out I will top it up."

A slight nervousness overtook Grace as the phone began ringing. Donna answered.

"Hi Donna it's …uhh.. Julia here." The correction could be made later. The conversation with Donna continued, warm and familiar. Grace could relax again.

Bruno opened his laptop for Grace to connect to the internet. Then the two men huddled at the benchtop and continued expanding the lists. They agreed that the shortest connections and flight times were Grace's sole criteria for the flights. She twiddled Dave's credit card between her fingers.

"This feels strange. I've spent all my lifetime fighting criminals, and now here I am like some Nigeria fraudster about to max out your credit card."

It was early morning when they decided nothing more could be completed that night. Bruno had painstakingly traced a number of options for routes into the northern Kenya region, avoiding the areas highlighted in recent reports of insurgent activity. He had emailed Martin some map images to review with his local knowledge. He had also checked Donna's lists and ordered all the medical supplies he thought they might need. He would collect them from the hospital in the morning.

Dave had prepared a complete budget and transferred a generous sum into Martin's bank account for vehicles and on-the-ground expenses. He had also ordered some US dollars for each of the team as cash reserves. The internet options were exhausted; the remaining items on the lists required real people and physical transactions.

Dave yawned, "I'm whacked. Bedtime for me. Goodnight you two."

Bruno moved to the big couch, sitting sideways and hugging his knees. Grace joined him, sitting at the other end, effortlessly sliding down to a cross-legged position.

"How do you do that? I can't even bend my knees that way."

"Yoga."

"Tell me a little about your real family. Or did I get some of the real story?"

"Sorry, all cover. You have to live with one story, otherwise you confuse the hell out of yourself. A slip is simply too dangerous."

"We really do have to start again."

At times Grace found her own life truths were so well-buried, she had to pause to answer Bruno's questions. Finally, he got up from the couch for a glass of water. "Would you like a drink?" There was no response. Grace was asleep.

———

Dave awoke early. He rolled to his side, trying to force his eyes to shut again. His brain immediately engaged with an instant flood of jobs of the list. He got up and passed Bruno's open door. He saw Bruno sprawled across the bed fully clothed, a gentle snore coming in regular pattern. No sign of Julia/Grace.

Dave showered and dressed quietly. As he reached the kitchen, he noticed Grace on the couch. She was tucked under one of Bruno's blankets, her head on a pillow, hair spilled over one side. Her face had transparency, almost innocence. Dave reflected on the doubts of their first meeting. What had triggered his distrust? He couldn't remember.

Grace awoke to the smell of bacon cooking. She opened her eyes with a start, disoriented. Dave appeared with a glass of orange juice. It tasted fresh and sharp, a little too sharp yet. Dave had laid a towel and a clean checked shirt on the arm of her sofa.

"Help yourself to the shower, and there's a shirt and some shorts if you fancy a change. Sorry, the ladies' section of the wardrobe is a little bare." His own words registered and stung back - Sue appeared then disappeared in a flash.

Bruno walked sleepily out to greet Dave. He drank from the orange juice bottle, emptying the contents. Throat dry and raw. He rinsed his mouth with some water, then went back to brush his teeth. He had just returned to the kitchen when Grace emerged from the bathroom in Dave's shirt. Dave saw an instant of similarity. Simone in Saturday dress-down mode. He smiled.

Grace started purposefully, "OK, what is first on the agenda today?"

———

By eight am the three were out the door: Dave to the bank, and Bruno to drive Grace to her apartment to collect her gear. Everyone would spend the last night in the apartment. Donna and Pete would arrive at Southern Cross on the ten thirty am train. Whoever finished first would collect them, then deliver all the passports to Aimie the PA at IBC. Aimie would handle the visa processing and return the passports to the apartment as soon as she could get them stamped.

Driving against the traffic flow, Bruno and Grace made good time to Box Hill. The cluster of tall apartment blocks provided excellent cover for an anonymous life. The neighbours were mostly Vietnamese immigrants, quiet, industrious and discreet. They took the lift to the tenth floor and Grace opened the outside door. The apartment contained two bedrooms, one with a locked door which Grace opened. A single suitcase sat already packed on the bare bed, along with a backpack for the trip. Grace quickly changed into casual jeans and tee shirt, stuffing Dave's shirt into the top of her pack.

On the bed in the other room Bruno saw the hat. Grace's alter ego now put into the past. He whispered, "*Goodbye Julia.*"

Grace was reaching for the light switch, when the lights went off of their own accord. The department clean-up had already begun, and soon no trace of Julia would exist on any records in the city.

She felt like a hermit crab, abandoning an outgrown shell, fragile and vulnerable, but free.

Chapter Nineteen – Nairobi

Bruno and Dave waded their way through the throngs at Nairobi airport. Joe, their driver, pushed through the wall of waiting taxi drivers and headed towards the baggage carousel. Dave had negotiated with Joe for use of his matatu for up to one week. Their plan was ambitious - only three days' preparation in Nairobi. Joe had smiled delightedly at the deal - he would earn more than two months' normal income in those three days.

Simone suddenly swept into view wearing a safari shirt and three-quarter length trousers. Slung casually around her neck she wore an aquamarine silk scarf, her only concession to colour. Over one shoulder she sported a very new-looking pack. She spotted Dave first, skipping through the bags and trolleys to launch a huge welcome hug from half a metre away. Dave staggered backwards a couple of steps, then reciprocated in a warm intimate hug which lasted until Simone spotted Bruno over his shoulder. Simone brushed a kiss across Dave's lips and raced across to Bruno.

Simone linked arms between the two men and led them across to Martin. Martin also wore crisp safari brown, making him look distinguished and official-looking. The men greeted him warmly, and Martin immediately felt at ease, absorbed into the close cluster of friendship. He felt refreshed; the business-class seats had made the journey relaxing. He spotted Simone's bag on the carousel and went to retrieve a slightly larger version of the backpack she had over her shoulder. The pack caused Dave and Bruno to exchange glances. It was so un-Simone.

Simone had been fired with a sense of excitement and purpose as soon as Martin had shown her Dave's email. It side-lined the normal trivia of her life in an instant. Martin responded to her excitement. The purpose put an energy back which he hadn't felt since before leaving Moyale. The two started planning and preparations. She had gone to the sprawling Decathlon sporting goods store and allowed Martin to choose suitable clothing for both of them. She had cried for Dave, feeling the raw wounds of his old loss and now a potential new one. During the long flight Simone realised that for once in her life she wasn't thinking about herself.

Tall white walls topped with iron lattice spikes signalled their arrival at the hotel. Two armed guards manned the gate, pulling the barrier arm up as they recognised Joe's matatu. Inside, the noise of Nairobi became muted down the gravel drive lined with hibiscus. Grace had chosen well, a great base for preparation: room for the vehicles when they arrived, ground floor rooms with direct access outside for loading gear. She had booked Pete and Donna into a suite, with a large lounge which would serve as the planning hub. Maps and lists were spread across the floor and table.

The new arrivals were introduced around the group. Dave suggested Simone and Martin could catch up on sleep, but both declined. They were keen to maintain the excitement of preparation. Sleep could wait.

The conversations were short. Consensus was reached in seconds. Simone smiled, thinking of the power plays and drawn out management meetings in her own office; this approach was so refreshing. Dave, Martin and Pete would go to Martin's friend in the Health Department office to start organising the vehicles, then to Red Cross headquarters for Pete to check the vehicles. Bruno and Donna would complete the medical supplies, while Grace would continue her research into the activity of the militants and risks around their routes. Simone had the job of locating the new vehicles for replacement with Red Cross. Martin had armed her with a list of dealers and a list of negotiating tips. He had also remembered the prices his department had last paid in bulk government deals.

Grace remained in the lounge with Donna and Bruno. She glanced across at the pair. She saw another Bruno again, meticulous and professional, working through all the possibilities. Donna brought a practical balance to the discussion. She had completed her early nursing training in the outback settlement of Warburton. She knew what could be improvised with limited resources, what the critical necessities were and what could be used to make do. They made an impressive team.

———

Grace had been nervous when Pete and Donna arrived at Bruno's apartment. Donna had accepted her as a friend, at face value, and now she was about to show a totally different face. Grace explained that the carefully-constructed life history she had whispered to Donna on the road to Ivanhoe was a cover. When she had finished Donna remained quiet for a couple of minutes. Then she reflected,

"I think I go more by gut instinct. It's more about the inner person who shines through any story. I got that person."

Grace felt the relief as she hugged Donna. She was shaking uncontrollably.

———

The sprawling fibro buildings of the Heath Department annex were a rabbit warren of small grubby offices, yellowing paper, dusty computer screens. Disinterested workers smoking or chewing betel nut lounged in doorways. Red-toothed grins followed by a guttural spit of red juice making ant-infested pools in the dust.

It took nearly half an hour to track down Martin's friend Ruben Wasai. Dave immediately recognised the Massai heritage in his tall lean build, if somewhat marred by the disproportionate pot belly.

Ruben's office contrasted with the chaotic paper piles in the other offices along the corridor. His had a semblance of organisation. Although files crammed his bookshelf, each file was neatly labelled with the name of an NGO. He held up his hands.

"I'm sorry Martin, once the Director got wind of it the price escalated. You know how it is. I know your principles, but if you want to move fast you need to talk to the Director. I believe probably two hundred US would move things along."

The group climbed the four flights of steps to the Director's Office. Peeling paint hung in flakes from the concrete walls. Partially boarded-up black holes indicated

238

two defunct lift shafts. Ruben opened the door to the fourth floor, revealing a total transformation. Carpeted floor covered a large reception area. Rosewood furniture with red velvet upholstery lined the walls, copies of Time magazine were stacked neatly on a coffee table. The receptionist's dress matched the scarlet red of the upholstery. Her dress neckline plunged to a large gold belt. Her fingernails, in the same scarlet shade, held her attention even as Ruben approached her desk. Without looking up she said,

"The Director is in a meeting for at least two hours."

Martin turned to Dave and whispered in his ear. Dave handed Martin a US note and Martin approached the receptionist, speaking rapidly in Swahili. She took the note from between his fingers, before knocking on the office door. Martin returned to the group, apologetically.

"I'm sorry, this is how it works in certain circles in Government - not all, but many."

The receptionist returned from the Director's office.

"The Director will see you in half an hour."

It was fifty minutes before the Director's door opened. A slightly more mature version of the receptionist emerged from the office. She walked straight to the stairs without making eye contact. Dave looked at his watch. The momentum of the rescue seemed to have been swallowed up by the hippopotamus of a man who now faced them. His breath reeked of whiskey, a bottle of Oban Single Malt stood open on his desk.

———

As they drove towards the Red Cross Compound, Ruben introduced Graham Wilkins, the Red Cross co-ordinator.

"Graham is an orthopaedic surgeon from New Zealand. He first came to Africa to hunt. He immediately lost his hunting appetite after he watched one of the party shoot a rhino from the vehicle. "That's not bloody sport!" he said. His intention to return home was thwarted by an urgent request to help with a girl who had been trampled by an elephant. He is still here fifteen years later - Africa is in his blood."

The compound stood in semi-darkness as the matatu pulled up at the front gate. Ruben went to the gate and called out. A uniformed security guard appeared behind the bars. The guard shook his head. Across the compound, a small scooter spluttered into life. The head light caused Ruben and the guard to squint. Graham Wilkin's incongruously gangly figure appeared behind the light of the scooter.

"Ruben - it's you - I had given up on you. Open the gate Tasi."

Graham was enthusiastic and helpful, the antithesis of the attitude they had received from the director. He pointed out to Pete the vehicles he intended to swap.

"There is one condition from our side. Now that the Director has given official clearance, we need to assess the situation up there for ourselves. So, I would like to come with you."

Dave nodded. "Please be ready by tomorrow night."

On the way back to the hotel Dave asked Pete how the vehicles looked.

"They've had a hard life, but they are all solid. Couple of tyres shot, but nothing major mechanically as far as I can tell. If Bruno and I can spend the day on them tomorrow we'll have them ready."

The lights of the matatu swung around the corner in the hotel grounds. Shining in the headlights were three new Landcruisers lined up in the driveway. Simone rushed out, spreading her arms towards her purchases. "Under budget as well!"

Over dinner the group had a catch-up on the day's achievements. They toasted Simone's record-breaking purchases. Dave brought their focus back to reality.

"Somebody must deliver the bank cheque to the Red Cross Manager who will sign the paperwork tomorrow, otherwise my credit card will be very sad."

"Pity we can't take the new wagons," reflected Bruno.

"Buying is the easy part - the registration and paperwork to follow would take a month, even with all the right palms greased." Martin still felt highly embarrassed by the exhibition at the Director's office.

Before the end of the meal, both Simone and Martin excused themselves to go to their rooms. The long day of travel had caught up. Dave stood and hugged Simone. "Thank you, thank you, and so wonderful to see you."

After dinner the group gathered in the lounge. Grace explained what she had found out from reports of the militants, and the areas where they seemed to be strongest. Bruno checked his maps for the best routes to avoid the areas concerned. After an hour or so Dave called a halt.

"Thanks everyone, let's have a quiet nightcap. You have done an amazing job."

Pete slumped in the sofa beside Donna, putting his arm around her. Bruno sat beside Grace and stroked the back of her neck. Dave looked at the couples and the dull ache became a moment of agony with fears for Maddie. Grace looked over and caught the moment. She kissed Bruno's cheek and walked across to put one hand on each of Dave's shoulders. She looked directly into his eyes.

"We are going to find her. We have the best team possible. She's going to be OK."

Her strength and conviction lifted Dave. He brushed his hand to her cheek. "Thanks Grace, it's great to have good friends."

Grace realised Dave had called her by her real name for the first time.

———

Dave awoke with a start. Late for the planned start. The clock on the bedside table read eight forty-five. He grabbed shorts and a shirt and raced down the hallway to Pete and Donna's suite. Simone sat at the table alone, bundled in a large hotel bath robe, hair tousled and eyes sleepy. She had just read the note on the table.

"We seem to be redundant this morning Dave."

Dave leaned over her shoulder. The list was neat and hand- written. *Donna's*, he thought. Then he read item three:

3. Donna and Me – camping gear purchase

It could only be Grace. She had assumed responsibility; everything left to organise had been allocated.

Dave and Simone sat at the big table and ordered some breakfast. Dave flicked through his diary, scrawled lists with cross outs on most items. Simone returned to her room for a shower. She arrived back in a waft of clean soapy freshness and Dave looked up and smiled. The French came instinctively: "Nous sommes presque prêts, mon cher amie." (We are almost ready, my dear friend.)

"Je suis tellement heureux d'être ici avec tu et Bruno. Je me sens utile pour un changement." (I'm so happy to be here with you and Bruno. I feel useful for a change.)

There was a knock at the door, preceded by the rattle of the breakfast trolley. A rich dark coffee aroma cut through the sweet freshness of the large fruit platter. Dave savoured the food while Simone caught him up on the story of Martin's good fortune, and his visit to Paris. "Si triste qu'Akeyo ne pouvait pas être avec nous."

For a moment Dave caught the dark haunting eyes of Akeyo. Emotion surged. Simone reached across the table for his hand.

"We have a priority to rescue another love first." The "priority" rolled with Simone's soft French accent. Eyes and hands held between the two for perhaps a minute.

Dave felt the strength of his friend, which galvanised him into action.

"Right let's get moving, we have a lot to do."

Chapter Twenty –Addis to Nairobi

The acrid smell of the burnt-out vehicle would not leave Rachel's senses. It had been Nat who recognised the Doctor's vehicle. Someone had wedged the number plate in a nearby tree. The vehicle itself lay crumpled into a contorted jumble of smoking, twisted iron, buried under the front of the bus.

They had driven into the town of Mega, trying to piece together the story. After an hour of questioning villagers, Abdul had found one of the survivors from the bus, a young woman and her child, both recovering at the house of a relative. Her hands were swathed in filthy grey rags, black patches of dried blood. The rail of the seat in front had slammed into her forehead, leaving her face bruised and swollen. She remembered little but her uncle had helped Police load two bodies from the car onto a truck to Addis.

They left the uncle with some clean bandages and iodine ointment for treating her hands. The group drove on in numbed silence to Addis. Rachel stared blankly out the window. A new mosque, wrapped in a spindly web of bamboo scaffolding, flashed past the window. It had an element of the essence of Ethiopia that Rachel had been keen to capture on the journey, but dull nothingness now swamped her thoughts. She felt Maddie slipping further from her grasp. She knew she had to face the reality of the new tragedy. She quickly quashed a momentary flash of anger aimed at the Doctor. She needed control for what lay ahead in Addis.

Abdul lead the way to the Doctor's compound in the wealthy suburb of Mekanisa. An elderly man swung open the imposing wrought iron gate. The two vehicles entered the compound which was surrounded by a tall mud-brick fence. Dominating the compound stood a large tent. The three-day mourning phase had brought a small village of people paying their respects. Pristine white gowns crowded the space. Clearly the Doctor was held in great esteem in many circles.

A screeching wail greeted the new arrivals. Rachel jumped, hair standing on the back of her neck. An elderly woman, blood dripping from scratches on her forehead, began beating her face and chest. Several other women joined the chorus. One came towards one of the brothers with a bowl and cloth. She knelt to wash his feet. He skipped away a couple of paces and she followed to repeat the process.

The sun cooked the air inside the tent, white walls of heat. Rachel felt faint and slumped into a chair, head in hands. The day had turned surreal, white figures hazy in the heat.

A cool hand touched her arm. The same woman who minutes before was wailing, now calm and concerned at her side. A small trickle of blood remaining from her ritual, ran down her cheek. She offered Rachel water, metallic and icy. She returned Rachel's smile then brought some food from the heavily laden table.

It took nearly an hour for Rachel to get alongside Abdul. She whispered in his ear, and he turned to one of the brothers to ask the question. The question prompted a sharp command, and shortly a young lean man dressed in jeans and tee shirt appeared. He led Abdul outside and Rachel followed. In fluent English he asked, "How may I assist you?"

Rachel quickly explained what they needed.

"Of course, my Uncle was taken to Menelik hospital morgue. I have a friend there who will be able to help."

The ride across the city took forty minutes. Rachel tried to keep her focus but found her thoughts continually drifting back to Maddie. *She will be safe. She must be safe.*

The friend appeared in the hospital corridor, a strong large woman, a senior doctor. She introduced herself to Rachel.

"Hi, my name is Ayana, how can I help?"

Rachel explained and Ayana led them through a labyrinth of corridors to a large room at the rear of the hospital. She spoke briskly to the elderly attendant seated in the middle of the large space. He shuffled over to a rusted filing cabinet, the only other piece of furniture in the room, returning to the desk with a battered folder.

The heavy metal door at the far end of the big room opened to a cloying waft of chemicals. Rachel took a step back, stifling a retching choke. She felt hands on her shoulders.

"Let me do this," Nat insisted.

———

Rachel lay back on the big bed. The tears came, firstly in grief for Steven Reid, then with anguish for Maddie. The call to Steven's family had been gut-wrenching, and she had cried with his parents. Now she felt exhausted and empty.

The team had moved into the Hotel D'Afrique, an old-style hotel with big clean airy rooms, a marble staircase hinting of earlier grandeur. Another of Abdul's contacts had given the team an entire floor of the hotel.

Having identified the body, Rachel had spent three further days chasing paperwork around Addis. This afternoon she had breathed a sigh of relief as she handed the logistics over to the New Zealand Embassy. She had also said her farewells to Abdul. She was moved by his parting words.

"You are the lioness, you lead the pride, but you must leave time for yourself." Sleep came slowly.

———

Maddie's smile lit up the room. She strode across to hug Rachel. Rachel felt the relief and a happiness she hadn't experienced in years. They hugged, tears mingled, bodies together close and shaking. Over her shoulder, Rachel saw Nat and Abdul dancing a slow jig, arms linked. The two Stevens burst through the door, beer bottles in hand. They handed bottles to everyone. Beer spilt across the white bed spread in triumphant brown arches. Others crowded through the door, balloons and streamers, music. The tempo built. A vibrant dance, bodies packed, everyone swaying to a beat. Rachel clung to Maddie, not wanting to lose her friend, again, ever. Maddie smiled at Rachel, then her head swung backwards at an unnatural angle, her mouth opened and a primal scream cut the music.

Lights played on the ceiling, cut into shadows by the swishing rotation of the fan. Rachel felt the cool air. She hugged her knees, staring at the wall. The pulse of the red digits on the alarm clock slowly registered along with the loud buzz. It took a long shower to cut the sound of the scream from her mind.

In the hotel foyer, Steven Wright greeted Rachel with an awkward hug. Started awkward, but held Rachel in firm warmth. For a moment she relaxed. She reached up and lightly kissed his cheek. "Thanks, I needed that."

Through the rapidly waking city to the airport, the three sat together in the front seat of the van. Shoulders touching. Rachel reached for the hands on either side and held them tightly. She felt their strength flow back through the contact.

Chapter Twenty-One – Nanyuki

Makalani rubbed his red eyes and picked at his betel nut-stained teeth. He belched a raw acrid residue of whisky, bottle empty beside his poolside chair. The watch on his wrist had yesterday belonged to the manager of the hotel, now dead amongst the bodies of his staff littered around the poolside.

An elderly man approached his chair. He knew Makalani's uncle, a powerful Turkana chief in Lowarengak alongside the lake. A man he could respect. *How had he not seen the evil in his nephew?* He also knew the quick temper and brutal retribution Makalani used to maintain control of his rebel gang. He waited minutes before Makalani finally acknowledged his presence. The old man kept his eyes downcast in a show of respect.

"Master, the families must collect the bodies of the dead so that the spirits can rest."

Another long wait before Makalani gave his consent. The old man motioned towards the gate. A crowd of perhaps fifty people rushed to identify the bodies strewn around the hotel grounds. There were gasps and sobs. A young woman bent over the corpse of her father perhaps five metres from Makalani's chair.

The staccato burst from Makalani's weapon buckled the young woman lifeless over her father's body. There were screams and the group began to run. The old man held up his hand and moved swiftly to place himself directly in front of the murderous barrel. He spoke calmly, this time eyes directly into the grinning face above.

"Master, you have angered some of the spirits here. I can only protect you if you let us lay our loved ones with their ancestors."

The menace of ancient witchcraft cut through the alcohol. Fear and uncertainty in the eyes betrayed the blustered response.

"You have one hour before I kill you all."

Two of Makalani's unit burst through the gate, giving the leader a convenient distraction from the eyes of the elder. He led them to the poolside bar out of earshot of the group. The group engaged in an agitated conversation before the two raced off into the hotel to gather the other members of the unit. Makalani waited in the foyer, taking another bottle of spirits from the bar on his way through.

Half the bottle had been drunk by the time the last of the group assembled. For some, there was anger at being disrupted from the pleasures of the hotel. Others responded with mindless drunken hilarity. It took another burst of gunfire into the ceiling to get attention for the briefing. White plaster dust floated down on the upturned faces.

The five battered Toyota pickups raced in ragged convoy. They travelled fast, forcing traffic off the oncoming lane. Warning shots rattled frequently from the lurching bandits on the trays. Dust billowed from the roadside as wheels slipped over the verge. Market day at Naro Moru slowed the convoy as livestock and donkey loads spilled across the road. The drivers honked horns furiously but progress slowed to walking pace. Goats streamed in braided currents around the vehicles. Makalani's vodka bottle hit a bony back causing a momentary flurry, bare road appearing for a few seconds. A high bicycle load of firewood creaked and weaved alongside the vehicles, cutting a swathe through the livestock.

The old man looked from the shadow of his small shop. He felt the disgust and spat into the dust. The bandits had ventured this far south only once before. He watched the face of the leader in the lead vehicle. The same face he watched plunder his store a few days ago. The face of a spoilt nasty child, grabbing from the shelves, smashing china and bottles. Driven by no cause other than greed, a bad man.

Good people in the village had been injured and robbed by the thugs. His oldest friend had died from shock after a savage beating. Greedy scavengers, vile *fisi* (hyenas). He spat again. What did they want this time? Then the thoughts connected. He must warn the Doctors. The Red Cross Doctors had helped many in the village, cleaning poisoned wounds and setting limbs, helping the sole local doctor with the huge stream of patients. He must warn them.

The old man pedalled fast. The bike creaked alarmingly down the rough track to the well out the back. From the well, he crossed a corn field to join the road. He reached the Mweiga Marram Road. People were streaming down the road, mothers pulling children in their white school shirts and blue shorts and dresses. Matatu crowded with market goers still oblivious to the impending threat. The bike creaked as he stood on the pedals, mud splattered bare legs. Hooded youths played their rap music outside the football field. Beat blaring. The bored eyes stared the same path to the hyena pack. He cranked around another corner. His breathing came in gasping pants. Pain in the damaged leg.

Three white trucks were parked outside the Medical Centre. A long queue snaked into the courtyard. The old man's warning quickly dissipated the queue, save a few where pain overrode fear.

———

Dave paced the small hospital compound, agitated. Puffs of angry dust under his heels. His conscience battling with the urgency of the race to find Maddie. He couldn't argue as both Bruno and Graham Wilkins pulled up their sleeves to wade into the queue of injured locals. Graham's priority clearly was more on his NGO responsibilities than the mission agenda. Although a fine and noble agenda, it wasn't getting them closer to Maddie.

Grace sensed the tension. She appeared at Dave's elbow, a light touch on his back. "The time is not lost Dave. We need to re-plan the route with the bandits so close. I have done some work. We…"

The creak of the old bike startled both and they swivelled simultaneously. The old man carefully pulled down the stand on his heavy bike. He spoke between wheezing breaths, "Bandits, close to the village, you must leave."

Inside the small hospital, Graham, Bruno and Aman the local Doctor were all working on patients. Gloves and gowns were blood-splattered. The three local nurses had already assessed priorities down the long queue. Donna and Simone were ripping bedsheets to bandage the lesser injuries. Hospital supplies of gauze had been quickly exhausted. Martin spoke rapidly to the old man.

Dave explained the situation but Bruno shook his head. "We can't simply walk away now, people will die".

Aman replied, "You are no use to anybody dead. These bandits are thugs and you will be prime targets. You must go. Go now and thank you for your help - you have saved lives. God speed."

Graham looked up from his patient. "You go, I will stay. Get out of here now. Thank you all and good luck." He turned back with finality to his patient.

Aman walked over to Bruno and took the sutures out of his hand and guided him gently towards the others.

"Thank you my friend. Go."

Martin nodded. "They are coming for us, we must go."

Dave lashed the old man's bike onto the spare wheel of the lead Land Cruiser. Martin explained that he would guide them to a safe place away from the town.

257

Outside the village, houses quickly became scattered. The old man directed them down a rough rutted track. Elephant grass hissed and cracked under the vehicles. They drove slowly, avoiding raising tell-tale clouds of dust. The vehicles rocked and jolted over deep dry mud holes. Acacia and thorn bushes lined a dry creek bed. Nearly an hour later the creek bed began to expose shimmering pools of insect-infested water. The track ruts began to splatter mud. A rough branch fence appeared, enclosing a small farming community. Women were layering bundles of brush to hide the vehicles. Dave wondered, *how had the news travelled so fast?*

Chief Nathaniel stood in the village compound. Tall and lean, he talked quickly to the old man then spoke to Martin. He smiled and turned to the others, speaking English with an almost Welsh lilt.

"Welcome to our mugundu, we have fifty people on our farm. If you need anything please ask. We are honoured to have you all and thank you for treating our Uncle."

As the group greeted Nathaniel, Dave noticed the old man quietly untying his bike from the back of the Landcruiser. He walked over with a smile.

"Please stay, have some food with us."

The old man partially bowed and simply responded, "Thank you." He clearly didn't relish the long ride home heading into darkness.

The women had continued laying brush against the fence and against the vehicles. From the outside of the kraal they had become invisible. Grace and Donna were engaging a large group of children in the camp set up process. Communication consisted of laughter and many hand signals, some effective.

Bruno sat down beside Dave, arm across his shoulders. He could sense the frustration in his friend.

"I have looked at the GPS and talked to Martin. We are not far from the Namunyak Conservation area. From there Martin has a contact in Namarei who can show us some tracks through the back of Marsabit Reserve. It will be tough going but it should only take a couple of days at most to get to Marsabit. Grace and Martin have talked to Nathaniel, and the bandits are pretty much leaving these rural areas alone."

Dave rubbed his hands. "I hope we are not too late…"

Simone walked over and sat on the other side of Dave, hand on his knee, light kiss on his cheek. No words needed to express the love and concern. Donna and Pete were raising garlic-lashed smells from the small camp cooker, two large billies steaming. Donna began explaining the food items to the old man. The pair laughed. Martin and Grace were engrossed in conversation with Nathaniel with the aid of many stick drawings in the dust.

Dave took in the scene. His head cleared. His skin prickled. A faint lump at the back of his throat. He was blessed with the support of this group. Nothing else mattered in this moment. Maddie would survive with this love flooding towards her.

———

Makalani's head blurred with pain, throat hoarse and raw. The young villager in the room stopped mid-sentence. Makalani screamed at him and lashed out. The young man leapt backwards only to be pushed roughly forward by one of Makalani's gang. It took fifteen minutes to get the man's story. Blood trickling from the side of his mouth. Makalani's pain turned into irrational rage. He fired his automatic into the ceiling of the ransacked bar. Bottles clinked as the gang fought off comatose sleep. The air rancid. Within minutes the vehicles lurched out of Naro Moru, drunken grinding of gears.

Wedged between Makalani and the driver of the lead vehicle, the young villager was terrified. He had felt pretty powerful bringing his news to the gang, now he felt small and childlike. Death so close with the hard barrel in his side, slamming painfully with each bounce. They drove with angry disregard, scattering morning goat herds, vehicles pounding over ruts. The rage virulent and contagious in the gang. A goat caught under the bumper of one of the vehicles screamed. A short burst of automatic fire finished the animal.

———

The young goat herders on top of the volcanic mound saw the vehicle lights from perhaps five kilometres away. They quickly conferred and the older boy picked up his stick and trotted back towards the village. He ran silently, an instinctive lope, avoiding the thorn bushes and rough basaltic rock. He could hear waves of the incongruous rap music drifting closer. Eminem. He had perhaps four kilometres to cover, but held the advantage of a straight-line run. Surely the bandits would want to arrive unannounced. Surprise would be one of their best weapons. The sand felt cool and good on his hard soles, and he eased into a faster pace. His shadow led him, long and black into the pink dawn.

———

Pete needed to pee. He gently eased himself up, careful not to disturb Donna. He looked at her peaceful face, the slow rhythm of deep sleep. He pulled back the mosquito net. The wall of the tent ripped in front of his face. The pink dawn light burst in. Somebody kicked his shoulder with a powerful force and he sprawled across Donna. She awoke with a start. "Stop fooling around Pete, I need more sleep."

She tried to push Pete off. Her hand felt warm dampness. She pulled her hand back and stared at the red. Her mind was numbed with sleep. She stared. Pete groaned. Donna screamed. Dave and Simone arrived at the tent simultaneously. The mosquito net over the two bodies had collapsed, a deep red cloak across Pete's shoulders. Dave ripped the net back and he and Simone gently rolled Pete off Donna. She was transfixed, eyes staring and not comprehending. Simone gently lifted her to a sitting position, arms around her shoulders, pulling her face into her neck. Both Dave and Simone then heard the sound, the faint clatter and the ping of lethal lead and copper hitting the vehicles.

Bruno, Grace and Martin raced around the camp throwing gear into the vehicles. Nathaniel appeared with a group of elderly and children and they crammed into the Landcruisers. Others from the compound had already slashed an opening in the rear fence. People were running with handfuls of possessions out to the fields. They lifted Pete into the back seat of one of the vehicles. Bruno held a large gauze pad over the jagged red hole. The brush stacked against the sides of the trucks flew as they accelerated across the compound towards the new gap. A few young people jumped on the running boards of the convoy, a couple climbing onto the roof racks. Dave looked back at the prone bodies in the dust. Amongst them the old man, still holding his bike as though he had fallen off moments before.

Grace drove the lead vehicle, with Nathaniel beside her directing. Simone, behind the wheel of the second truck, had Donna close beside her, shivering. Between gear shifts, Simone gently stroked her arm. Dave followed in the rear truck, with Bruno desperately attending to Pete, trying to stem the flow of blood. Martin handed Bruno items from the medical kit. All the vehicles were filled with the sounds of children crying for mothers and mothers crying for children.

———

Makalani strode from his battered pickup truck. He felt power, a true leader now. The pain in his head drove the remorseless anger, he had no fear. Already behind him the gang were firing at the compound despite his arm in the air and angry signals to stop. Surprise had been totally lost.

Left alone with the vehicles, anger replaced the young villager's fear. Waiting for the last of the bandits to disappear out of sight, he opened the bonnet of the first truck and systematically smashed every component in sight with a large rock, finally ripping the leads from the battery and burying them in a mud hole. He repeated the process for all but one vehicle. Now was his chance to learn to drive.

The ragged red edges of the morning sun crept over the hill behind. Makalani followed the long shadow he cast ahead. Then he stopped. At the head of his shadow were three sets of red eyes. Three proud lionesses, jaws still stained from the night's kill. The anger turned to deep primal fear in an instant. The lionesses caught the scent of his urine. The sets of eyes held him transfixed.

Makalani raised his gun, his eyes blurred, the trigger producing nothing but a metallic click. The mothers of the pride were gliding towards him. Power in the rippling shoulder muscles, teeth bared. Two circling to each side, one in the middle. Makalani looked around desperately for others of his gang. The automatics had fallen into silence.

He turned to run, he knew he had made a fatal move but he was out of rational control. He saw the shadows of the others also running. Running back to the safety of the vehicles. He could smell the lions' carnivore breath.

———

The young goat herder watched the bandits from the safety of a small cluster of trees. The anger in the group had returned but now more in hopeless frustration. They were marooned forty kilometres away from town. The heat soared, crushing the dehydrated brain tissues further. Heads pounded. The leader appeared isolated. He sat alone alongside one of the trucks, a beaten man. The herder walked a long loop back to the compound. Inside he spotted his younger sister, her pristine white school blouse marred with a black-red hole. She lay in the dust. He carefully carried her to their hut. His eyes were dry, teeth clenched in hatred. Another cycle of hate had started.

———

Dave sat in the shade. Nearly two hours had passed. The passengers had gradually dispersed to compounds and villages along the way. The comfort of relatives. Only Nathaniel and his wife were left. They had lost a son. Dave tried to find words. His mind racing, confused. His quest seemed selfish in the light of the carnage caused. All his wealth could never bring those lives back. He could only manage a soft "Sorry" as Nathaniel led his sobbing wife to the nearby hut of a relative.

Donna had recovered some of her strength and nursing instinct, working alongside Bruno helping with Pete. She worked efficiently but her face was an impenetrable mask. They had inserted a saline drip, hoping to reduce the impact of blood loss. Out of the rocking vehicle Bruno had also managed to clamp one of the arteries, but Pete's condition remained dire. Bruno looked over at Grace with renewed respect. She and Simone had assumed leadership. They were poring over the map and GPS with Martin.

"Right," started Grace, "Priority one is to get Pete back to the nearest medical facility, then Nairobi. He needs blood. We are not too far from the B5 down to Nakuru then the A104 down to Nairobi. Simone will drive that vehicle with Donna once Bruno has done everything he can. Martin should go with them to help with navigation and communication. As soon as Simone gets cell phone coverage she will request medical support, and notify our insurers. The rest of us will head north to Marsabit. Any other thoughts?"

Her assurance and clarity gave everyone a lift. Bruno spoke first.

"I have done everything I can for now. We need to move."

Dave looked at Donna, then said, "Bruno needs to be with Pete, at least until we get medical help. We should stay together until we get that help. Grace is right, Pete is our first priority for now."

Simone said quietly, "That is brave and generous Dave." She moved over to his side, taking his hand. "Allons vite."

The three vehicles reached Aga Khan University Hospital in Nyahururu less than two hours later. Dave and Martin rushed in and returned with doctors and a trolley. Bruno quickly briefed the doctors as they wheeled Pete in. It took forty minutes before Bruno reappeared.

"He's in good hands. Blood supplies are on their way from Nairobi with an ambulance."

Bruno sagged with relief, both for his friend and the release of tension. He could not remember how long it had been since he had been so hands-on in an emergency.

Grace moved to Bruno and embraced him. She whispered quietly, "I am so proud of you." He simply responded "Likewise."

"Let's find some food - I'll check with Donna."

Dave headed into the hospital. He returned shortly afterwards with his arm around Donna.

She smiled through her tears, "Thank you all."

During a very subdued lunch, Martin and Dave slipped away to report to the local Police. They quickly found the Police were dealing with dozens of similar incidents all around the district. It became obvious that action was limited by resource and an uncertainty in responsibility. Despite offering a little sympathy, the police simply did not want to know. They assured Martin that "The appropriate authorities will be fully briefed". Martin raised his hands in a gesture of resignation. He knew the system too well. Their time was too precious to waste here. He turned to Dave and pointed towards the exit.

They re-joined the group, who had already reorganised the load to free one of the vehicles for Simone and Donna to stay with Pete. Farewells were brief, tight with emotion. Ahead stretched over three hundred rough kilometres. Martin had already talked to their guide who agreed to meet them at the junction of the Illuat to Korr Road.

Late afternoon they pulled into the town of Baragoi and Martin quickly located a petrol supply. They cranked an ancient hand-pump to fill the diesel tanks from rusty drums. Bruno filled a plastic bottle to check the quality of the fuel, not clean but no sign of water contamination. The filters would have to cope. A small roadside stall provided warm soft drinks as they refuelled.

Deep sand nearly buried the road. Local buses with the tinny sound of music blaring slithered down the tracks towards them. Plastic containers piled high on the roof racks tilted perilously from side to side. Parallel tracks meandered on both sides, threading through low desert scrub. Bruno stopped the lead vehicle to lower the tyre pressure and repeated the process as Dave pulled the second vehicle in behind. A small group of wild camels trotted nonchalantly across the track ahead.

"I think that was the junction we are looking for!" Grace yelled, glancing at the GPS. But no-one could see the guide.

"Let's wait for the others. I will have a look up this road." Bruno had already started to walk through the thicket lining a dry river bed. On the other side trees still obscured the view. He climbed the bank and perhaps another hundred metres up the road he could see a sign with a motorbike propped alongside. Almost ten minutes later, he got back to the vehicle.

Grace looked anxiously up the road. "No sign of the others yet."

Bruno looked back. The road showed no tell-tale plumes of dust. He tried to recall the last time he had checked the rear-view mirror. Five more minutes passed before Bruno finally said, "Something must have happened. We need to head back - but I think our guide may be waiting over the river."

They drove across the river bed and reached the sign and the motorbike. The faded sign read "Africa ECO Services Ltd Camp 1". Sitting on a log in the shade was a happy-faced young man, dressed in safari shorts and tee-shirt.

"Hi my name is Elia, you must be Martin?"

Bruno quickly explained the situation and the three headed back down the track. More than five kilometres back down the road, Elia finally spotted the other vehicle slewed sideways across one of the parallel sand tracks. Bruno carefully navigated between the scrubby bushes to pull alongside. Spurts of sand were shooting from Dave's shovel at the front of the vehicle, his face masked in sweat-glued sand. The shovel made a loud clang as it hit rock.

"I thought there was a sand mound, but it was rock, which bounced us onto this rock. Hell of a jolt. I think the steering is shot."

They cleared enough sand to see under the front wheel. Bruno shook his head. "The tie rod and knuckle joint is completely shattered. If Pete was here we would stand a chance of a repair but I think we are down to one truck."

The selection of equipment to be loaded into the remaining truck took some discussion. Bruno added the two spare wheels from the disabled truck onto the roof rack. They left a pile of abandoned gear on the sand. Dave noticed Elia a few yards away on his cell phone. The gear would quickly find a new home. It took some effort to swallow his concern and joke, "You shouldn't have let the learner driver take the wheel Bruno."

The last rays of sun glinted on the horizon as the truck came into the village of Korr. Elia suggested camping in the grounds of his church, the Africa Inland Church.

"It will be hard to find the trails in the dark and the Pastor is my uncle."

It had been a long tough day. Bruno and Grace started preparing a meal as the others set up the tents. Elia had disappeared into the village, promising he would return at first light. With the dishes packed away, Dave noticed the faint light at the door of the church. A single electric bulb illuminated the porch, the body of the church had faint orange shadows. Dave found a bench at the back. Two candles flickered dimly at the tiny altar. *Sue*. Sue had been a practising Catholic, although the practice had been limited to supply trips to town which coincided with Sunday Mass. Father Brian occasionally drove his battered Subaru to minister to the scattered outback followers. Dave always kept a good single malt whiskey ready for his visits. It would last two visits at best.

Sue maintained her faith like a rock in her life, simple and immovable. In their early years they had discussions about issues of faith. Issues like creation versus evolution. Dave's logic always seemed to win the argument, but Sue remained unmoved from her rock. In France Dave had explored the views of Muslim friends and found many of the tenets of good life, caring and respect for others had direct parallels with Christianity. He had settled for a rough bush agnosticism with the simple human values distilled both from Sue and friends whose values had gelled.

He could feel Sue close in that warm darkness. He jumped as the bench beside him creaked. The Pastor's white shirt glowed a translucent orange. He introduced himself. Dave commented on the Australian vowel inflections in his English.

"I was trained in Melbourne. Four wonderful years, almost gained a degree in AFL, and Carlton beer."

Dave chuckled and relaxed. The next sentence had him sit bolt upright.

"She is alive, the one you seek. The sisters have moved her to the shores of Lake Tukana near Loiyangalani. Go back to South Horr and head eighty clicks to the lake shore. The sisters are waiting."

The bench seat creaked again and the Pastor was gone. Dave sat, emotional and trembling. He rubbed his face. Was he hallucinating? Sue whispered softly in his ear: "*Believe.*"

Dave heard Martin snoring gently in the tent, but he couldn't sleep himself. He wrestled with his thoughts until the sun rose. Outside Elia was already brewing coffee. Dave asked, "Where did you disappear to last night?"

"I had a meal with my Uncle and slept at his place."

"Was he there when you got there?"

"Yes, he had been waiting for me."

Dave clenched his fists, then asked, "Can you get us to Loiyangalani by Lake Tukana?"

Chapter Twenty-Two – Nairobi

Rachel Steenkemp sat tensely in the red plastic chair in the hospital foyer. The week had been a nightmare of frustrations and increasing pressure from her producer. She disliked Bill Struthers intensely. Bill saw her unerring ability to deliver good quality content as her only asset. Her stories always sold well. The costs of this project were mounting and the race story had died at the border, less than half-way through. Rachel could sense the inevitable. The raw emotion of her losses strangled her usual drive. Maddie's gentle face constantly haunted her, along with the agony in the voices of Stephen's parents.

The media story of the injured Australian tourist had been low-key, almost hidden in the press. The Government desperately tried to limit the impact on the tourist trade. Reports from the unrest in the north were silenced quickly. Her media contacts knew little more than the few lines in the news release. Her gut instinct led her to the hospital.

Two women emerged from the doors of the ICU ward down the corridor. One tall, elegant, European, the other pretty despite the reddened eyes and strained face. Rachel stood. The pair approached. She met the eyes of the tall woman, a warning flash, fiery and defiant. Rachel knew from Bill's phone call that the rescue team from Australia included three women. *These must be them.*

"Hi, I am a friend of Maddie Jacobs. Are you ladies part of the rescue team from Australia?"

"Friend?" The accent was French, the tone guarded.

"I love the woman. She is one of the most extraordinary, strong, sensitive human beings I have ever met."

Rachel's shoulders sagged, and she sobbed. That instant distilled the priorities of the situation - career, money, Bill Struthers, withered into irrelevance.

"Anything I can do to help?"

Rachel began shaking uncontrollably.

The two strangers embraced her in the middle of the busy corridor.

———

It took nearly two hours for the three to fill in the jigsaw. They had moved to the quiet foyer café of Rachel's hotel. It took Donna to suggest the next action.

"Pete is stable and over the worst. I know my way around here now - you two go back. I'm fine. Get moving."

Simone looked at Donna. She had grown enormously in her estimation over the last few days. She had found someone whom she could regard as a close friend. An indomitable and cheerful soul, with a huge reserve of strength. Simone had also seen the depth of her relationship with Pete. They were parts of a single unit, different but complementary, gilded with mutual respect.

———

Rachel's afternoon flew. She found both Nat and Stephen and explained her plan. Both were relieved to be heading back to their families. As Rachel was about to go back to her room, Nat handed her a package.

"It's all the footage from the race. You will make better use of it than Bill will."

Nat also handed Rachel the small video camera. "This was Stephen's little pride and joy."

The package galvanised a plan. In the phone call that followed, Bill Struthers made one of the poorest financial decisions of his life. He sold the footage to Rachel. Bill put down the phone with a smile. *Stupid stuck up tart, good riddance, she's even paid me for the worthless junk. No bloody idea. Time for a celebratory beer.*

———

It took some time for Rachel to adjust to Simone's driving as they headed out of Nairobi. Simone had perfected the French driving style of approaching the car in front at speed then overtaking at the last second. Finally, Rachel relaxed. She knew she was in the company of a very powerful and competent woman.

Although Simone had entered the GPS location that Bruno had sent that morning, she had carefully traced the route on a new paper map. She wasn't entirely comfortable with electronics. It wasn't until she reached the outskirts of Nyahururu that she asked Rachel for directions. For four hours they had sat in comfortable silence. Rachel offered to take over the driving.

"I am fine."

Simone's mouth set in a thin line of determination. She drove herself in the same manner as she drove the truck. The truck began to slither into sand drifts. Simone abruptly stopped and swung her door open. The blast of hot air caught Rachel by surprise. She reached for her own door handle, but by the time she had opened her door Simone was back in the cab.

"We need the four-wheels now, the hubs are locked."

The vehicle slid back into the sandy tyre tacks on the road. Simone eased up the speed, expertly sliding into the smooth curves. The controlled slides relaxed Simone. She felt the movement on the sand instinctively through the wheel. Her face relaxed with the sense of fun. Rachel noticed the shift and cautiously opened the conversation.

"You drive well - you must have a lot of experience driving in these conditions?"

"Non, never before…but I did train briefly as a rally driver. I had a boy-friend with a beautiful turbo Subaru. His car became his mistress, I merely ranked as his society trophy to boast to his friends. To be fair I think I also was more in love with the thrill and fun of his car. Then I crashed, and the car and boyfriend were no more. One of many brief flings. My life is a mosaic of dangerous flings."

The sudden opening-up took Rachel by surprise. A right-hand curve squeezed her against the door, sunlight catching an elegant plume of sand spraying from the front wheel. An animal bounded from the roadside, half-hidden in the plume. She lost the thread of her response and silence washed into the gap.

A few minutes passed before Rachel turned to Simone and quietly asked: "What brought you here? It seems so far removed from your normal life."

Simone replied after a long pause.

"Firstly, it was Martin. A man who arrived from another continent – no, another planet. The man who married the woman I most admired and respected. Someone who had so little and who suffered so much, but had more simple wisdom than I would ever hope to have. She became mother, sister and friend to me and saved me from my own stupidity - at least briefly. Someone like me needs saving continuously. Then Martin brought something else - dignity and respect. He brought the view of who I was from the words of Akeyo his wife, my friend. It was the person I want to be. Martin brought a wonderful curiosity for the things I dismiss daily. It opened my eyes again. Most importantly he brought the love of my mother back to me. I valued so many trivial things that never gave me time with her. I shunned her because I blamed her like a child for all the things that had gone wrong with my life."

Simone paused as she drifted the heavy truck into a slightly tighter bend. Tongue between teeth in concentration. She realised the words that she had spoken crystallised an insight she hadn't consciously registered.

"Then there was Dave. Another person I respected enormously. A person whom I regarded in my heart as a friend, but have never taken action to continue that friendship. When his wife died I didn't go to the funeral because I had a dinner party that week. A bloody stupid dinner party."

Simone slammed the steering wheel with her palm. "By some incredible coincidence in my life, Dave asks Martin for help. Help saving someone he now loves. Martin is in my house. It is a gift for me to grab, to do something useful. I realise everything I do is purely about me. Drop all the things that yesterday seemed important and simply help someone. I felt so free. I dropped so much baggage in an instant."

The tail of the Landcruiser twitched slightly. Simone corrected with a flip of the wheel.

"Does that answer your question Madame Reporter?"

The last question had an edge that caught Rachel off guard.

"Simone, the reporter resigned – no - probably chucked away her career yesterday. For me also it is about helping someone I love and respect."

Simone glanced across, holding eye contact, validating the truth. Her tone lightened.

"Tell me about Madeline."

Rachel was caught off guard again, her voice shaking, tears rimming. Again, Simone caught the truth of the moment.

"Umm. I think it's her unexpected depth. She is always the energetic bouncy fun person, but she is more. Much more. She is very thoughtful and deep thinking, and seems to be able to capture the essence of things very succinctly. Maybe a bit like Akeyo, the wisdom of hard knocks. She is very straight, no games, no hidden agendas. Fiercely competitive though, and she knows her technical stuff intimately. The love for her boys is absolute. Her love for Dave is something special. I really hope she is OK."

Simone took her hand off the wheel. Her arm did not quite bridge the width of the Landcruiser bench seat. Rachel briefly squeezed the offered hand before the truck lurched over a rut.

It had been dark for an hour when they pulled into South Horr. Simone had been assured that fuel was available somewhere in the village. It took three passes up the main street to spot the pile of rusty two hundred litre fuel drums beside a tiny wooden booth, which also offered Coke and mobile phone top ups. The village appeared deserted, no-one to open the padlocked hand pump.

Rachel could see that Simone was shattered. She directed her back down the street to the rough blue building labelled 'El Almo Motel'.

"We need food and some sleep, then fuel first thing in the morning."

Simone nodded tiredly.

Two elderly men, white haired, orange betel nut gums, sat on red plastic crates outside the doorway. Both were spritely and smiling in the dim light.

"Welcome ladies to our finest hotel. Fifty US dollars for one night," said one.

"Twenty is all I have sorry." The notes were already in the shirt pocket.

"Room number one inside the door." The proprietor stood and led Rachel inside. Room number one was the only room.

"Toilet and washroom out the back."

The toilet introduced itself with a distinct odour from some distance. The washroom featured a bench with a cracked enamel bowl and two large Coke bottles filled with brown water. A chicken clucked its way out from under the bench.

The women quickly prepared sandwiches from their cool box. Simone gave the entire contents of Room One a generous dose of insect spray. Rachel found some clothes pegs to close the largest of the holes in the mosquito nets.

Rachel smiled at Simone. "Would you like the first shower?"

"Non, apres vous Madame."

"No no, I insist, after you."

Both giggled and the ants were not disturbed on the cake of soap beside the enamel bowl. Within minutes both women were asleep, their own sleeping mats covering both the sagging mattresses and the myriad of dying insects from Simone's spray assault.

———

Rachel opened her eyes to streams of orange light criss-crossing Room One through cracks in the walls.

"Did you order room service?"

Simone groaned sleepily, "I do have croissants, almost fresh".

The only hurdle to a swift departure, was the chicken, which had taken up roost in the toilet. It took Rachel several attempts to dislodge it from the cistern top. The El Almo Motel had created a sense of ease between the two women. Rachel had admired the fun way Simone had coped, clearly a huge gulf from her normal hotel experiences.

It took nearly an hour to locate someone at the fuel kiosk. Meanwhile Simone had found some food at a small shop, including a freshly baked loaf of bread. She added cheese and some tomato to start the journey with the taste of fresh sandwiches to supplement their earlier single croissant.

The road took a steep drop into a dry river bed, sand turned to rock. Simone quickly passed Rachel her sandwich. The loose rock started a forward slide. Simone accelerated to gain control and the vehicle slewed into a deep sand patch at the bottom of the slope. Simone changed down to low ratio and the truck slowly ploughed its way across to firmer ground.

"Nice work."

Rachel handed the sandwich back to the outstretched hand. Both women ate their sandwiches in silence as the road settled into a more sedate deep sand track. A few more minutes passed and Rachel turned to Simone and asked,

"Tell me about Dave, you have known him a long time?"

"Long time…"

Simone drifted into a flood of memories and a long silence.

"Over twenty years, we studied together. Maybe I should say Dave studied, and I, I floated around. We shared a cottage together, we were four together with Bruno and Akeyo. When I first met Dave, I found him rough, I thought coarse, a country boy. But how wrong the first impressions can be. Underneath that layer he had so much more character. He often could be so gentle, thoughtful. We were the same age, but he remained solid as I was flimsy. He always respected our friendship. I was often nasty, a child. But he forgave me every time. He helped me out of some stupid situations, bad men in my life. Maybe not bad men, bad choices."

Simone drifted into a long reflective silence.

"I think there are some rare people in your life where trust is absolute. You can always come back to a deep friendship on the same terms you left off maybe years before. And there was a long gap but he invited me to his wedding. The same girl he loved when we were studying. I came a few weeks early; Dave and Sue were in the middle of wedding plans but they made time to make me welcome. The family accepted and included me completely. Real family. Fun. I could see in Sue everything I wasn't; she and Dave completed each other, a team. We talked, we drank wine, we reminisced and we laughed. I laughed like I hadn't laughed in many years, in fact since our time together in Thure. One night, Sue told me how Dave had described me to her. She described a person that I didn't recognise. That person I thought I could never be. But Dave saw something different. For those weeks I became that person. I went back to France and my own life swallowed me again. I looked at my own friends and realised most I didn't even know. The conversations I had with Dave and Sue were deep and to the soul, no barriers. I could count only two of my own friends where I could ever attempt such conversations."

Simone turned to Rachel.

"I'm sorry, I am not sure I am answering your question, I am talking more about myself."

Rachel leaned across the cab and touched Simone's arm.

"Thank you, it takes courage to talk the way you do. And you have answered my question. I feel privileged."

Rachel turned to look out the side window, reflecting on her own life. She caught the spike of her broken marriage. Like a snake in the dust outside, always following, always ready to strike. Why did it always have such a bite after all these years? The conversation had been at the airport. She had arrived back from a long assignment in South America, Bolivia. She was exhausted. Simon's timing was thoughtless and cruel. He had driven her home and outside the apartment he had simply said, "I am not living here anymore, we will talk later". She had stood watching the street where the car had disappeared for nearly half an hour. Numb from tiredness and shock.

The "talk after" had been fuelled with rage, fired by friend Sharon and too many cocktails. In her heart she didn't really feel that way, but the hurt and alcohol fired words. Too much damage done, nasty things said. In the sad quiet that followed, she saw her own total neglect and regret but Simon had already moved on.

She turned back to Simone and said,

"Isn't it strange how the worst things in ourselves are always the most prominent in our self-assessment. We always seem to have our fingers on the self-destruct button."

Simone nodded.

"But sometimes something like this comes along, totally out of the ordinary, something extreme. It cuts through normal life like a bolt of lightning, and you ask "what is really important?" Then it is not about myself, it is simply helping a dear friend. I only matter in what I can contribute to that. It is a new value."

"Yes, I think I got that with Maddie, someone who had become a special friend. What yesterday seemed most important became insignificant, like my career...." She pictured Bill Struthers fuming at his desk.

"I think we are getting close, I am sure that is the lake on our left. I think I will say a silent prayer for Madeline and for Dave."

Chapter Twenty-Three – West of Bendigo

Bruno paused (as he always did) as he drove through the gate of the Institute. Pete had burnt the name plate into a beam of jarra timber: *"The Maddie Jacobs School of Hard Knocks"*. He beamed with a huge sense of pride. Grace had to nudge him to finish the last kilometre up the ghost-gum lined drive.

They were finishing a long drive back from Melbourne. They had been at the graduation of Kath Wilson. Now Doctor Kath Wilson, Doctor of Marine Biology.

Bruno still remembered the day her uncle delivered her to the Institute. Face pale and scratched, eyes vacant. Catatonic with drug withdrawal. A human train-wreck. Although Donna had become something of a specialist in drug rehabilitation, the first few months had required twenty-four-hour support from all the team.

The first glimmers of hope came on the 'Walk to Somewhere'. Together Bruno and Pete had devised the 'Walk to Somewhere' in conjunction with two local endurance athletes, veterans of both the Marathon de Sales (an ultra-marathon across the Moroccan Desert) and the

Valley of Death run. The two athletes would lead a small group from the Institute on a totally self-supported one-hundred-and-fifty-kilometre bush walk through tough country. Bruno would track the group in a four-wheel drive support vehicle, always well out of sight, but always ready for emergencies.

The first night started with a bush camp. Jacques and Bridget, the leaders, would lay the ground rules in very clear terms. To this stage Kath, despite recovering physically, remained shut down emotionally and verbally. Donna and Grace had taken some care with the psychological councillor to assess her readiness for the walk; they still had some nervous doubts.

As the briefing finished, Kath abruptly stood up and started running out of camp. Bridget raced after her, then promptly collided with her back as she stopped in a clearing, head leaning backwards.

"I wanted to see the stars," she whispered.

At the half-way mark after four days, Bridget did a circuit of the swags before bedtime. Kath sat on her swag holding one foot up to her knee. She quickly hid it as Bridget approached, but Bridget had seen the large raw red blister patches. She gently took Kath's foot. Kath hadn't said a word of complaint all day, but clearly walking caused her agony. Bridget had seen many walkers pull out with less damage than Kath's feet had sustained. Kath looked up and pre-empted her.

"I'm not stopping. Only a bit of pain, but beautiful country to focus on, the pain is irrelevant."

Bridget spent an hour helping Kath clean and cover the raw patches. She became so concerned she later slipped away from camp to trot the three kilometres back to Bruno's camp to discuss the situation with him and the medic.

Bruno concluded, "It's her call, we take too much away from Kath by pulling the pin on her."

Bridget watched Kath walk the next day. She strode out, showing the odd wince as her foot turned on a rock. She even stopped to point out a young mother roo with a joey. A different Kath had emerged.

Bruno had chosen the finish camp well. The camp nestled in a deep shady billabong in a small rocky gorge. A small waterfall trickled cool water down a rocky overhang. The group were all in the water as Bruno arrived for the finishing ceremony. He looked at Kath's eyes and the sullen dull look had been replaced by a light and a strength.

He felt the welling of pure joy. He and Grace had helped shift something again.

Bruno always finished the ceremony with a tribute to Maddie. He always managed to revisit the shift he had felt himself when Evelina recounted the story of Maddie's heroism at the presbytery.

———

The nuns had warning of the rebel group heading up the hill, intent on sacking the church. Still desperately in pain and unable to stand, Maddie had insisted Evelina take her to a position beside the big gate. Armed with an ancient shotgun from a farmer in the congregation, Maddie had Evelina wedge the gun on the hinge of the gate-post. Her shoulder would not withstand the recoil of the weapon - it took all her strength to reload and fire. She desperately resolved to buy some time for the sisters to retrieve some of their possessions, especially the important treasures from the church. Evelina refused to leave her. She sat beside her, ready to hand her shells. The first rebel vehicle screeched up the hill. Maddie waited until the lights almost reached the gate. Both barrels exploded. The vehicle lights died, the windscreen exploded in a shower of glass. The vehicle engine screamed in reverse. A crunching crash as the tray slammed into the wall across the alley. The parked vehicle was silhouetted in the headlights of the second rebel pickup as it appeared over the brow of the hill. Maddie desperately tried to reload the shotgun. Again, the air-splitting boom, both barrels peppered the vehicles. Maddie frantically signalled Evelina to leave. Evelina was not prepared to take that sacrifice. She dragged the mat on which Maddie lay across the yard. Out of the darkness appeared the shadowy form of a donkey cart. Two old villagers effortlessly lifted the mat onto the back of the cart, hiding Maddie under a pile of corn sheaves. Evelina trotted alongside. She turned on her cell phone, lifting the sheaves, to check on Maddie. Her eyes were closed, the face pale, breath shallow with small gurgling noises. Evelina panted a short prayer and covered her face.

Nearly fifteen minutes later the night sky lit with an orange glow. The clatter of reckless machine gun fire splattered uselessly into the night sky. Maddie had created the window to safely evacuate the entire contingent. Evelina feared the cost would be Maddie's life.

———

Bruno looked into the eyes of the group as he concluded the story.

"And that incredibly strong woman is the inspiration to the Maddie Jacob's school of hard knocks. I see that strength in each of you. Everyone has exceptional, untapped reserves. This walk has shown the strength you can all muster. Think of the choices in your life where you can use that strength."

———

Bruno and Grace had both felt a sense of pride as the small group of Doctorate Graduates had processed across the stage. Kath had taken her papers, then asked the Dean if she could say a few words.

"I have come from a pit at the bottom of humanity to celebrate today, thanks to three extraordinary people in my life: my Uncle Ken Wilson, and Bruno and Grace from the Maddie Jacobs School of Hard Knocks. Thank you for my life."

———

Bruno and Grace had arrived back from Kenya restless. Nothing in their old worlds seemed to fit anymore. Bruno had suggested doing something completely different:

"Something in the bush. Maybe something to prevent young people ending up like those you encountered in your job Grace."

Grace responded enthusiastically: "Yes, but what? It would be neat to do something different. Something meaningful."

"Do you remember the story Dave told us about Maddie's mentor? The guy who introduced her to dirt bikes? Actually sowed the seed?"

"Yes, vaguely."

"I was thinking about the kids you worked with. Especially the ones doomed by rough starts. Maybe there is some way of helping break the cycle. Alternative choices. Disciplines but with fun things, like four-wheel driving and enjoying the bush. Get them started on experiencing something other than booze or drugs or video games or whatever. Maybe some sort of adventure camp, but developing skills as well."

"We will need funding and all sorts of resources," Grace paused, "but yes, I would really love to do something like that. But how on earth will we start? "

"Team Kenya. I will ring Dave and Maddie first thing in the morning. I know Pete and Donna will have some ideas. I can sell the apartment, must be worth something by now."

———

Eight years on and today they had another focus. Africa, an annual pilgrimage. The Africa trips were always preceded by a steady stream of visitors. Those whom Bruno and Grace anticipated eagerly were the graduates. They would always leave with a smile and a pile of cash from their wages.

Pete and Donna would always drop by with a few local businessmen, leaving their completed beer cans with notes tucked underneath, sometimes one thousand or more. Fundraising seemed effortless, which always humbled and astounded the pair. The local community had a strong connection with a small town on the other side of the world. They had seen the church, the school and now a small laboratory and clinic grow from their efforts. The community had a sense of pride in the contribution to "their" African town.

This year Dave had been uncharacteristically vague about the plans. Normally his emailed lists of requirements covered page after page, but this time the list only included the usual supply of medicines.

Bruno had a last check around the large airy lounge, taking a ritual parting look at the life-size painting of an eland in harsh desert country above the fireplace. For both of them this painting encapsulated the feel of their Africa.

They were sitting on the veranda when Donna and Pete arrived to drive them down to Tullamarine Airport. As they loaded the car, Donna handed Grace a beautifully wrapped box. These gifts had become a tradition for their Africa trips, and Grace knew it would be something thoughtful, useful and usually expensive.

"Don't open it until you are on the plane, and I have another surprise for you at the airport."

The airport check-in queue snaked slowly towards the prim young lady at counter 18D. Donna slipped quietly into the airport crowds, taking her phone out of her pocket.

Bruno paced nervously, anxiously waiting for Donna to appear. Pete looked at his watch - half an hour to boarding, hopefully not too big a queue through security. The trio turned towards the big departure board above the gate.

"Here's the surprise!" Donna put her arms around Bruno and Grace's waists, twisting them to face the new arrival.

"I have come to help you guys for once," said Kath Wilson. Bruno and Grace looked at each other before reaching out to hug Kath. Grace wiped away a tear. Bruno turned to Donna.

"It's perfect. It's the complete circle. You are amazing Donna, thank you."

———

The plane doors closed. Bruno felt the familiar sense of excitement. He turned to look down the aisle where Kath sat several rows back, just in front of Pete and Donna. She smiled and gave him the thumbs-up.

Grace had the long box on her lap. "I don't deserve whatever this is, I have been spoilt beyond words already."

Bruno reached across and tore the wrapping. "You deserve everything and much more. Rip it open."

The gift was a lightweight, six-hundred-millimetre Nikon lens. Again, Grace's eyes flooded. Her little digital SLR had a great short seventy-millimetre zoom. Eight trips to Africa had produced hundreds of wide savannah shots with small dots, pixelated leopards, distant rhinos, blurry elephants. If only she could produce a shot like Maddie's extraordinary close-up shots. The lean budget of the institute had plenty of things to spend good money on without being frivolous. Donna had delivered another perfect gift.

———

Kath was nervous, more nervous than excited. She turned her new passport over and over in her hands. She had never been out of the country. Africa seemed a bit wild as a first trip. The travel health clinic had scared her. The list went on and on: malaria, typhoid, rabies, hepatitis. The needles made her nervous, as if the past would suddenly catch up and envelop her. So many needles. And the warnings: pick-pockets, kidnapping, Somali terrorists. *Shit why didn't I choose Norfolk Island or somewhere close as a first flight? I'm there for Bruno and Grace. A small payback to them. Courage girl!* But it didn't work, simply hollow words. The fear lurked, barely below the surface, waiting to snatch her mind. *Big girl Kath, you've come too far for this shit. Be strong. Strong.* Her nails were digging into her hand.

Bruno looked back and saw the passport twirling in the hands. He moved beside her, into a vacant seat. "Move over, Tender Foot." They shared this joke from the 'Walk to Somewhere'. The shredded feet, and the courage. Bruno squeezed her hand. Reassurance. She wasn't alone.

"Thank you so much for coming. It is huge for Grace and me. It is a tribute to us that you are here. You are an extraordinary woman. No one can take your power away - you have earned it fair and square. Anything you are worried about on the trip?"

He had intuitively closed the wound. They talked for an hour. Bruno talked about the Africa he loved, and she got the sense. The excitement returned, the fears calmed.

When Bruno got back from his seat Grace was asleep. He carefully removed her new toy from around her neck.

Nairobi Airport bustle had a friendly familiarity for Bruno and Grace. For Kath it felt so different, such a huge leap from the orderly familiarity of Melbourne. She also felt comfortable in the company of the pair who knew the routine so well. She began to enjoy the experience, the difference. She had arrived in Africa.

Chapter Twenty-Four – Marsabit

The sun presented almost perfect light. Deep golden light.
A stabbing white thorn shot out of green. Blue haze
slurred the hills beyond. Light about to envelop the crater.
Raw scrub, black basalt rock, black shadows at their base,
creeping across the dry dust. A flash of movement behind
a grizzled acacia. White tawny flank and the flash of a red
eye, brief meteor reflection of the sun. Then the moment
the crater swallowed all the black, jagged red on the far
rim.

Martin's hand swept the broad-brush strokes of colour,
quickly adjusting tones on his palette. He felt the scene
through his hand, alive. Orange turned to black. He flicked
on the small light in the back of his van. He picked up his
fine camel hair brushes and began overlaying fine intricate
detail, white thorns slashing across ochre. The half-
imagined eland, head turned to the sun, sweeping horns
and strong body. Framework of a few brush strokes. The
stars like myriads of pinholes puncturing a dark dome. He
laid down his brushes. Sounds of the night desert finally
penetrating his concentration. He uncoiled himself from
his seat, took a few steps backward. The canvas glowing in
bright moonlight.

His eyes narrowed, shutting out detail, then focussing back. *Does the canvas speak by itself? Is the light and colour as I saw it?* Few canvasses survived these minutes. Martin ruthlessly discarded imperfection, but tonight it worked, everything he had seen had been captured. He carefully placed the canvas on soft cloth in a large box bolted to the van wall. The ride home could destroy a night's work. Brushes were rolled in damp cloth, and the palette board wiped. Everything had its place in the van, neat racks and rows of paints and brushes.

A mixed palette of colour joined the other smears on the steering wheel as he finally sat. Tiredness tightened his eye lids. Evelina would see his van lights as he reached the township. Mother Evelina now, five years already since Madeline had passed away. Evelina had taken to leadership with grace, never losing her bubbly sense of fun but leading with gentle steel. Tonight, she would have prepared corn cakes and rich goat stew. They would eat together and look at the canvas propped on the table. Evelina had the casting vote. This work may still end up on the pile of canvasses to be painted over.

Some years ago, Evelina had suggested the switch from water colours to oil. "See the richness now, this is our country, this is more the feel of that land," she had said as Martin's first oil canvas arrived in the kitchen. Martin hoped that Evelina would see what he had felt about tonight's work. He didn't want to lose this one.

The food smelt good, but Martin firstly had to clean his hands with turpentine then wash them in the warm bucket of sweet-smelling water on the bench outside. One whiff of turpentine and Evelina would bar the door. "That smell is not compatible with God's good food. Try again, better this time."

With soap finally overpowering turpentine, Evelina began saying Grace. Before they sat, Martin carefully placed the canvas against the wooden crate on the table. Evelina smiled but judgement could not be passed until they had finished eating. Martin delivered two cups of strong sweet tea, Indian tea with condensed milk. Evelina took a sip of tea, then stood and took a few steps backward, pausing before walking up close to take in the detail of the painting. Finally, she said, "This one has new light. There is a change I have not seen before. I can feel the night descending; the thorns are real. Yes, this one is worth celebration." She tipped her cup in a silent toast.

Martin trusted Evelina's critique absolutely. Somehow their unique love and communication allowed her both to see Martin's vision and to assess whether he had achieved it. Her own curiosity had led her to hours of research and

Martin knew her knowledge of art had grown enormously. She could quote styles and techniques of painters from old masters to modern African painters.

Early that morning Evelina retired to her small sparse cell, the same room she had slept in since joining the order. She would be up at five am leading the morning service, Martin would sleep till ten in his compound outside the convent fence.

Martin's battered van made its way up the hill to the market garden. In a modest way he had tried to realise Akeyo's dream of a garden oasis in the desert. He had invested in a deep artesian well that drew a reasonable quality water supply from an aquifer in a dormant volcanic fissure. The garden produced a variety of vegetables to supply the local restaurants. Marsabit had developed a steady restaurant trade once the road to the north had been sealed. Tourist buses now created a regular demand, breaking the long haul between Addis and Nairobi. Jobs in the garden were keenly sort after by locals. A retired army colonel ruled the work force of twenty with strong but fair discipline. He had become Martin's right-hand man.

Martin approached his foreman. "Where is the truck for the tomatoes?" An unusual problem had arisen with an over-supply of tomatoes. A planting which under normal circumstances would have only serviced local demand had produced a bumper crop. Martin had found a solution when he discovered that the local butcher planned to head south in his empty truck to collect a load of meat. However, with the fruit already picked that morning there was no sign of the butcher or his truck.

An hour of searching around the town finally located the butcher with his truck in the local workshop. Martin interrupted a heated argument. The butcher was yelling, "I will pay you everything for the repairs as soon as I return and sell the meat!"

The mechanic responded, "You will never pay. Last time you did not pay for months."

Martin eventually intervened. "I will pay you for the repairs today, and we will halve the freight cost for the tomatoes."

As he left the workshop, Martin saw a tourist bus heading into town. His presence would be required at the restaurant. Local restauranteur and friend Armin kept a wall display of Martin's paintings, which sold well with foreign tourists. Armin's banner promoting him as 'Internationally-acclaimed Kenyan Artist' embarrassed him somewhat, but he couldn't deny that the exhibition Simone had arranged at the Musee d'Afrique in Paris did qualify him for the "international" claim.

The bus disgorged forty red-faced, safari-suited, camera-slung American tourists. The journey had been a long one. Clearly neither Armin's cuisine nor décor were up to expectations. Most opted for Armin's Coke and hamburger lunch special option. The noise level escalated rapidly.

"How much for the one with the camels?" the voice rose above the general hubbub.

"The price is as marked on the painting sir," Armin responded politely.

"I'll give you five bucks, US of course".

Martin moved over beside Armin at the table. "The artist has exhibited at the Musee d'Afrique en Paris. The collection sold for a record forty thousand euros. The artist donates all the proceeds to the local school, so not only do you buy an international quality artwork, you contribute significantly to local education."

Martin's perfect French pronunciation and his clear authority had other heads in the group turning sharply. The noise level dropped.

"Well that is something. In that case I will have those three there and the little one with the antelope. Prices as marked of course."

By the time Martin left the restaurant the entire wall had been cleared of paintings.

He drove up the hill to the school. He felt relieved. The problem the headmaster had raised about major maintenance work, had been totally funded by today's painting sales. He looked forward to catching up with the head master, a well-educated and witty man. They talked for over an hour, enjoying food Armin had supplied from the restaurant.

The afternoon provided some peaceful time in the rambling airy room that served as his studio at the rear of his house. Racks of paintings lined the walls. Three active works sat in a circle around the mosaic paint-splatted table in the middle. He changed into overalls that were once blue, a blue relegated to minority colour by rainbow splatters of oils.

Last night's painting demanded attention first. Some detail missing - he could see something emerging which wasn't quite captured. The paint had been over-worked, colours merging. A slash of the palette knife took it back to bare ochre stain. He wiped the palette clean and remixed colour. Fresh crisp colour. The bare hole built up detail again. Brisk strokes. He stepped back and looked again. It worked.

He turned his attention to a work for the school. A representation of local legends. The headmaster had told the stories over many hours. Martin had jotted down notes and made small sketches as he spoke. The big canvas almost filled a wall. The detail had to be precise to be true to the stories. Martin had watched some of the school juniors painting their own stories. He had adopted some of the style, but somehow it didn't quite work, colours not bright enough to excite young minds. He brushed a deep band of Indian red then cut figures with the palette knife deep to canvas white. Simple forms started to emerge. He stepped back, the legends began to speak to him. It started to flow, clean brush strokes, no overlaying, primary colours, precision knife-cut figures. It grew quickly. Martin felt the excitement of flow.

The first legend was a true story of the region, Ahmed the Elephant. A Bwana Tembo, King of Marsabit, a living legend, tantalisingly rare sightings enhanced the massive ivory of his tusks. Born in 1919 he roamed the high forest of Marsabit National Park, by 1970 his story had grown to such stature that President Jono Kenyatta declared him a national treasure.

He was assigned his own entourage of protectors, but unfortunately even they were unable to save him. Sometime earlier a bullet had penetrated his stomach causing peritonitis. He died in 1974 majestically propped up by his huge tusks.

The brush strokes swept fluidly into the next legend.

The snake man lived in the mountains. He marked trails in the sand, deep trails that made rivers. Rivers that sucked the water away from the plains, leaving nothing but dry desert. The fire gods deep in the volcanos grew angry with the change in their land. The trees were dying, all the animals who depended on the water were moving away. Nothing left to hunt. No food. They sent their fire and ash into the sky, raining down to kill the snake man. The ash cooled to make hard black rock. But the snake man had hidden deep in the mountains far away. He took the rain with him, so the land remained dry. Only the sand and black rock.

The fire gods sent more molten rock into the sky; these rocks were soft. They formed shapes and grew into strong animals - the eland who could survive with little water, other desert animals, and plants formed from the soft rocks. Soon there was life again in the desert.

The fire gods had spent every bit of their force. Exhausted, their fires died, deep holes in the hills. But the sun remembered the fire, the colour of orange and red. Each morning and evening the sun would touch the hills with the colours to thank the fire gods for their sacrifice.

Smells from the kitchen registered with Martin and interrupted the flow. Evelina had learnt that direct interruption was impossible. Subtle spicy smells would gradually register with Martin's stomach and release the brushes. Once again, the pair sat at the wooden table and began to talk into the next day.

Tonight, Evelina struggled once again with forgiveness. Many times, she had said the words, then something would happen to open the wound again. Her little sister. Those eyes looking at her with that adoring love. Love for the big sister who carried her everywhere, wiped her nose and her bottom. Talked to her, made little toys, leaf boats to float down the drain. Held her, cuddled her neck. Evelina could still feel her warmth. *Why, why, why had they taken her?*

The trigger today had been the arrival of some of the young rebels back in the town. They had escaped a justice system that struggled to find witnesses to the deeds, struggled to distinguish identities from the uniform dark glasses, jeans and hoodies. Free and arrogant. The dark windows of their vehicle as evil as the eyes behind the dark glasses. The bass beat of trash rap music, loud and defiant.

The Government had called them rebels, but beyond a few slogans, the cause was a mystery, a lie. The actions were simply thuggery and theft. Bandits with the same disregard for life that took her dear sister. Evelina talked and Martin listened until the hatred subsided. Evelina found peace again with the warm hands that held hers, the past put back in its place.

Martin awoke at nine am, aware he had a meeting at the Clinic. He and Evelina were trustees for the Clinic. He would pick her up on the way. Today the board planned to approve the new development plans for the small laboratory. The laboratory would be equipped with tests for typhoid replacing the inaccurate and outdated Widal blood testing.

Typhoid killed an unnecessary number of local people. The board planned to tackle the problem by taking tests to the people. They had sponsorship to train local youth in basic nursing skills to visit remote villages on bicycle to collect samples. It also helped reduce the number of street-loitering youth, giving purpose where employment opportunities were few.

They were also going through a lengthy process to get the clinic incorporated into the National Health Service. The process sorely tested Martin's patience. Fortunately, his experience from many years in civil service allowed him to pick and fight only the winnable battles.

Evelina stood outside the Presbytery gate. Her presence lifted his spirits further. As with all her responsibilities Evelina took the governance of the Clinic very seriously. She spent hours on the internet informing herself of key issues in health. She frequently surprised the young doctor with her knowledge. Martin often wondered if in fact she ever slept in that small cell of hers.

A short ride down the dusty streets brought them to the clinic building. It was a squat concrete structure, fresh green paint lifting the dour architecture. It stood unique from the surrounds with its clean lines and well-maintained grounds. Outside was a familiar vehicle. The door had a logo from one of Martin's paintings. Golden orb of sun, silhouetting a proud eland head. "Marsabit Wildlife Experience" announced the elegant script beneath.

Old friends greeted each other warmly inside the director's small office. The director arrived and placed a tray with a pot of tea and five battered mugs on the small table. The meeting agenda consisted of three items. The mugs of tea were still hot when Martin closed the meeting. The doctor excused himself to attend to patients and left the others to a leisurely catch-up. Tomorrow the group had an anniversary to observe.

The sun already brightened the eastern hills as the Landcruiser headed out of Marsabit. The heavy tyres hummed on the smooth tarmac surface. Martin sat in the back with Evelina, eyes on the desert. Much loved painting sites flashed past. Deep in reflection. The pain had blunted its sharp edges with time but still rested deep in his gut today.

Evelina glanced across at the man she loved. She felt his pain. She had no conflict with the love, it manifested without breaking any taboo. He had become the father and brother that she had lost. They gave her comfort and strength in her purpose. They shared everything and had no secrets.

The road entered the turn-off to Sololo, the memories flashed with more jagged edges. There was no track where they turned off the highway. The vehicle began to lurch across the rough rock, winding through acacia and thorns. Only the GPS truly remembered the route, the surrounds had little distinction. Martin had forgiven himself for the struggle to find the site all those years before.

They reached the place. The pile of grey basalt rock was dotted with new rocks. Smooth river rock, that Martin painstakingly painted each year. Splashes of colour in the desert sameness. The group all held new rocks. Evelina spoke a short quiet prayer. The four rocks were placed. Martin felt the warmth of the hugs, and the three left him to his thoughts. Evelina sang an old village song quietly, a children's' song:

They walked the long path to the well
The water was cool and they drank
The gourds were heavy on the trail
But they were strong and the village came closer with every step
Mami was happy with the good water'

Dave and Maddie walked perhaps fifty metres west to another monument. A black and twisted shape, rusted metal. Both briefly touched what once had been motorbike handle bars. They had found the wreck the second time they had come with Martin. They still wondered at the thread of pure chance that linked them in this vast desert space.

Chapter Twenty-Five – France

The desert peace of a few days ago seemed a world away. Charles De Gaulle airport resounded with bustle and noise. Simone struggled with the familiar sights, now feeling so different. Her head raced with plans of change. Her calendar had been ruthlessly stripped of social engagements - those that were recurrences from pure habit, those that she had added for possible business connections, those that were the remains of aristocracy clinging to the past. She felt revitalised and focused.

She opened the door of her apartment and dropped the packs in the hallway. She explored the space of her home with a new vision. She looked at the large abstract canvas over the lounge table. She had never felt a connection to it but had been convinced by an art critic acquaintance that the investment would become valuable, once the underlying themes the young artist was exploring were understood by a wider audience. She remembered the intellectual elitist arguments that went with the discussion. Nonsense. It spoke nothing to her gut. She took the painting off its hook.

She explored the rest of her home with the same new filters. In the office her hand lingered on the framed photograph of the group outside the Thure cottage. No longer simply a memory from the past, it had new dimensions, a new life. It would be joined by new photographs from Africa. She sat down on the office chair and reached for the phone. Without conscious thought she dialled her mother's number.

The phone call provided a kaleidoscope rush of experiences, feelings and excitement. She felt like a child gushing the experiences of her day to her mother. She tried to express the rawness and space of the African plains, the adventure of the rescue, the new friendships and the change in her life. Her mother heard the change resonating in the conversation.

It lasted an hour, followed by a long comfortable silence. Simone found herself asking, "Mother, what would you like to do next weekend?"

"I would like to go down to our old summer house in the Loire Valley. It has so many fond memories and it has been so long."

Simone remembered the old farm house. She had run around the grounds surrounding the chateau in her bare feet as a child. The family had often driven down through Chartres or taken the train to Tours. The chateau had been owned by an uncle of Simone's father, a delightfully eccentric old man, now long dead.

It took Simone several passes to find the small lane through the woods to the old grounds. Vegetation dangled low over the narrow lane. Simone had to stop several times to drag tree branches from the path. Looking to her right she noticed a pile of stone blocks, all that remained of a the once grand gateway. The elegant wrought ironware of the gate itself leaned drunkenly on one side of a tree. They could drive no further. Simone helped her mother through the gate. Tall grass dissected two paved lines, leading them up the driveway. They walked some distance before the spires of the chateau appeared above the grass. The building still had some majesty, despite the roughly boarded windows and crumbling blockwork on the walls. Simone turned to her mother to gauge her reaction. She was smiling, the memories cutting through the ruins.

Walking fifty metres further they could finally see the old summer house, behind the chateau. From a distance it looked the same, square and squat, rambling back into its own courtyard. Simone's own memories came flooding back. Childhood wandering through the cool green oaks, rabbits and squirrels in the woods. The walk down to the old jetty and the uncle's old river boat on the Loire.

Her mother made her way to the river bank, a favourite picnic spot. She trampled a small circle in the long grass. "Dejeune ici ma chere."

Her mother lay back in her circle, eyes on the blue sky and fluffy cumulus above. She had lightness in her being that Simone had not seen for years.

Simone walked back to the car to fetch the long crispy rolls, ham, tomato and cheese, along with a rug. Trees and views tugged happy memories as she looked around. The cherry tree, her mouth red with fresh cherries, throwing some down to her dear Papa.

They ate their food in silence, soaking in the peace of the Loire water, green forest and blue sky. Simone poured her mother a small glass of wine and a slightly larger one for herself. As she sipped, she looked over at the roofline of the chateau. An idea took shape. She turned to her mother, eyes locking, the idea was transmitted and understood. Her mother simply said, "Oui".

Simone stood and left her mother enjoying the space. She strode towards the farmhouse. So familiar, windows shuttered, doors with a few rough planks boarding them up. The planks disintegrated to brown powder as she pulled one. A rabbit bolted from the hallway, briefly startling both. She slipped into the cool darkness of the house. Shafts of light from broken shutters lasered the darkness. She waited for her eyes to adjust before making her way into the kitchen. Familiar copper kitchenware still hanging from the walls. She tapped the walls, firm thuds, still solid. She explored the old house for half an hour. Familiar corners triggering more memories. The huge old fire place where she sometimes used to hide from her brother. She looked up into inky blackness.

She emerged into the bright sunlight, eyes clenched. Again, she waited for the adjustment. She walked back to her mother. "It is essentially sound, does need a little work to be liveable. Plus, a complete clean out. I am going across to look at the chateau now. Would you like to come or are you happy here?"

Her mother seemed quite content, so Simone wandered across to the chateau. The wall of the back courtyard had completely collapsed, leaving a huge pile of broken blocks and rubble. The huge oak doors were hanging loose, swinging in the light breeze with a metallic squeak. She cautiously entered the hallway, wall linings streaked with white-grey guano, the pigeons responsible cooing gently in the high hallway balcony above. The wall lining drooped from the walls, ancient yellow hessian and crumbled plaster. The staircase, despite still sweeping majestically up one end of the hall, had rotten timber beneath the dank-smelling carpet. More black mould than original red. Shutters hung limply at sagging angles. Glass shards spiked inwards from windows, ready to join the small piles of glass on what was once beautiful Persian carpet.

Her inspection took an hour, despite not risking the climb to the upper floors. Somehow the decaying state of the building fired her imagination further; the plans were growing with the challenge.

As she approached her mother, Madame Lelievre laughed. Her white blouse smeared with the brown of rotten wood and torn at the shoulder, face and one arm blackened from her fireplace inspection, and her skirt torn from a jagged window pane. Simone assumed a haughty air and walked straight past her into the Loire up to her waist amongst the lily pads, then collapsed onto her back. Laughter as reckless as the plan she had hatched.

She was still laughing as she walked up the river bank. Her mother held up the picnic blanket as she shed her dripping garments, then embraced her with the blanket hiding her nakedness.

They talked quickly as they walked back to the car. Simone outlined the dream that was unfolding. Her mother responded enthusiastically.

"It is the perfect wedding venue. Weddings are a growing business in rural France, excellent revenue prospects. I would love to help."

Simone turned with admiration and a sudden realisation that there were so many things she didn't know about this remarkable woman beside her.

Simone's immediate saviour was the unruly piles of gear she carried around in her car. She manufactured an ensemble from the contents of her gym bag coupled with selected garments from a bag intended for dry-cleaning. Her resultant style only caused a slight raise of eyebrows from her fashion-conscious mother.

In the village they found a small hotel. After some persuasion, the proprietor opened the shop next door to sell them a few overnight essentials. Simone made a few phone calls to cancel her appointments for the next week. Madame Lelievre's phone calls were tracking through a chain of relatives of her late husband.

Most of the tables in the small restaurant were full when the two women came down for dinner. They sat engrossed in animated conversation. Simone barely noticed the synchronicity that they were operating in. The thousands of arguments of the past became history. There was also a moment of predestiny when the young man at the next table turned to Simone's mother.

"Excuse me, I couldn't help overhearing, but I am a real estate agent in the village. Last year I helped a potential buyer make an offer on that chateau, so I have contact details for the owners. I am happy to assist you if you wish."

By Wednesday of the next week the two distant cousins, now based in Canada, had accepted an offer on the chateau and grounds. Jon Pierre, the real estate agent, had proved an efficient and professional operator. The dream now had bones of reality and began moving at whirlwind pace. The owner of the little boutique in the village had also become a friend for life after supplying a small wardrobe for both mother and daughter.

Four months flew past. The wind had a wintry bite. The farm house had a warm homely feel, with the new central heating unit pumping real heat and the big open fire adding the ambience of dancing flame. They opened a bottle of wine to celebrate their move into the renovated ground floor of the farm house. Simone had set up her bed in the lounge while her mother slept in the library. Clean smells of fresh cut wood wafted upstairs as Jacques their builder completed work on the renovations. This evening Florence had joined them. Florence was one of the few friends who had survived Simone's cull.

Florence brought enthusiasm to the project and a design flair that would grace the chateau while preserving the essential history. She also brought additional capacity which allowed Simone to juggle her old life and her new dream.

Meanwhile her mother had astounded her with her meticulous oversight of contracts to rebuild the complex. A succession of tradesmen were dismissed for inferior work. She finally approved the third stone mason, a man with old school skills and attention to detail which allowed careful replication of the original historic style. Work progressed steadily on the structural work on the chateau but there were many months ahead. Madame Lelievre's neatly scripted booking ledger already had the first wedding booked for the summer.

The three women were about to toast the fourth partner of the venture.

Simone had heard the voice on the phone and been transported back to Africa in an instant. Rachel, someone for whom she had developed deep trust and respect. It meant a new dimension to the plan, an exciting and complementary one. Her mother had seen the excitement and trusted her judgement completely.

Madame Lelievre had also implemented a morning ritual, so simple, but everyday reconnecting to the microsecond in which the venture was born. They would walk to the highest mound in the grounds and watch the first rays of sun light the chateau spires, then turn to the Loire where it swept around the forested corner. A moment of tranquillity absorbing the essence of the place, and the simple pleasure and peace it encapsulated. For herself she also whispered a short prayer of thanks for the reconnection with her daughter.

———

Florence dropped Madame Lelievre at the market gates then drove the small van a few streets away to park. They met at the saucisson stall, their routine first stop. Florence loved the market. She always arrived back with special treats for all, including the decadent chocolate caramel that Jacques devoured in spite of Madame Lelievre's attempts to issue incentivising rations. The regular items were quickly sourced, then the pair wandered through the craft stalls, looking for decoration for the new room upstairs. They operated in cooperative sync. Florence's spray of dried flowers would be counter-balanced by Madame Lelievre's stark black and white photograph. *Garçon sur la Plage*. An hour quickly passed. They reached a small coffee stall and sat in the red plastic chairs.

Florence returned with the coffee to find Madame Lelievre engaged in conversation with a well-dressed, sharp-featured man. He stood and introduced himself as Philippe. His hand was firm and warm despite the morning chill. She listened to the conversation, quick-witted fun banter interspersed with a quiet listening and thoughtful response. Her instincts trusted him, the matchmaker in her gut suddenly suggested Simone. Madame Lelievre had similar thoughts but they parted company inconclusively.

Some weeks later the pair encountered Phillippe on the same plastic chairs. He appeared genuinely pleased to see Madame Lelievre again, but this time Florence led the conversation. She had some prime facts to determine and started rather too bluntly: "Your wife trusts you to shop at the market?"

"My wife died two years ago. I am afraid the market is more of a compulsion and a bit of an escape for me."

"I am so sorry, forgive my assumption."

The hurt was painfully evident, so Florence immediately softened and diverted into an outline of their project, trying to convey some of the passion they held for it. Once again, she found an easy interested listener with the ability to ask searching questions. Florence ended the conversation with an open invitation to visit the chateau.

Phillippe showed up one morning the following week. Madame Lelievre met him at the gate. She had been showing the stone mason some old photographs which captured detail on the original stonework. They chatted at the gate then drove the short distance up to the chateau in Phillippe's car. The grand tour took nearly an hour. Phillippe was fascinated by the integrity of original design that Madame Lelievre had painstakingly researched. She discovered that Phillippe had a background in engineering, and began to make suggestions to the builder for reinforcing the old walls.

Phillippe was fascinated by the woodwork. The original heart oak glistened like glass when worked with modern tools, quickly blunting planes. He ran his hand over the beautiful old wood, relishing the smooth texture and inherent strength. Madame Lelievre explained that the core of the chateau had been built in the fifteen hundreds.

Painstaking hours of manual craftsmanship, joints beautifully fitted with wooden pegs. The new glazier had been forced to make cardboard templates to cut the glass for the arched window frames, each pane unique. Some of the original panes remained, the fluid glass over centuries thickening at the bottom. Trees with contorted trunks through imperfect surfaces, and glass edges ragged where they had been pinch cut with pliers.

Simone scarcely registered the stranger her mother brought to the lunch table. New engineer perhaps? The international transaction she had been working on had stalled in a Hong Kong bank. Incorrect swift code. She glanced at the stranger again, gym trainer assessment of his body. Relatively fit, he moved gracefully, a little soft around the abdomen, strong arms, sensitive fingers, maybe a musician. What was his name again? Swift code may have been the customer branch number rather than the client's main bank. Catherine could follow that through - what was the time difference to Hong Kong? It needs to be cleared before close of business on Wednesday otherwise the whole chain of transactions would stall.

Simone's lack of presence was scarcely noticed in the conversation at the other end of the table. Phillippe enthusiastically contributed ideas to the build and both Florence and Madame Lelievre were deeply engaged, the food untouched. Madame Lelievre stood to dish the salad. She looked at her daughter, the old self in those dark eyes distracted, unaware. She tapped her shoulder and motioned her to the window. The window-framed forest sprouted light greens buds of summer life. The Loire, silken and silver caught the midday light.

"Breathe it in," whispered her mother.

Simone caught the old self snap back just in time. She breathed deep to her belly, and slowly expired. The scene outside the window demanded her presence. She breathed again. She pushed the nagging issues into the necessary trivia bin at the back of her mind. She turned to Florence and Phillippe and smiled.

"I'm so sorry I've been so distracted. Very rude. My apologies."

The smile caught Phillippe by surprise. He held eye contact and saw the new person. Lunch became an uplifting break from Simone's intense work day. The farewell kiss had a momentary pause, a closeness they both felt.

Simone worked three days on her old business, then three days on the chateau project. Sundays had a routine of relaxation and a traditional lunch. Workmen and their families were invited, and the builders had constructed a long trestle table in the partially completed chateau hallway. Wood chips and the smell of freshly cut timber complemented the aromas from the shared food.

The village had a growing sense of pride in the project and a respect for the women who were guiding it. The network of local people had now filled a complete page of Madame Lelievre's wedding booking ledger. She proudly announced to Simone and Florence that they would break even on the project before the end of the first summer.

Simone looked at her mother with renewed love and respect. At ninety-two years old she continued to astound her daughter from a well of talents and energy.

Phillippe became a regular visitor for the Sunday lunches. He also contributed an unexpected skill as a chef to the weekly dishes. Simone looked forward to the conversations with this man who seemed to offer new dimensions with each meeting.

A month out from the first wedding, Madame Lelievre called a rare meeting of the owners and the head tradesmen. They stripped the incomplete projects back to a list of absolutely essential tasks to properly host the first event. Lights appeared at the work sites at night. Wives appeared with meals for the workmen late at night. The gardening team trimmed hedges and the flower gardens were groomed.

Unbeknown to everyone Madame Lelievre had organised a second event two days after the wedding, to celebrate the re-opening of the chateau. The invitations had the entire village abuzz. The chateau had emerged from its scaffold and plastic shroud with new clean stone work and freshly painted windows.

Two days before the wedding all the work tools were hidden away in the old barn. Madame Lelievre gathered the entire work force on the mound in the chateau garden. Her words were simple:

"Thank you all. You have created beautiful history beautifully. You must all take pride - it is yours as much as ours."

The wedding day passed without any major glitch. All food preparation had been placed in the hands of the caterers, marquees lined the grass courtyard, roses decorated the gate pillars. The three women looked over their estate with pride.

The day of the celebration party dawned fine and sunny. Phillippe arrived early to help with the food but Madame Lelievre had deliberately left everything in the hands of the same wedding caterers. She had also delegated everything to ensure she had no direct responsibilities for the day.

Today there were no formalities. Madame Lelievre thanked every individual workman and woman personally, with a small gift. The food and wine were superb, the day drifted into night and a string quartet started to play. Phillippe appeared beside Simone and held out his hand. They started to dance a slow waltz. The waltz became a slow-moving embrace.

Madame Lelievre caught Florence's eye, they both smiled. Just before midnight, the old lady started the walk down the path to the farm house, twinkling led-lights like stars draped along the hedge rows. The pain in her stomach was more insistent tonight. Still she took in the beauty and peace of the setting with every breath and step.

The party continued until the sky above the forest turned rosy pink. Florence's husband raised a glass of wine to his wife. Phillippe and Simone, sitting opposite, joined in the toast. Simone took Phillippe's hand, said goodnight and started to lead him down the led-light path.

The lights in the library were still on. Through the window Simone could see her mother in the tall-backed chair. She lay forward on the desk asleep. Simone quietly entered the room, put her hand gently on her mother's neck to wake her. The neck was cold, lifeless.

Chapter Twenty-Six – Africa

Maddie resisted the urge to slap the big red ant crawling up her arm. She glanced down as she felt it cross the red mountain range of the scars on her wrist. She had been holding the Nikon for more than an hour.

The gazelle stood at the water's edge, alert ears twitching. He lowered his long neck, ready to drink, then raised his head. An urgent sense of danger. A ripple in the water. Maddie saw it and pressed the shutter button: ten frames per seconds burst. The giant Nile Croc lunged, filling the view. Grace flinched as the teeth leapt towards her six-hundred-millimetre lens. Another burst from the camera. Blood spread in the water. A squealing plaintive call. Then there was nothing but the concentric circular ripples in the pool.

It was all over in twenty seconds.

Maddie had been there for an hour and a half. She tried to replay the shots, but her damaged wrists cramped. Slowly she pulled herself up to a crouch position. Now furiously brushing the red ants and feeling the stinging bites. Placing a large thorn bush between herself and the water she gingerly got to her feet. Cramp now bit her calf and shoulder simultaneously. She pulled her water bottle from her jacket pocket and took a long swill. Rehydration salts bitter in the drink despite the claim of lime flavour on the packet.

She started to hobble back towards the camp then froze. The black mamba lay directly in her path, coiled, sunning itself on a large river rock. She cautiously slipped the camera off her shoulder. The focal length for the big lens was too long. She took a few sliding steps backward. The beautiful head slid into focus, seemingly touching distance. The mouth opened, slight sideways move to frame the head against red clay. Two beautiful shots. A bonus for nearly two weeks' work. The first week had been working up the river trying to find the hunting ground of the big croc. Nightly camps with long searches for the tell-tale red eyes in the dark. Many crocs but not the legendary big male.

Today's shoot would be the last - she had completed the brief. Amazon paid well, this work becoming part of a world-wide series simply entitled "The Kill". She had included some dramatic macro work of insect kills, not in the brief, but she felt sure it would gain her an edge in the final selection.

"You finished Maddie?"

The quiet voice came from her right but she could not see Jonas at first. The expert bushman had been quietly guarding her position, out of sight of the river, but ensuring she wasn't surprised by animals coming down to drink. She saw his wide smile, and returned it, with a thumbs up. Jonas pointed at the images excitedly. He passed the camera back and broke into a short shuffle dance around her to celebrate. Maddie caught his hand to swing him around in a tight circle.

The smell of coffee reached them before the camp appeared. Michael had an instinct for arrival time back to camp. He looked up from his laptop, rows of meticulous detail on elephant sightings. The data completed his survey for the park and would add to his thesis.

"Hey Dr Michael, study time finished, coffee time now. We need to celebrate the big croc kill!" Jonas shouted.

"I knew Jonas's instincts would find you the perfect croc slide. Let me see the pictures." Michael responded. Maddie passed him the camera.

"Beautiful. You will have to send me prints to add to my collection. My Maddie photo wall."

Lunch celebrated both jobs successfully completed and the end of the trip. Michael had baked a pile of corn cakes,

Maddie added a rich spicy guacamole sauce, Jonas had soaked some thinly sliced biltong in madeira. The combined result had an interesting flavour, complemented by coffee heavily sweetened with condensed milk. The three ate in appreciative silence.

Camp pack-up had a familiar routine. Maddie did a last sweep of the camp for rubbish. Michael had already buried the edible scraps and burnt those that were combustible. Maddie took routine before and after photographs of every campsite. The only visible impact was the flattened grass imprints of the tents. They kept the camp load away from the river until Jonas had checked for hippos and crocodiles, then quickly loaded the boat and launched into the chocolate water of the Chobe River.

Maddie kept her camera at the ready with a wide twenty-eight to two-hundred zoom. Jonas started the motor. Immediately a trail of bubbles announced the broad rounded backs and bulbous heads of a small hippo pod as they broke the surface. A large male opened its jaws with the long yellowing tusks caught in Maddie's frame. At the river's edge a small herd of elephants was guiding a tiny infant up the slick clay bank. Two trunks gently nudging and lifting either side. Maddie was swivelling like a rear gunner in a Lancaster bomber. Jonas would spot the next target long before it appeared in Maddie's lens.

Maddie never tired of the river. Same sense of wonder and excitement, nearly one hundred trips. The only thing that had changed was the more ruthless culling of the string of images - only the unique and elite survived.

Suddenly she lurched backward off her seat. Michael grabbed her arm and camera as she sprawled onto the tents packed between the seats. Jonas had spotted the stream of water very close off their bow. A large hippo in a half-submerged charge. A safe distance downstream, he eased off the throttle. Maddie reclaimed her position in the bow and Michael passed the camera back. She gave Jonas a thumbs up and a shaky smile. The tents and Jonas's instincts had saved her many times before.

Two hours down river Jonas began using the current; fuel was running low. Maddie felt the familiar pangs of disappointment as the first lodges started to appear on the river bank. The transition from wilderness peace to civilization. Normality. "Her" river out of reach for another time. Reluctantly she packed the camera away.

They unpacked the boat alongside the jetty at the ranger station. Maddie couldn't keep the tears from her eyes as she hugged Jonas. She knew he held the key to much of her success in this part of the wild. This little man had given generously and she loved him for it.

Michael drove her the short distance to Kasane in a battered park truck. They said their farewells outside the rental office by the large Spar supermarket. Michael was keen to get back to his wife and children. He left almost abruptly with a casual wave.

Maddie packed the car and went to the supermarket to buy drinks and snacks for the journey. The rental car responded to the key with a sluggish whirring. She pushed back in the seat, taking a deep breath. The flow of Africa. As if on cue the rental agent appeared carrying a battery.

"Sorry, I forgot to charge this one."

Within a few minutes the key produced a much healthier sound, one which offered more promise for the six hundred and fifty kilometres ahead to Maun. For the first time in weeks, Maddie glanced at her watch. Three fifteen. Her resolve to complete the drive today slipped in an instant. She would overnight in Nata, three hours away. Six hours on the Kalahari after a long day was simply not possible today. In the dark it could be lethal.

Maddie came alive behind the wheel. This road mesmerised with long straights, two lines merging at the distant point on a horizon that remained unreachable. Scrubby bush and trees lined the road, limiting view across the plains. Piles of elephant dung offered frequent distraction. She had learnt that the undigested contents would contain long thorns lethal to car tyres. Elephants and giraffe occasionally appeared from the scrub, but her wildlife lens was packed away. The routine freed her mind.

The children. Little Kati. The spirit was in little Kati. Eight years old going on twenty-eight. She will have organised her doll for the flight, best dress. She will be wearing something new. Something she would have nagged Dave about until he relented. Probably nagged at least twice. Despite her much-loved doll, she was a tomboy. Open for anything. At her school she played rugby league with the boys. She played hard and tackled low. Energy-charged and constantly curious. Seeing her face gave Maddie the deep enveloping sense of love in her breast. She held it for a couple of kilometres.

The boys would also be on the flight with Dave. Both eager to escape from boarding school to the places they loved around the lodge. They would be bombarding Dave with plans for adventures. Maddie keenly felt the anticipation of reuniting with their gruff teenage love.

Then Dave. His touch. The gift. Every time he responded with unique way of making her feel special. How he had changed since they were reunited on the Lake shores of

Tukana. Evelina's determination had triggered something deep inside Dave. He had found generosity and humility. They had moulded together and the children had cemented the mould. Now the anticipation of meeting again was tangible. She shivered.

Nata appeared in the orange of the dropping sun. She pulled into Nata Lodge a few kilometres outside the township. The lodge staff greeted her with warm familiarity. One of her elephant shots had pride of place above the reception desk. She shunned the tourist gathering in the dining room for a quick sandwich and fruit in her room. She hadn't transitioned far enough from wilderness peace to face tourist banter.

Breakfast arrived with dawn light. The lodge was still quiet as she drove out to the sandy road. Overnight rain had left deep puddles. She stopped for petrol on the road back to Nata before turning west onto the Kalahari highway. The dawn light reawakened the sense of wilderness peace. The rain continued. Sweeping grassland interspersed with dense bush and large rain pools. Tyres hissed over the damp road surface. A large concrete Aardvark loomed on the roadside. She smiles as she remembers the romantic weekend. Dave had whisked her away there when she was just pregnant with Kati. It created space for the demands

of a new-born to come. Their time. Beautiful light for
some stunning shots.

Cattle and goat herds began to announce the arrival into
Maun. Large red billboards shattered the grassland space.
Maun, gateway to the Okavango, sprawled into view. She
had spent many hours in the far corners of the delta
wetlands so the town had fond connections.

Maun Airport was abuzz with tourists but with her own
flight less than an hour away she quickly slipped through
to the anonymity of the departure lounge.

On take-off the small neat block compounds of Maun
town-ship quickly disappeared. The waterways of the
Okavango snaked in a glistening array under the wingtips.
Swampy ground with palm tree islands stretched for miles.
Water plants and vegetation amongst the network of
waterways created a mosaic. Maddie could barely make out
the southern bound of the delta, the Thamalakane Fault
and the Boteti River. Familiar places from past expeditions.
Memories accompanied by a catalogue of special images.

——

Twenty-five hours. Kati lay fast asleep in the seat
alongside, doll neatly propped in the baby seatbelt
attachment the hostess had provided. The boys were

watching their tenth movie. Dave looked at the children. The boys still travelled with the same enthusiasm and excitement. He finally closed his eyes.

Maddie drifted in. He could feel her hand on the back of his neck, that first signature gentle caress. It felt so good to be going back. The boys were excited. David hadn't yet settled into boarding school routine and was desperate to get 'home' to the lodge in Kenya. Peter was a little harder for Dave to gauge, his teenage monosyllables leaving large gaps in communication.

Maddie and Dave talked every day. Maddie's satellite phone was perhaps the greatest gift for both of them. Maddie came alive through the search for the image which captured the essence of the environment. Her enthusiasm was contagious. For both of them it was a break from the relentless fundraising and management efforts required to maintain their diverse trusts. Before collecting the boys from school, Dave had completed the annual review with Bruno for the School of Hard Knocks. Now they could relax with some family time.

The other foundation had been their friends. Every year they had honoured a commitment to keeping in touch with friends. Both couples, Bruno and Grace and Donna and Pete, had been stalwarts in all the projects, but they always

took time out to enjoy an adventure together. A
celebration.

Dave began happily reminiscing as he drifted in and out of
a light sleep. A memory made him chuckle. They had
completed the guest house for the safari business, and
were greeting the first group of guests. A group of farmers
from southern USA. Despite their very clear advertising
that the safaris were purely for photo shoots, this group
arrived with a large trunk of firearms.

"Photo shoots – yeah we understand the code," they
winked.

They settled the group into the guest house and returned
to their own house to decide how to approach the
problem. Sister Evelina was visiting and hatched the
master plan with her usual devilish sense of fun.

They briefed their safari manager Joseph. He was the only
one likely to be able to maintain a straight face. Next
morning, he handed the group their chosen weapons out
the back of the lodge facing the steep volcanic slope.

"Gentlemen, before you may shoot any animal there must
be a sacrificial shooting. Local tribal custom requires that
this sacrifice must be a religious leader of high standing.
Please take up your shooting positions."

At that point Sister Evelina in full regalia appeared from behind a cluster of acacia. Walking slowly and holding her bible to her face she turned to the group.

"Lord have Mercy on you gentlemen."

The tour group turned to each other in confusion. The firearms were quickly put down.

"No way. That price is too rich for me. Do you have any alternatives?"

At that point Dave emerged with a bottle of Kentucky corn whisky and the alternative.

———

Even Peter couldn't contain his joy and excitement as Maddie appeared at the arrival hall, arms wide for the onslaught. Dave joined the four with a loaded luggage trolley. The warm embrace with Maddie lasted a long time. Kati pulled at Maddie's skirt. "Mummy, my turn now and dollies."

They loaded the truck and Maddie threaded through the traffic on the familiar route to the tall white walls topped with iron lattice, their Nairobi base. The staff greeted the family like the old friends they had become. The familiar room deactivated the children, and they were in bed asleep in minutes.

Maddie and Dave lingered on the large couch, touching and talking until Dave drifted into a deep sleep.

The family left Nairobi early, starting the long drive home. Joseph greeted them at the gates of the lodge, then helped them unload. The boys and Kati were immediately diverted to a baby elephant. Joseph had found her close to her mother, shot by poachers in the deep bush up from the lodge. Kati became immediately captivated. The little elephant had an immediate affinity with her. Joseph handed her a feeding bottle. Kati stroked the large leathery ear, looking directly into the wide long-lashed eye of her new friend.

The familiar clean wood of the kitchen welcomed Maddie and Dave. It felt good to be home. The children would be occupied for hours catching up with their familiar haunts around the lodge. Maddie took Dave's hand and led him up the hallway to celebrate their special reunion.

The familiar rhythm of the Lodge started late next morning. A Swedish group was due to arrive. Maddie called to the boys,

"David, you can go with Joseph if you like. Peter, you can drive the second truck. Joseph is taking the group up to the grasslands on the top ridge track. See if you can find old One-Tusk and his family."

Both boys had developed an acute awareness of wildlife signs and behavioural rules. Last summer, Peter had spotted the old elephant bull who frequented the top of the crater rim before Jacob their tracker had seen him. Jacob, although secretly delighted the hours of patient teaching had paid off, pretended to sulk.

"You'll be taking my job soon."

Dave and Maddie firstly did the rounds to check on the lodge staff. Maddie then sat at her desk to check the calendar. Two weeks out she had pencilled a large circle with four names inside: Grace, Bruno, Pete and Donna. Another big anniversary coming up.

Dave pulled up to the clinic, taking a ritual few seconds to reflect. The squat concrete building gave him a lot of pride. It felt like one of the best things he had achieved in his life. The time he, Maddie and the other four had worked on the building gave him a huge sense of satisfaction. They had created something real and useful with their own hands. But they had also immediately given it back. Ownership rested with the staff and the town. It took only a few words about the next project for the local people to offer support.

The project had also given him deep respect for Martin. Martin had worked through the bureaucracy of the building process, masterfully side-stepped road blocks, and was now tackling the affiliation with the National Health system. They had become close friends, enjoying many long conversations. They had solved many problems of the world in theory but in practice together they had genuinely impacted some real priorities in the town. Today it would be great to catch up with his old friend.

Nina, the head nurse, greeted Dave at the door. Her tall and willowy figure towered above him.

"Dave - welcome back, so good to see you again."

Without pausing for his reply, she continued, "Oh, for the laboratory project, my nephew drives a concrete truck down in Nanyuki. I have persuaded his boss to allow him to deliver a full load of concrete, maybe two."

"Well done. How on earth did you manage that Nina?" Dave queried.

"Many old lovers owe me much. Do you have some time Dave? I have a few ideas for Bruno when he arrives."

"Of course Nina."

"You remember Bruno's suggestion of developing a priority list for the top routine medical issues here? Well, I have completed the list, and would like Bruno to set up some training for us. Do you think that would be possible?"

"I will ask Bruno. Anything else?"

"The new nurse Kalina, has to go. She is too young, too idle and lives on her phone. She has no compassion and no skill. She is not a nurse. I have passed my recommendation to Sister Agnes."

Sister Agnes, now in her late seventies, provided the administration support to the clinic. She still worked tirelessly and dealt with staff issues in a gentle but firm manner. She always resisted removing staff.

"The promise of a person is only developed by a good teacher. If the person is failing the teacher is failing," was her stock response when faced with dealing with removing a staff member. Dave always trusted Nina's judgement and usually undertook the role of convincing Agnes. Often, he would enrol Evelina in providing a suitable biblical quote to support the argument.

"I will talk to Agnes. What else is happening in the clinic?"

"The clinic is overflowing with patients. A typhoid outbreak in one of the northern villages. The dry season has left little water and one small local well became contaminated. Almost the entire village has been affected. Twenty extra beds in the recreation room. We are running very low on typhoid antibiotics."

"I will ask Bruno to add that to their list. Thank you Nina, and now I do have some other work to do."

Dave retired to the small staff kitchen. His laptop was open on the bare wooden table, connected to the wireless network. The connection speed allowed a slow sip of tea between pages. An email from Rachel caught his attention. The response from Simone had him even more excited. The timing was perfect.

The morning passed quickly as Dave loaded the truck with supplies from familiar stores around the town. Each store held a group of familiar faces and catch-up conversations. It was late afternoon before the truck started the dusty few kilometres back to the Lodge. Close to the gates two of the safari trucks also appeared from the track coming down from the crater. Maddie waved. Thumbs up, a successful day.

Dave found himself tense and distracted during the ritual sundowner drinks with the guests. He was dying to pull Maddie aside and share the news, but she was ensconced behind a wall of cameras and laptops, analysing the day's shots. The Swedish group's excitement from a rare encounter with a cheetah forgave his grunted responses. The children appeared and gave Dave an excuse to head back to the house.

A garlic and onion aroma greeted Maddie when she finally extracted herself from guest duties. She embraced Dave from behind as he stirred the pasta sauce. Her embrace released the last of Dave's tension. He could deliver favourite meals and his surprise news at the same time.

———

Bruno was uncharacteristically grumpy. The truck was filled with travel cases, not the usual array of camping gear. He had anticipated new territory for their camping safari, maybe somewhere totally remote, new wildlife. This journey had the hallmarks of tourist luxury.

"If you are taking me to some flash touristy resort, I will never forgive you," he grumbled out the window.

Dave smiled. They had worked hard and had fun over the last two weeks. They had levelled the foundations for the lab, mostly by hand, built the boxing and laced the reinforcing.

Dave had been impressed with the tenacity of Kath Wilson. The young woman had uncommon strength and determination. He had watched as Donna bandaged her blistered hands. She kept on working. Bruno had told the story of her feet on the "Walk to Somewhere". Dave was intrigued, so he and Maddie had made time to take Kath to all their secret places on the reserve. She responded with enthusiastic curiosity. There was always a gift in sharing places they loved, but the payback with Kath had been generous.

Kath had also worked with a group of local youth Evelina had invited to the church. She had won them over with her straightness and her openness with her past. It started with an impervious wall of reflective sun-glasses. Heads down. Feet shuffling. Kath sat and waited, a full ten minutes. Eventually she said:

"What's happening? Nothing. That's all silence can bring. Nothing." Evelina translated, although for most the English version was clear.

Kath began to talk about her past, ruthlessly, without excuses for herself or her behaviour. She talked directly, face to face with each of the group, pausing only briefly for Evelina's translation.

"My life was shit. It was driven by the need for the next fix. I would do anything, absolutely any bloody thing. Now I can decide. I choose what I do and what I don't do."

Some of the sullen eyes behind the dark glasses in the group began to see a reflection. Kath walked to the first guy in the group.

"Please show me your eyes. I want to see you."

She asked their names and their stories. She didn't push, she listened. Gradually the dialogue grew. There was common ground in music. Kath recognised some artists and rapped some passable impressions. She had broken the ice and could see herself in each face. Despite the difference in backgrounds the commonalities were emerging. At the end she felt a sense of pride when she asked,

"Who would like to continue tomorrow?"

All put up their hands.

They had left Kath to stay in the house, and share the next safari tour, "And look after Sheba please," little Kati had requested.

Nina's nephew had delivered the concrete on time. The base and wall pillars were complete. Nina had hijacked Bruno to start the training program, so he escaped some of the hard-manual labour. Pete was disgruntled when Dave called a halt on the project.

"We have never left a job half-done, so let's at least get a roof on."

———

Both Pete's and Bruno's mood improved when they arrived at the small grass airfield outside Nanyuki. Small planes were haphazardly parked around the field. This could still be somewhere interesting. Dave had often promised a trip to the wild Skeleton Coast in Namibia, an area that appealed to Bruno, although and perhaps because he knew so little about it.

He became more intrigued when he saw Martin and Evelina already strapped in the back seats of the Cessna Caravan. "Please - I hate surprises – where are we off to?" he pleaded.

"France," said little Kati innocently, forgetting her promise of secrecy.

Chapter Twenty-Seven – Melbourne

"What on earth was his name?" The apartment looked
familiar. Almost a year in one place. He had been here for
perhaps three months. She should remember his name.
The room spun half a rotation. She needed to pee. Her
head collapsed over her knees on the toilet. She pushed the
door shut.

"Sebastian? ... no he was Cape Town".

The toilet walls spun again. She awoke to the smell of
vomit. Out through the kitchen window a grey sky
reflected her mood. She didn't remember wrapping the
towel around her body. She had cleaned her teeth twice,
but her mouth felt bitter and sour. Johann would be
waking soon. Johann, of course! The jug burbled and she
poured a hot tea. The tea worked. The jangle of the alarm
startled her.

Johann appeared at the kitchen door, rubbing sleepy eyes.
He shook his head and continued to the bathroom. She
heard him swear. The end was near. Again.

She went to the spare room and sat on the bed. She heard
the door shut as Johann left. She pulled down a suitcase

and her backpack. It took fifteen minutes. She sipped cold tea and tried to write a note. Another fifteen minutes and she dropped her keys on the table beside the note. The note said "Sorry."

Cool air greeted her as she opened the door and stepped outside. She looked back at the apartment. It looked familiar. She felt nothing. She dialled a cab. It took nearly a minute to answer the driver when he asked, "Where to?" Then she heard "Airport please." The response came instinctively. The airport bustle felt comforting. She felt hungry and sat at a familiar café.

"The usual?"

She wondered what 'the usual' would bring. The plate contained avocado and tomato smashed on toast with the salty tingle of bacon. The taste awoke something, then the thought slipped away.

She flipped through her phone, shredding contacts. Then she stopped and dialled the number. A friend she could always trust. No bull. The voice caught her throat, unable to respond with more than a slight choke. The voice knew her being. It was ruthless but with compassion. A chink appeared in the mist, something real again. I am still in this body she thought, somewhere there is still me. She turned off the phone.

A large lady at the next table caught her eye and smiled.

"Where are you off to dear?"

"Australia."

She hid behind the large coffee mug that had arrived, killing the conversation. Australia, where on earth had that come from? But she knew. It was unfinished business. It had hung around her neck like the proverbial albatross.

Across the concourse the sign said "Left Luggage". She wheeled the suitcase across, paid for the key and rammed the big case into the steel box. Nothing but clothes and past. Recent past, wasted past. The key dropped into the stainless waste bin with a slight metallic ting. The recent past was locked away where it belonged. She felt the lightness of the burden lifted. There was still possibility.

———

Rachel's mother's house sat in a row of identical solid Melbourne brick villas. Same intricate wrought iron lattice work on identical verandas. Flower baskets competing with neighbours for colour and style. Comfortable lounge chairs for hot summer evenings. Rachel lingered outside with the sensation of familiarity cocooning her. The doorbell brought her mother's forgiving love into her arms. Inside they talked. Rachel slept and they talked again. She wanted forgiveness for the cruel endings to strings of relationships. Her mother forgave. She wanted answers for her life drifting off the rails. Her mother smiled and made cups of tea. It was nearly a week before there was nothing left to say. They sat in silence, then her mother said,

"I loved you from the moment I first held you. I love you now. You start again on the same footing, but this time you stay true to yourself."

The cool dark room at the back of the house would always be her room. On the shelf above the clothes drawer Rachel found the big Pelican hard case. She knew what it contained. The impossible dream. She brought the big bag onto the kitchen table and began sifting through the footage. Smiles came with the memories. Something came alive, the creative instinct. She knew the end of the story; she had to tie the threads together.

It took a few days to track Nat Papadopoulis down. He had started a small production studio in South Melbourne. They had all the editing and sound gear she needed. He offered a generous price for the production work. Still incomplete content. The follow-up story was missing. Rachel sat at her mother's kitchen table again, working out a budget. It came close to fifty thousand - she perhaps had twenty. She ran her ball point pen around the missing budget amount and her mother leant over her shoulder. She explained the shortfall. Her mother opened a drawer full of neatly-filed papers. She came back to the table.

"My retirement fund can cover that - you were going to get what's left anyway."

Rachel protested, but there was no budging her mother's resolve.

The first weeks started in creative flurry. Rachel's budget had not accounted for her own living costs, so despite her mother's protests she took on some advertising production work. She worked as much as possible at night so she would not disrupt Nat's studio. The weeks turned into months.

Weekends were taken up with trips to gather the follow-up content. She filmed on a camera she borrowed from Nat. The reunions were emotional and the story became personal. Rachel came alive again, she started to care about people, a care she was ashamed to admit she had lost. She also started to trust advice from Nat. He kept the content tight and focused without losing the obvious personal involvement. He shared her passion.

It seemed a lifetime since she had bid Nat farewell at Nairobi airport. Then he had been more of a junior colleague with touches of personal care which were a little awkward. She had a reputation for cool professional distance. Those little personal touches were the memories which drove Rachel to trust him with this project.

The memory of Nairobi Airport sent a shudder down Rachel's spine. She had arrived back there feeling lost. Despite the friendship she had developed with Simone the others in the group were wary of her. Bruno in particular had clearly told her that paparazzi were not welcome. She was deeply hurt; she had abandoned her job to help someone she regarded as a friend. Only Simone saw the true motives; she had allowed the few precious segments of footage by the lake.

Rachel arrived back feeling totally alone. There was a bitterness which was uncharacteristic but which rapidly became her driving companion. She had dumped the case containing the footage at her mother's house and immediately started looking for work as far away as possible. She joined an independent war correspondent in Kabul. He turned out to be a thrill seeker living on an edge which constantly terrified her. His stories focused on the sensational, while Rachel became constantly haunted by the local women weary of war, wary of intruders, ever seeking the normality of family and peace. She escaped to Morocco to produce a gentle travel documentary. A few months in a tumultuous relationship with the presenter and an escape to Johannesburg, and Sebastian.

Rachel took a deep breath. Sebastian recalled the worst of her relationships. She held her breath, struggling to subvert the memories. *How could she have become such a bitch?*

Nat spotted the turmoil in her eyes and gently touched her arm.

"Time for our favourite latte café."

Rachel let her breath escape with a slight whistle.

"Demons Nat, yes, coffee time."

Nat had a sensitivity which Rachel had never appreciated on their past assignments. The first time Rachel was invited to his home for dinner, she could see the closeness of his family. Nat always made time for friends popping into the office. Good friends with lots of laughter. Rachel felt quite humbled that she was now regarded as one of those friends. Something reliable and solid in her life.

They had also reached the point where Rachel's initial budget had been exhausted. Nat came directly to the point.

"I need to pay the guys, but there is a stack of other work. If I had someone to manage the office stuff and the sales contacts we could cover the costs. This documentary is going to be great and will sell, so if you are prepared to share the IP and help around the office we can finish the rest."

Rachel didn't hesitate. She had seen this point looming and was determined her mother would not risk more of her savings.

"Thanks Nat. Offer accepted."

Rachel continued with some of the advertising work as well as extending her hours in Nat's tiny office. She worked up to sixteen hours a day, sustained on pure adrenaline. She felt alive and the creative development of the project excited her. Her short nights passed in deep dreamless sleep. Sundays she spent on quiet activities with her mother, walks in the park with picnics when the weather allowed.

They had returned from a Sunday stroll along South Melbourne beach when Rachel received a call. The accent was French, it was Simone. The voice was friendly and familiar. Rachel felt a momentary emotional sob, a ghost disappeared. They talked for an hour, giggling over memories of the Hotel El Almo.

"You remember the dream I had of a chateau in the country? Well that has come alive, and it is almost finished. Are you still interested in the idea of setting up a video production business? We are doing big weddings, and all of them are paying well for quality video. It would be a great base for more creative work."

"I would love to, on two conditions. One, that my mother can join me, and secondly, that I can complete the current project so I can pay for a partnership on equal terms."

"Perfect."

Rachel was excited as she explained the plan to Nat. His eyes lit up.

"A number of businessmen in the Greek community with European connections have been pestering me to set up an operation in Europe. This could be great."

Rachel baulked for a second, feeling her dream was being diluted, then saw the value and the karma of the joint opportunity. Nat had the ready-made production expertise.

The future vision drove Rachel with a passion and focus she had never felt before. Nat managed the production with a rigorous eye for detail. Transitions were seamless, sound sync was millisecond perfect. The two young editors could see the quality and responded with their own responsibility for perfection.

It was Wednesday, and Rachel had been working since six am. She decided she needed a break. She left the studio to buy some food at the little deli down the road. On impulse she left the shop and headed towards the sea. In a few minutes she had reached the path alongside South Melbourne Beach.

There was a cool wind, with few people about on the beach. A sturdy ex-life guard of perhaps seventy-year vintage emerged from the surf. Black swim cap and dark googles scrunching a face reddened with the cool of the sea. Stomach extending over black brief swim shorts. Rachel smiled. Classic Melbourne beach, it gave a sense of familiarity.

She sat on a bench and took a bite of a prawn roll. It tasted good. She was thinking about Nat's suggestion of entering the International Documentary Awards. They had no substantial budget for marketing so it might be an opportunity. Then again if it didn't get a mention, or worse a bad review, it would be a wasted entry fee.

The big man had reached his towel on the beach. He looked up and smiled and waved. Rachel waved back.

"You should give it a go," he called. "The sea is refreshing once you get used to it."

Yes she thought. It was easily the best film she had ever produced. Was that because she was so emotionally attached? It would need to be tested in the real world, but the conditions for entry called for unaired footage.

The big man climbed the steps from the beach, towel wrapped around his ample waist, ancient St Kilda Surf Club tee shirt damp on his body. He stopped on the pavement to brush his sandy feet. He looked directly at Rachel.

"You know, sometimes thinking is counter-productive; you need to get into action and trust your instincts."

Rachel started to respond, but he was gone.

———

Nat's wife adjusted his bow tie. He fidgeted, nervous and excited. His three children stood in awe of the cavernous foyer of the MGM Grand. The two boys, small replicas of Nat himself, his daughter in a beautiful gown that Rachel had gifted her. The child was competing with the refined young lady. She couldn't resist a run and slide across the polished floor. Her brothers followed with yelps, before remembering their stern briefing, walking sheepishly back to the three adults.

Rachel remained calm. She knew the competition. The finalists included a BBC Wildlife series, a Swedish production following the rain deer herds of the far north in Lapland, and a Canadian production examining the dwindling Arctic ice cover. Global issues, beautiful videography. World class. Did they even deserve to be in this company? She caught Sherine's eye. Nat's wife Sherine, a yoga teacher, brought a gentle serenity into the partnership. She caught Rachel's doubts and made a downward calming sweep of her hands.

"Breathe. It is out of your hands, you have done an amazing job. Relax."

She had said the words as they left their hotel suite minutes earlier.

Their table was in the front row. Their tiny contingent was dwarfed by the three tables taken up by the BBC Team. They shared with some of the Swedish film makers. Nat quickly engaged in technical discussion with their lead editor. The graphics designer seated next to Rachel was animated and talkative. He gave high praise for the technical quality of their work. Rachel deferred the praise to Nat. She tried to breathe deeply, half-listening to the flow of conversation but distracted. Once again, she caught Sherine's eye over the table.

Her small hand gesture circled the space. 'Be in the moment' it signalled. Rachel looked around, took it all in. She took a sip of champagne, another breath. The graphics man was in the middle of a sentence, she tuned in.

"...you have captured the human qualities. Stripped away the usual bullshit. I really love the style and the message is straight to the heart. I find it refreshing to find something that tells a story but is not trying to save the world, it is simply showing the world as it is, real people, real emotions along with a dramatic story."

He paused to take a sip.

Rachel looked at him. Something gelled in the words. She felt a well of pride. Seeing the reflection through another pair of eyes, the vision she had always had. It had worked. It had worked! She was happy, she could go home happy anyway, any outcome, it didn't matter. Instinctively she reached over and touched the back of his hand.

"Thank you, that means more than any award."

Their conversation was interrupted by the announcement of the first entertainment. The Dixie Chicks. Rachel had a musical friend who loved the Dixie Chicks, but she couldn't remember if she had ever actually heard the sound herself. The table was directly under the stage. The energy of the three ladies hit Rachel in the chest. She felt every beat. Her foot and fingers started to tap. Her neighbour was tapping the table so hard their champagne flutes toppled. They both laughed, the sound of laughter lost in the mix. She was in Las Vegas with the Dixie Chicks metres away. This was happening. She looked across at Nat's children; the thrill was in their eyes, it added to her own.

The night flew. The technical production awards were lost in conversation with her neighbour. She almost missed the announcement.

"And the Runner Up is, from Melbourne Australia, 'Wild Ride Africa'.

She raced around the table grabbing Nat in a hug from behind as he embraced Sherine. The children were dancing. Nat turned to her, his eyes streaming. They held the embrace for a long time before heading to the stage.

———

The three children were lined along the window seat in the hotel suite, devices in hand. Fuzzy Dixie Chicks images to greet envious friends in the Melbourne morning. It was nearly two am.

Nat and Rachel sat, drinks in hand, staring at the cheque on the table. To Nat it brought relief from the nagging financial worries; he felt free and light. Rachel had insisted that all Nat's debt be totally cleared, with bonuses paid to all the team before they split the proceeds. There was still a generous amount left for each. They had barely sipped their drinks before Nat's phone began to ring. Call after call.

Rachel went to the window, staring at the lights below. *It's a gift,* she thought, *something to be given back.*

Chapter Twenty-Eight – The Chateau France

Transformed! Simone looked around the big dining room with pride. The technician was tidying up after finishing installing the big screen. It lit up the room, covering the dark moody portraits on the wall. Rows of elegant couches filled the space behind the giant oak dining table. Small ebony side tables sat at the arms of every couch. Simone relished the preparation. She was about to showcase her new life to dear friends. People who mattered. She wanted the presentation immaculate.

Rachel appeared at the doorway.

"Wow! Amazing job Simone!"

She had arrived two weeks earlier, and they had worked tirelessly with the preparations.

"Time to celebrate, I'm so excited. When do the others arrive?"

"I'm about to ring Bruno to check. They should be on the train by now."

——

The landscape blurred with the TGV speed. Bruno sat, head to the window. Familiarity yet distance. He tried to recognise towns and villages flashing past. It was no longer home, but there was a pull. A cottage, a long-walled garden stretching from the back. Flowers and neat rows of vegetables. His father kneeling on the old tattered cushion, pulling weeds. Hands rough but gentle, firm and warm around his city hands. Soft hands. His mother was coming down the path. Smell of rich coffee, croissants and fruit on a wooden tray. The sun warm at the bottom of the garden. The scent of garden cut by the aroma of coffee and croissants. Croissants warm and crisp with tomato from the garden and rich jambon from the patissierie. His mother smiled. Forgiving smile, too few moments with her son smile. Sadness.

The warmth of Grace's body pushed him into the window. Her lens rested across the back of his neck. She was capturing a different view, beauty blurred by speed. Bruno relaxed into the familiar warmth and wrapped his arm around her waist. The ghosts lingered until the ring from his phone interrupted his thoughts.

———

373

Simone paused before making the next call. Butterflies fluttered in her belly as she dialled. To have Dave as a guest in her new world was special.

———

Dave drove slowly. He and Maddie had opted not to take the TGV with the others. Dave wanted to share memories of France with her. The green of the narrow road turned to grey stone walls of a small village, sharp turn left under the church eaves. The round grass space of the village heart punctuated by a fountain, yellow and grey-green with lichens on old stone. He relished the sense of rural village life. He had deliberately chosen a twisted route of minor roads. He drove absorbed in the surrounding history of flower baskets and ancient arched doorways. He was at peace. The rest of the family in the car were asleep.

This was the France of memories and half-memories of similar scenes. His mind drifted back. He was in the old green Citroen, heading somewhere. Akeyo was singing, Bruno adding bass harmony from the driver's seat, almost on key. Akeyo was in the back seat beside him, a curve in the road had her slide across the seat. She kept the warm contact at his side. Her hand slid across his belly under his shirt, briefly and electrically. He caught the hand as it slipped out. The dark slim fingers contrasted with his

374

farmer's square hands, delicate, fragile, as fragile as the person beside him. He sank into the dark eyes. Akeyo finished the song and slid back to the far side of the seat. Sue somehow slipped into the seat between them, finger to her lips. Tolerant but warning. Dave looked at the familiar blue eyes, a different feeling, but somehow merged with what he had previously felt. The seat was empty, then the curled form of Maddie took their place, scars cruel, red and ragged on her face. Eyes pleading. Dave clenched the wheel hard and focused back out the window.

He tried to recall the words embroidered on the tapestry in Anne McLeod's apartment. Slowly they came back:

"Your feet are the anchors to the earth of your own land. Your head drives discovery of new places. Your heart links the people in the places you find. Your soul follows threads woven by your ancestors. Your actions define the lessons you have learned."

———

Bruno raised his voice above the noise in the carriage.

"That was Simone, she is looking forward to seeing everyone. And Martin, she has a scene she would love you to paint."

375

Martin smiled, then looked across the carriage. The closeness of Bruno and Grace brought a momentary sense of loss. Evelina reached across and pulled his hand.

"Look at that beautiful bridge. Those arches and stonework. It is straight out of a history book."

Evelina's excitement was contagious. Her entire life had been spent largely in an area of semi-arid desert, perhaps one hundred kilometres across. She had already digested the guide book on her lap.

"I think that is the Loire, we are almost there! I would love to see all the chateaus, especially Villandry and Chenonceau. There are so many beautiful places here. I am blessed with choices I never dreamed possible."

The deceleration of the train pushed Evelina back into her seat and she giggled, childlike in her wonder and excitement. Martin absorbed some of her joy. With the joy came a deep sense of occasion, understanding that he too was a beneficiary of Akeyo's love even now.

He pulled a small sketch pad from his bag. In the few minutes before the train came to a standstill, he sketched an impression that captured the emotion. Only Evelina would share that image and see.

———

Donna sat beside Evelina for most of the journey. She absorbed Evelina's meticulous research, firing her own interest. She was excited. History had never registered in her experience, but this was something close, real and tangible. She was here, like a guest appearance in a fairytale. Pete was asleep. Pete had his own frame of reference and it was solid, reliable and immovable. Sometimes Donna sought the magic elements outside that frame, outside the reliable comfort. She felt slightly embarrassed as his snoring peaked. The kids made jokes. Donna's nudges made no impact. Evelina absorbed her in amazing recollection from her guide book. Pete drifted into the background. She tried to engage the children, but the electronics held sway. She peeked over Martin's shoulder at his sketch.

It was a picture of the children. They were in a circle, arms raised, hands interlinked, reaching up. Donna didn't understand. To her it was about the closeness of old friendships, the group, their own history together. The children's time would come.

———

Pete awoke. Head angled high on the seat-back. He was looking directly to the sky. Strange cloud. Looking carefully Pete could see a donkey. The sun had dipped to provide an outback desert orange on flat ice-sheet stratus. Four figures in white, dashes of white, finely sculptured. Two women one tall, one crouched on something, could be a bicycle he thought. Puffs of red behind. The two other figures, one lean and tall, one-legged stance, the other old and bent. The stratosphere wind swept the scene into purple then grey. Two jet stream trails criss-crossed the grey desert plain. Pete rubbed his eyes, then closed them again.

———

Simone and Phillippe wandered through the orchard down below the chateau. Simone stopped to pick some lush white raspberries. She slipped one between Phillippe's lips. She had shared generously with Phillippe, so he felt he knew the group intimately before setting eyes on anybody. Simone had inherited her mother's graciousness. Before the funeral she had spent hours talking to her mother's old friends, researching family records. Her mother grew in her estimation with each discovery, things she had never been aware of, things she had ignored. She was left with a commitment, light on her shoulders but blanketing every

378

past doubt. She had pride and she wanted to share. She finally felt safe from herself.

They had worked together preparing for the occasion. The chateau grounds and accommodation were pristine. Fit for a special celebration.

———

Simone lead Evelina to her room. Evelina's eyes lit up. She turned to the window, running her fingers down the long satin drapes, then stood entranced at the view of the green forest framed in the arched windows. She followed Simone to the bath and ran the warm water from the bath taps across her hands. They returned to the bedroom and Evelina twirled joyously in the space. She reached to embrace Simone.

"Are you sure you have not taken me to heaven prematurely Simone? You know I still have much work to do, but thank you. Thank you. I will remember this for the rest of my life."

"A small gift for everything you have done."

Simone smiled, wondering why such a simple gift gave her so much joy in the giving.

Rachel was nervous. She had not seen Bruno since their abrupt parting at the lake. Her confidence in her work waivered with doubts about exploitation, especially as seen by Bruno. Simone had tried to calm her anxieties, but Simone had not seen the completed work. Even she may see differently. She had telephoned Nat who in turn handed the phone to Sherine. Sherine had been direct.

"I know it's a beautiful masterpiece, Nat knows it's a masterpiece, you know it's a masterpiece. There is nothing to change. It is done, you have presented it with a wonderful compassion. Go out to the woods, look through the canopy to the stars, and breathe the air."

Rachel was doing exactly that as the lights of Dave's rental car slashed through the darkness.

The huge dining room lighting was subdued. Rachel was standing under a small spot-light. She held two pages, neatly typed. She cleared her throat, looking down at the pages. Then she stopped. She lifted her eyes, firstly to Bruno. Bruno held her gaze, firmly. She repeated the process with everyone in the group. Last was Evelina, her dark skin making her nearly invisible in the deep chair.

There were only her eyes, two flecks of white. Rachel focused as best she could against the light. Evelina leaned forward. Her smile caught in the cross-light. She lifted her hands towards Rachel, palms upward. The palms spread outward, embracing the group. Eyes locked into the smile. For a second Evelina was the embodiment of the love in the group. Rachel dropped the two pages to the floor, smiled and began:

"Friends. I hope I can call you friends. You certainly feel like friends."

Her eyes turned to Bruno, and he smiled with a slight nod.

"These have been ten years of hard work for me. Hard work, because much of the time I was fighting myself. I would say falling off the rails. That is if I had any vestige of rails to fall off. This is the story which you all know from different angles. Some of you from the most deeply personal angles."

She turned to Dave, and held his gaze briefly.

"It was also deeply personal to me, to me it was the story of a dear friend. It didn't start that way. It started as a mere job. A job which I was sceptical about. I thought it was to be a light-weight production, which if lucky would have made air time after the late-night news. I didn't know the extraordinary woman that would emerge. The guts, the tragedy and the strength and the real legacy. I struggled to balance my own feelings to present something that was worthy, compassionate and not sensational for sensation's sake. The sensation had to be the sensational people involved, which includes all of you, and of course Maddie."

"It has won an award, but the only award which is meaningful to me is your acceptance or appreciation or approval. Please forgive me if I cannot deliver on any of these. If not, I will have not served Maddie. Thank you."

———

The bike started as a small distant speck in the middle of the screen. Dust plume elegantly spraying either side. The sound built until the bike passed, seemingly inches from the camera. Rachel had seen the scene a thousand times, but tonight she was hit by the memory of Stephen Reid, crouched behind the lens, looking for the perfect angle. *That is perfect to me Stephen, thank you.*

The camera bounced as Rachel followed Maddie through the dust. Maddie's flashlight and a dull grey dawn sky. The Korean Camp was half a kilometre away. Little Hye-Won was already up. She had fallen multiple times on the previous stage and was walking painfully. Maddie had learnt that she had only previously ridden on road, and little of that on dirt. With the help of a driver who understood some English, Maddie began a lesson in off-road technique. It lasted nearly three hours. What Hye-Won lacked in experience she made up for with tenacity. Maddie worked carefully through basic techniques, always smiling and helping lift the bike out of deep sand every time Hye-Won fell. Only once Maddie was satisfied that Hye-Won had mastered a few techniques did the two return to their own camp for breakfast.

Rachel asked: "Why on earth would you help a hopeless-case competitor in a race like this?"

Maddie looked directly at the camera: "She taught me a lesson which is more valuable than any bike skills. This was a tiny repayment in comparison."

Rachel felt the thrill - she had captured the essence of Maddie in that moment. She looked for reactions in the others. Dave nodded and smiled. She turned to Martin, his eyes transfixed on the screen.

———

Martin could see the land. More, he could feel the land. Partly it was his painter's view, but deeper was the land where his family fought and struggled to grow enough to eat. The land Akeyo had tried to trick into producing. It had attachments to his being which were as much part of him as his hands. His hands that linked the beauty of the land to the essence the land embedded in him. He had the distinctions of different lands. Lands so green, contrasting the desert sparsity. Lands with different histories. Like the place they had experienced today, intricate man-made gardens so rich they mocked the lean rows of vegetables in his own gardens. He saw difference. Martin also saw the art in the craft of Rachel's work. A fellow artist in different media.

The lights came on for an intermission. Martin walked directly over to Rachel.

"Rachel, you have captured my land perfectly. I struggle every day, brushstroke by brushstroke, to get that sense. Your camera work is masterful."

Rachel thanked him then caught Dave's eye. She walked over to him.

"Dave, what did you think?"

Dave paused, turned to Maddie and then back to Rachel.

"I saw nothing but Maddie. Every word she spoke felt like it was directly to me. I'm super proud of the Maddie you captured, so selfless, so strong and such incredible tenacity. I knew her ferocious competitive spirit but you showed the balance of generosity. No wonder I love this woman so much."

What he didn't say, is the way he felt her pain, real pain in his own body. That he had relived every second of anxiety, doubt and fear.

Bruno walked over to join the group.

"Why were you so worried I wouldn't approve Rachel? You did an incredible job with such a sensitive touch. What did you think Grace?"

Grace wiped her cheeks. "The story was so captivating. I really loved the sense of freedom in the desert. That view of Maddie as a tiny dust speck in that vast space. I was there with her. That sense of something wild, untamed and exciting in that experience. Pure adventure..." Grace trailed off, "and the mastery of the production, seamless flow, beautiful moving panoramas."

"I would like to give that Ralph Hettingen and Richard Wills a solid kick up the backside", Donna chimed in. Everyone laughed.

"Seriously Maddie, you beat the guys at their own game. I would give my right arm to ride the way you do. Girl power without the ego and noise. Lead on Maddie, I will follow you anywhere."

Maddie smiled. "Donna, you do more work on the ground than anyone. You are the one I admire."

Rachel clapped her hands. "Thank you so much everyone, but there is more. Can we start the second half?"

————

Evelina giggled as the first images of herself appeared. The sound broke the tension in the room. Maddie's wounds were stark. Rachel had focused on the damage, then showed the pain in Maddie's face as Evelina walked her slowly around the muddy courtyard, quietly encouraging every step. The physical damage had not weakened Maddie's spirit - her eyes said it all.

There were universal tears in the room as they watched the scene of Dave gently hugging the wasted body that was Maddie's shell.

————

Pete turned to Donna for the first time in their relationship with silver slashes down each cheek. Open emotion rather than the gruff sleeve-wipes of the past. The story had shifted something in Pete. He turned back to the screen.

———

Maddie started to speak. The voice was a whisper. Nat had worked for hours on the sound, picking the fragments and assembling the message:

"I don't have long. There are things that you all need to promise me you will do. Sister Evelina's Church was destroyed by fire. You need to rebuild it. You need to rebuild the Presbytery; these sisters do great work there. You need to provide better medical facilities for the town…."

Rachel had been at the back of the group, unable to focus the camera on Maddie herself. By pure chance she had chosen to focus on Dave's face. She caught the moment that Dave accepted the challenge. It was so subtle, yet it said everything.

The film switched to a prologue starting with an early race interview with Ralf Hettingen. Rachel asked the question,

"What do you think of Maddie's chance in the race?"

The response was curt.

"She will be lucky to survive the long stages. These races require strength and stamina, and she is up against strong world class riders. Unfortunately, women do not have the strength of the men, her window will be short."

He turned away from the camera, clearly disinterested.

The follow-up interview showed a substantially portlier Ralf Hettingen. With a wry smile he acknowledged,

"An extraordinary tough lady. She has even managed to extract a large number of euros from me. She works as hard with her fund raising as she did on her bike. She certainly used those euros more effectively than I do with my accumulated toys." He gestured to a gleaming Ferrari behind him. "Her foundation has made a huge difference to many people."

Donna clapped.

The interview with Kath Wilson showed Kath strong and calm.

"Maddie has more strength than anyone I know. What she has done through her foundation has changed my life. No, saved my life. I had zero future, she has offered an unlimited future."

Grace squeezed Bruno's hand. "The greatest thing we ever did", she whispered in his ear.

Evelina's smile lit up the screen.

"She survived death by a miracle. She remembered every single act of kindness from the community and repaid each a million times over. She repaid many miracles."

Maddie's words ended the film: "When you are given a second chance you see the world in a different light. Things that seemed so important before are often simply trivial. There are good people everywhere. People risked their lives to help me. It is the least I can do to attempt to give something back. In a way my crash was the greatest gift of my life, next of course to Dave and our children."

———

Dave turned on his sofa seat. He pulled Maddie into his arms and held her. The clink from the first bottle of '*Mon Lapin*' started the celebration.

———

High above the chateau, a French impressionist was experimenting with a new painting style. He had finally grown tired of stinking cats. At least that was the lie he told himself. The truth was, he had learnt to listen to the stories of others.

Acknowledgements

My daughter Karen Gault for her (almost) impartial first reading and keen insights.

My wife Barbara Gault for her meticulous proof-reading and support throughout the project.

Michelle Elvy for her professional review, suggestions and editing.